# Coming on the Clouds

## by
## Carolyn Atkinson

ISBN-13:978-1502520180
ISBN-1502520184
Cover and interior art by Betsy Smith
Author Photo by Dana Niemeier
CarolynFAtkinson@gmail.com

## Acknowledgments

I am truly grateful for all of the encouragement from my friends and family who read this book as a work in progress. I am indebted to my "Farm Family" who have been such an integral part of my life and this project. I also would like to thank my daughter Michelle who provided invaluable editing and insight. She will be a great English teacher one day.

And surely I am with you always,
to the very end of the age.
Matthew 28:20
NIV

# CHAPTER ONE

··· ◇ ···

"Just promise me you guys!" Josh pleaded. Jessica and George had been studying in an alcove in the Bush Science library when Josh burst in with his proposal.

"Why are you so concerned about this anyway?" Jessica said.

"I listened to a sermon series at my church about the mark of the beast and it made a lot of sense to me. In Revelation it says that there will come a time when the only way to conduct commerce will be by using a mark of some kind on the right hand or the forehead. Think about how fast technology is expanding. Is it really so farfetched to think that the government will want to track our spending and whereabouts? Think about it - more and more of our movements and associations are being watched. I just heard yesterday that the president wants to track citizens by their cell phone GPS, and what is the real plan for Homeland Security? That and a lot of the other things they were talking about - a one-world government, worldwide banking, political changes in the world- it sounded like it could happen, and in our lifetime. The Bible says that if we take the mark of the beast we are doomed. Of course talking about it now makes me sound a little bit paranoid."

"A little bit?" George laughed, "How about a lot!"

"Yeah, I know, and I realize that I would be the last person you would expect this from, but what if it happens?"

Jessica considered what Josh was saying. He was right that what he was saying was unexpected, but she knew he was sincere, and that his faith was important to him. She and George had been very involved in their youth group as high school students, but neither of them had really connected to any ministry since they had been at college. Josh had become involved with campus ministry as well as joining a local church. He tried to get George and Jessica to come with him but they had a hard time breaking away from their studies.

"Ok, say it does happen. Say we are asked to take the mark, what are you proposing that we do?" asked Jessica.

"Well, I think we should find a way to get together and just drop off the grid. We would have to get rid of cell phones and computers and whatever other technology is around at the time and go live off of the land. Do you think you could do it?" asked Josh.

"That's a lot to commit to. We may be married, have kids, and jobs - we would just walk away?" Jessica asked.

"Yes," Josh said gravely, "Of course you would bring your family if they would come. But if they refused, you'd have to walk away."

Jessica looked over at George. When he turned to look at her she felt like she was suddenly in a time warp, transported back to when they were six years old and playing together in the backyard of her home. She was inside the tree fort with her dolls having a tea party, and he was outside, fighting off imaginary foes with his light saber. She and George had been best friends since birth. Their families lived two houses apart and their mothers met in Lamaze class. They grew up together and since neither had siblings, they formed a sibling-like bond. When they were deciding on colleges it only made sense that they would go to the same one. They had settled on Rollins College in Winter Park, Florida, only a few hours away from their home in Stuart. What they were talking about made her feel like kids again, ready for an adventure. Jessica smiled at George.

"So what do you think Poin?" she said, using the name the three friends called each other. Other students had always thought they were nerdy so they decided to embrace the nerd in themselves. They used the name as an abbreviation for Poindexter, the archetypal nerd. George and Jessica had met Josh shortly after arriving at Rollins and they had clicked. They were all chemistry majors and all kept up on world events so they spent most evenings studying together, discussing chemistry and solving the problems of the world. Josh had grown up in Raleigh, North Carolina. George and Jessica knew that he had experienced a difficult childhood, but Josh didn't talk about it very much. He liked to keep things light and fun and was well-liked at school. When they walked around campus male students greeted Josh with fist bumps and female students greeted him with smiles and winks.

George looked at Jessica thoughtfully for a moment, then he turned to Josh. "Where would we go? Have you thought about that? We can't just go camp on someone's land, we could get arrested. How would that help the cause?"

"Well, yes, I have thought about that, actually. My grandfather was a farmer in North Carolina. We used to go there in the summers. My dad was supposed to inherit and work the farm, but he didn't want to be a farmer and he and my grandfather had a falling out. When my grandfather died about 10 years ago, my dad walked away from the farm. He still pays taxes on the property but we haven't been there since. I don't know what it is like now, but we could go there."

George thought about the three of them living on a farm with their families and friends and imagined a kind of summer-camp feel. He looked at Jessica and recognized that look she got as a kid when she tried to talk him into something their parents wouldn't like.

"I can see it in your eyes - both of you," Josh said. "This isn't some kind of fun time we are talking about. We would probably be hunted by the government, have to hide and do without the basics of life. I don't want you to say you would do it unless you are really serious. Because I am very serious."

George turned to Jessica.

"I'm in, how about you?'

Jessica looked long and hard at George, then at Josh. There was something about Josh that made you believe in him and trust him.

"I'm in," she said.

Josh nodded gravely. He left without saying another word.

"What did we just agree to?" said Jessica.

"The force is strong with that one I would say," said George with a very serious look. Jessica punched him in the arm and he laughed.

"Don't worry about it Jessica," he said, still laughing. "What he is talking about is never going to happen. This is America!"

# CHAPTER TWO
... ◇ ...

Cock-a-doodle-doo!

As she hit the alarm on her Device Jessica groaned. How could it already be time to get up when she was still so exhausted? Then, like every morning for the last 15 years, she remembered. The worry, the knock on the door, the pained look on the face of the policeman, the confusion on her five-year-old daughter Karen's face – they all washed over her anew. It reminded her of the movie "Fifty First Dates" she saw when she was a kid. She was Drew Barrymore having to relive her pain every day. Jessica looked at her left hand. Two wedding bands flanked her small diamond solitaire engagement ring. She had added Michael's band 15 years ago. She left a few tears on the pillow and got up to start a new day. Pulling on her bathrobe, she grabbed her Device and headed into the kitchen of her two bedroom townhouse.

As Jessica entered the kitchen with her Device the lights and the small kitchen screen turned on and the coffee maker started. While she enjoyed the smell of the coffee brewing she tapped her Device to bring up the newspaper on the kitchen screen. Scrolling through it she decided that no news may actually be good news after all since there didn't seem to be anything positive in the whole thing. Textmails came up with another tap. Some were ads, some were interesting quotes sent to her from e-friends, and some were work related. Those she saved for later. She responded to the textmails with her Device and checked the time. Remarkably, she had already been up for an hour – where did the time go? It was almost time to clock in and she hadn't even dressed. There was just enough time for a quick breakfast, a fast shower and then it was time to work. Jessica quickly ran a comb through her pixie-cut dark hair, frowning at the grey that was just starting to creep in at the temples. She was glad that she didn't have to waste time on makeup and transport since she did all of her work from home.

Jessica entered her office area with her Device and the desk screen lit up. She set her Device next to the keyboard on the desk, activating it, and brought up her work site. She clocked in and checked her textmails and to-do lists. She still felt a little sleepy but having worked in the same company for 20-plus years, she felt she could probably sleepwalk through her day. Well, maybe that wasn't completely fair, Dacon Chemicals was producing new products all the time and she did have to keep up with the growth or lose her position. This was especially true since she enjoyed the agricultural component the most and with the decline in American farming, the need just wasn't as great. She had to make sure that she had information that was interesting to her customers. Jessica's territory was the southeast, but she had never really traveled far from her home in Stuart, Florida. She studied information on the new pesticide that was being released the next month, textmailed a few questions to the main office and leaned back in her chair. She felt she had accomplished a lot for a morning and clocked out for lunch. As she left the office the light turned off and the screen darkened, awaiting her return.

In the kitchen, Jessica scrounged in the refrigerator for lunch. She settled on a peanut butter and honey sandwich. She put the honey on sparingly; it had become quite expensive due to colony collapse disorder, a topic that interested her since she worked with agricultural products. The bees started disappearing in 2005 for unclear reasons. There was a lot of speculation that it was a combination of pesticide practices and genetically modified crops, but no one ever really knew. Some rural areas could still maintain hives, but not on the grand scale of yesteryear. Honey was scarce and therefore pricey, but she craved it more than chocolate. She used the last of the honey and realized that there was very little else left in her fridge. Turning to the screen, she brought up the grocery list she had been accumulating, added a two-ounce bottle of honey and sent it to the store. As she was finishing up she heard a ping and in the corner of the screen was her daughter, Karen, waiting for Jessica to accept her call.

"Hi, Mom!" came Karen's voice through the speakers. "How's it going?"

Karen was a beautiful girl, twenty years old now and in college at the University of Florida. Her light brown complexion and almond-shaped eyes made her look slightly exotic. Jessica always felt that her daughter got the best of her parents' features but Karen complained about her curly hair which today she had twisted up in bun. Karen was studying History, but at this point she was unclear about what she wanted to do with her degree. Jessica always reassured her daughter that following her passion would eventually lead to a career.

"Pretty good, I'm just taking a break from the grind. How about you?" Jessica asked.

"Nothing terribly interesting is going on here. I am really enjoying Early American History. The Founding Fathers were so amazing! Why didn't we learn about them in high school?" Karen asked.

"Well, just before you went to school it was decided that there was just too much history for students to cover, so they started at 1880 – with the Progressive Movement. I fought it because I felt it was politically motivated, but I lost. When I was in high school we learned it all, and though it was a bit rushed it made more sense to me than starting over a hundred years in. I agree with you, by the way, the Founding Fathers were inspiring. Some would even say enlightened. In fact I heard your grandfather give a sermon on that one time."

"I would have liked to have heard that," said Karen.

Actually Karen had never heard her grandfather give a sermon. She wished they could have visited her grandparents more, but Karen knew her mom was doing the best job she could as a single mom, just getting by. Karen had promised herself long ago that when she was older she would make time to visit her mom. Her kids would know and love their grandmother.

"When do you think you can get up here to visit?" Karen asked. She knew that her mom didn't have any plans to visit, that she didn't make any plans at all, but Karen never stopped trying.

"Well, you know I have a lot to do here," Jessica stalled.

"I know, I know, but I miss you and you still haven't met Taylor. We have been dating for six months now!" countered Karen. She didn't want to push too hard knowing that the mere discussion of a trip was enough to trigger an anxiety attack in her mother. But the alternative was to just let her mom rot in her townhouse her whole life. And what kind of life was that? One look at her mom's expression made her realize that she was already on the brink of an attack so Karen knew she had to drop it.

"Just tell me you will consider it. OK?" Karen said.

"I will," said Jessica, relieved to be leaving this conversation. "Tell me about you- what is new on campus?"

"The usual, a lot of political discussions and parties, I doubt much has changed from when you were in college. There seems to be a rising distrust of the World Government, although I am not really sure why, I haven't seen any real changes to warrant it."

"In that case you are right – nothing has changed since I was in college! Of course we didn't have the World Government then, but we knew it was coming," said Jessica. Well, some people did anyway.

"Hey Mom, I've got to go," said Karen, checking her Device for the time. "My next class is in fifteen minutes, and he actually takes off points for being late. How high school is that? It makes me want to take all e-classes, but I do like the interaction in the live classes. Anyway, I love you Mom – I will talk to you soon."

"I love you too, sweetie," Jessica replied and the corner went black. She allowed herself just a moment to be sad that Karen was off at school and she was here alone, but then it was time to get back at it. While she ate her lunch she faced the kitchen screen, turned on the news in one quadrant and brought up her social site in another. In the third quadrant she brought up the garden show available today and in the fourth she pulled up her textmail. Glancing at the news on G-TV she watched the hosts debate the topics of today but barely paid attention. Clearly the World Government stance was going to win – it did every time. Jessica still remembered the days when the debate was live and heated, with both sides represented. She understood that the old type of programming was dangerous in that it incited discontent and even riots, but she missed it just the same. The ticker tape on the bottom of the screen read: *woman kills, cooks and eats ex-husband's pets.......more bodies found in rapist's home-in the living room and backyard, neighbors unaware of problems........mother encourages 3 y/o daughter to smother her 1 year old sister stating that "it would make her life easier".....* And on it went. The evil in the world was just overwhelming sometimes.

Jessica looked over at the social site to check on her e-friends. She scrolled through their updates and their pictures, laughing at some and questioning the wisdom of putting some of them up for all to see. Jessica had an elaborate online social network, a product of living a solitary life. Sometimes Jessica even fooled herself into thinking that she really knew these people, even though she had never seen any of them in real life. For all she knew they could be completely different than the persona they portrayed online. It was only natural to make yourself just a little more interesting. Sometimes it seemed like the site knew her too well. The ads for dating sites, wrinkle removal and gardening supplies made her feel a bit uneasy, as if they were looking at her profile a little too carefully. Karen said her ads were mostly for engagement rings, birth control and marijuana. Jessica tried to see the humor in it.

Jessica updated her site from her Device with pictures of Karen sent from school, some funny quotes that had been sent to her, and pictures of her garden taken last week. Actually she was down to a couple of peppers a woody looking tomato plant with no tomatoes, a decent looking rosemary bush and a healthy assortment of weeds. The pepper plants looked weak, with very few leaves and just a couple of peppers which threatened to bend the whole plant over like the Christmas tree on her mom's favorite Christmas show –

A Charlie Brown Christmas. It was a pretty pathetic garden really, especially when her job was in the agricultural field. One reason she had chosen this townhouse was because of the backyard which, while not very big, had very good sunlight and water access. Also, it was fenced and the garden could be hidden from view which was important because there was an ordinance against food gardening in urban areas. This was supposedly to protect property values, but Karen thought it was overly controlling and designed to make people even more reliant on the government. Of course she didn't want to pay a fine, so she hid.

"Today I will definitely get out there and weed after work," she said aloud. She would be working late since she had taken such a long mid-day break but she could fit it in. As she grabbed her plate she knocked over her water. Hastily she grabbed her Device to keep it from getting wet. That was a close one. She had already been reissued a Device by the government this year after she dropped hers in the toilet when she was trying to clean and talk to Karen at the same time. Loss of the signal sent an automatic report to the closest agency and they delivered a new Device within an hour. It was scary how dependent she was on her Device. Without it she couldn't access her screen, read or even turn on the lights. She had spent the time relaxing in her garden and had just started to enjoy her freedom when the new Device arrived. There was no charge for replacement, which made Jessica think of a quote from Albert Einstein "Sometimes one pays most for the things one gets for nothing." Still, it was such an improvement on the technology of her youth when they had three remote controls for the TV, separate screens for the computer and the TV, a home phone and a cell phone, credit cards, debit cards and cash, emails and texts, books, newspapers and e-readers and ring of keys. Over time all of these had merged into one Device that had become so vital to commerce that the World Government had seen it as a necessity and provided it to every citizen. She cleaned her dishes and put them away and it was time to get back to work.

Jessica returned to the office and to the sales portion of her day. She reviewed her client list and noted a few who should have already placed their next order. She textmailed Jared Brown, a farmer in North Carolina who had been her client for at least ten years.

*Hey Jared, how is it going with the Malhindran? Are you about ready to order again?* she wrote. A few seconds later his response popped up on the screen.

*You are so right- I completely forgot to order – can you put me down for the same amount as the last order?*

She answered immediately: *Absolutely. How is the product working for you? Do you have any questions?*

*Malhindran is a miracle weed killer! If you are ever up this way I would love to show you the fields – we could feed you some great vegetables, my wife is a wonderful cook – just let me know!*

*I will definitely textmail you if I am in the area. That sounds delightful.* Jessica really would love that. After ten years of textmails she felt like she knew Jared and his family. His wife and four kids felt like cousins to her. She sent them e-cards on their birthdays and included them in her Christmas card list. That was one thing from past decades she was unwilling to give up – Christmas cards. Sure, most people sent their cards by textmail now and yes, that was better for the global environment, but there was just something about writing with a pen on paper and putting the stamp on it that made her nostalgic for the times of her youth. She cherished the few that she received in the snail mail, or s-mail as it was called now, and kept them with her Christmas decorations. Many of them were Winter Holiday cards which made Jessica a little sad, but she saved them anyway. Not so, of course were the ones from Michael's parents, Lebron and Sasha.

The day that e-Winter Holiday cards come from a Southern Baptist minister is the day I completely give up on this society, she thought. Jessica suddenly realized that she was daydreaming and that she had forgotten about Jared. She quickly textmailed him the invoice, and within seconds he had Device-approved it and she sent it off to the warehouse. This sale alone had made her day productive. Her employer respected her organization and diligence and rewarded her accordingly. She was one of the highest paid members of the sales team which had allowed her to send Karen to college without relying on the Government option of Homeland Service after graduation. Few people could afford to do this, what with the 75% income tax and the escalating costs of tuition, but she lived modestly, didn't travel at all and spent little on herself. She didn't own her apartment, but then again, no one she knew did. Housing was available from the government and was already paid for by taxes so to own a home you have to have inherited it or be quite wealthy, neither of which was all that likely. Jessica remembered when she first started working she got a paycheck with money taken out of it and then the balance of taxes was paid on April 15th. Now all of the money earned by global citizens went into the World Bank and the money that they were allowed to keep was credited to their bank accounts. While this system was much more efficient, kept people from hiding income from the government and got rid of the need for paper money, it still seemed wrong to her. Her daughter's generation had known no other system, so the idea of dealing with cash and checks seemed archaic to them.

She sent textmails to two other farmers with information on the new products coming out. She knew that the products would help them have more productive crops and she felt proud of the work she did to help them. Farmers were great to work with, so down-to-earth – literally! She knew Jared really meant it when he asked her to visit, he wouldn't just say that. Maybe someday....

At the corner of the screen was another ping and a young dark-haired man was pictured, awaiting her call approval. She tapped her Device and smiled. Her groceries had arrived.

"One minute, I will be right there Daniel!" she said, clocked out and headed for the door, Device in hand.

"Hey, Jessica," said Daniel, holding out his Device. She tapped the corner of it with her own Device, transferring the information, and quickly reviewed the bill.

"Looks good to me," she said and tapped her approval of the expense.

"Want me to bring it in for you?" Daniel asked. He knew she

would say no, but it was his job to ask. Daniel had been delivering to Jessica for the last five years and, while she was always polite, Daniel always sensed that she was uneasy with him. He hoped it wasn't anything he had said.

"No I've got it, but thanks anyway," said Jessica, taking the small box from him. "See you next week!"

"Have a good day, Jessica," said Daniel, and off he went.

Jessica took the groceries into the kitchen and unloaded them. She looked over her purchases and put them away, mostly in the freezer and the cabinets. She popped a frozen meal of chicken and rice into the microwave for dinner. Jessica really liked to cook. She loved the food smells permeating through the house and when Karen had been here she had done quite a lot of cooking. Well, maybe not the kind that Jared's wife did, with fresh products, but those were too expensive for her. Frozen and boxed meals made cooking a lot easier, especially now. It was hard to get into it once Karen was gone. Cooking for one was a drag. Karen was always trying to get her to invite people, especially men, over for dinner but she just didn't want to. Karen didn't understand. Even Jessica didn't really understand. After Michael died she had immersed herself in work and in raising Karen, severely limiting her time for socializing. Then after Karen became more independent Jessica found that she actually feared the face-to-face socializing that had been easy and fun for her in her youth and young adulthood. At this point in her life she would have to admit that she had a social phobia of sorts. Even the interaction with Daniel had been stressful and she had never let him come in – even after years of weekly deliveries.

Oh well, I guess I am just messed up, she surmised. But I can't say I am unhappy, so why rock the boat? Jessica ate her meal in front of the news on the screen, cleaned up, found her workout clothes in the dryer and put them on.

Jessica went into the living room with her Device and the wall screen lit up. She reviewed the new shows offered and chose one, keeping the news in one quadrant on silent and adding a workout show in the other quadrant on silent. She set the textmails and phone calls to ping her Device and started the show, a somewhat gory murder-mystery show that Jessica liked because the actor and the actress had such a great chemistry, although the explicit sex scenes and vulgar language made her uncomfortable. It didn't seem to bother other people so she figured she must be unreasonably sensitive. Then she started the workout recording and began her workout, using a few weights and a mat. Jessica was still in good shape for her age, which she credited to her regular workout routine and not eating junky foods. She occasionally glanced at the news program and the smiling hosts. How they could talk about serial killers, natural disasters and famine with a smile on their faces was beyond her. She read the ticker-tape below: *Soldier kills 12 and wounds 35 in a shooting rampage at navy base, 8 y/o boy abducted on his way home from school, molested, killed and dismembered......,man killed after complaining about a barking dog....*, she glanced back at the workout routine recording, checking her form as she did, heard two pings denoting new textmails, all the while following the plot of the murder mystery. Jessica thought multi-tasking was a wonderful thing but by the end of the routine she was glad to just be able to focus on two programs. She was glad she didn't follow sports. Jessica had lost interest in watching sports once football was banned after the flurry of lawsuits over injury. Some of her e-friends talked about having eight programs up on a screen at once. Having finished her mystery show, Jessica moved on to a nature show, letting it fill the whole screen. Well, most of the screen, the bottom third ran the commercials simultaneously with the text running below. She used to find it distracting but now she was used to it and even preferred it over the frequent interruptions. Some of the ads were very risqué, but since her Device was set to adult there was no screening. But seriously, do adults really need to be bombarded with ads for impotence medicines, breast size enhancers, tampons, condoms and vibrators? Over the years she had become desensitized and hardly even noticed it any more. What she couldn't get used to was the product ads placed within the show. Sometimes the link was pretty weak, like in the mystery she had just finished when the actress offered a cup of coffee to the actor out of nowhere and he took it, sipped and proclaimed it to be the best he had ever had. "Folgers," she had said. "The very best". The ad companies must think we are all idiots. That was one reason she enjoyed the nature channels, since it is awfully hard to introduce coffee to a bunch of penguins. Also, it harkened back to her educational roots, her biology major. She thought back fondly to her college days and the deep discussions with George and Josh. She hoped that Karen was developing similar friendships.

The nature show ended and Jessica was exhausted. It amazed her that she could be this tired and yet not have left the apartment once. But all in all it was a good, productive day. She headed up to her room, glancing into Karen's room which was exactly as she had left it, changed into her pajamas and hopped into bed. She switched her Device to the Reader mode and continued the book she had begun last night. Jessica tended to read adventure books about wilderness exploration which even she found odd considering she sheltered herself so severely. After just a few pages she felt too sleepy to continue. She set the textmail and phone to the emergency-only setting which alerted the incoming callers that she was not taking calls unless they pressed the override, causing an obnoxiously loud alarm. As she drifted off to sleep it occurred to her that she never went out to the garden.

# CHAPTER THREE
··· ◇ ···

Cock-a–doodle-doo!

Jessica was confused. She was dreaming that she was walking on the beach with Michael, holding his hand and looking out over the sunset. Among the sandpipers scurrying along the sand there was a large rooster.

Cock-a-doodle-do!

Jessica awoke smiling at the funny intrusion into her dream caused by her "farmhouse" Device alarm. Then, again, she remembered and wished she could go back, just for a few more minutes, to the company of Michael. Grudgingly she sat up, stretched and padded down to the kitchen. As the lights came up and the coffee began its brew cycle, Jessica had a sudden feeling of anxiety, as though she had forgotten something. She reviewed the previous day in her head, looking for mistakes, but found none. These periods of anxiety seemed to be coming more frequently, and for no apparent cause. The kitchen screen was lit and Jessica chose the GTV AM News Report from the lineup of options. The two anchors, a young blonde woman and a handsome dark-haired man, smiled from the screen, seeming to look her right in the eye.

"Good morning! I am Annette Jennings and this is Stephen Bennett and we are here with the latest news, sports and weather for the Central Florida area! So Stephen," she said turning toward the handsome man, "How is the weather shaping up for those baseball games this weekend?"

Jessica went to the refrigerator, took out the milk and grabbed the cereal from the pantry. The cereal she had ordered was a little more money than the other cereals but this one was advertised as the healthiest – containing all of the vitamins and minerals she would need for the whole day. It kind of made her wonder why she even bothered to eat for the rest of the day. She thought about Jared and his wife sitting down to breakfast. What would they be eating, she wondered. Fresh shelled eggs and maybe even bacon from real pigs? How decadent that sounded. She was thinking about whether they made their own bread, and how that would smell baking when the newscasters words broke through her thoughts and made her blood run cold.

"So Annette, if I understand you correctly, there has been a breakthrough in the fight against identity theft, is that what you would say?"

"Absolutely, Stephen, you certainly have that right! This new implantable chip would serve to verify that the Device the person is holding is actually theirs. As we all know, Device use has revolutionized the world by providing access to information and consumer items to everyone on the planet, but Device theft and unauthorized use has been rampant. This small chip would be injected in the skin of the right hand of the user with a small tattoo with one of the ten regions - ours would be NA for North America of course - overlying it to verify its placement. This chip would allow the device to be used only by the true device owner. Isn't that incredible?" Annette turned back to her co-anchor with a smile any dentist would be proud of.

"When will this advancement become available?" Stephen asked.

"It will be available in the next few weeks free of charge to anyone who wants to improve the security of their device, and who wouldn't want to do that!" Annette gushed. "In other news.."

Jessica suddenly felt like she was in another dimension. There was a buzzing in her ears and she felt a little light-headed. Sitting down before she fell down seemed like a good idea. She wondered if George and Josh had seen the report. George she had kept up with, of course, but not Josh. Jessica pulled up George's number on her Device and stared at it. Was she over-reacting? Would George just laugh at her? It had been 25 years – would he even remember?

# Chapter Four

···◇···

Brrrring, brrrring, brrrring

George's eyes opened and he grabbed for his Device before the alarm woke his wife sleeping peacefully next to him. She didn't have to wake up for another thirty minutes and she took her sleep very seriously. Becky mumbled something that sounded like "Don't cut the green one!" and then was quiet again. He smiled at her sleeping form. She often said these quirky things when she was in light sleep. Sometimes he told her about them later and they both got a laugh out of it.

As was his custom, George lay quietly in bed reviewing his day before heading for the coffeepot. Five e-patients this morning, follow-ups of course, followed by rounds in the hospital and afternoon clinic patients. After that he really had to get to the gym – his weight loss program was not going so well.

"Time to make the donuts!" he thought to himself and got to his feet. His father had always said that when he left for the hospital in the mornings when he was a kid. He never thought to ask him why. His dad didn't even like donuts.

As George entered the kitchen with his Device the lights came on, the coffeepot turned on and the kitchen screen lit up with new show offerings. He chose the news, knowing that what he was getting was more filtered than the coffee, but at least he would learn if anything major had happened in the world. He also brought up his day's schedule and textmails. There was nothing surprising on the news, so he turned off the screen. George knew when Becky came in that she would want to keep the screen filled with something in each sector but he preferred silence. He had a theory that the bombardment of the senses with constant input was the cause of the increase in depression, anxiety, and other mood problems seen these days. He even wondered if the prevalent behavior problems in children as well as adults could be linked with constant stimulus. He would love to see a study done on this, but who would fund it?

George took a few items out of the refrigerator and started breakfast. Becky would be up soon, and she would wake the twins when she got up. She was the one who got them out of bed, dressed and ready for school. George couldn't believe they were already in the first grade. Becky was such a great mom, and a truly great person. He was so lucky to have met her after he lost his first wife, Samantha. Becky was ten years his junior, so sometimes he felt like an old man around her, but she never seemed to be bothered by the age difference. Plus there's nothing like a set of seven-year-old twins to keep you young. Maya and Mark came running into the kitchen as if on cue and gave him a hug. He looked down at the tops of their heads, Maya with her dark brown hair in neat braids and Mark with his unruly black hair, the cowlick in front identical to his own at that age. George remembered when he was in college he tried to get that cowlick to behave, finally opting for the close cut that was fashionable at the time. Now his receding hairline made it a moot point.

"Daddy, Daddy, Daddy," they sang out together, "What's for breakfast?"

"Nothing until you are dressed and ready for school," he replied.

Becky came into the kitchen looking like she could have used just a bit more sleep.

"Come on back to your room you little hoodlums," she teased, with mock exasperation. She gave George a hug and a kiss and went off to supervise.

George put four breakfast burritos in the microwave and hit sensor cook. They were perfect every time. What a great thing. He did worry about the amount of processed ingredients he was pouring into their developing brains and bodies, but no study had ever really shown a connection between processed food and disease. Of course that was no surprise since the studies were funded by the companies that produced the products. Just as he set the plates on the table Maya and Mark came dashing in with Becky close behind. As they wolfed down their food George made a note of the fact that neither of his children looked as fit as he and Jessica were at their age. They weren't exactly fat, just kind of doughy looking.

Becky herded the two off to the car with their backpacks, making sure to slip their Devices into the zippered shirt pockets specially designed for them. Becky called out to him "Be right back!" as she followed them out. And it was silent once again. George checked his Device and saw it was almost time for his first e-patient. He lumbered to the bathroom for a quick shower and shave and got ready for his day.

George entered the office he and Becky shared. They had a partner desk with back-to-back screens in case they needed to work at the same time, though that was rarely needed. He saw his e-patients in the morning and then headed out, while she did her errands in the morning and had her office hours after he left. It was a system that had worked for many years now.

The screen pinged. In the upper corner quadrant was his first e-patient, Terry Garfield, looking impatient. Terry turned 80 years old last May and he did not really do well with this new way of providing medical care.

"Doc are you there? Doc?" Terry yelled into his Device. "Confound this piece of junk. I don't think he's there," he called out to someone off of the screen. George guessed it was his daughter.

"I am here Mr. Garfield," George said. "See me on your screen?"

"Oh, hi Doc! How are you doing?"

"Well, I am fine, Mr. Garfield, but how are you?" George quickly reviewed the lab work that came up on one quadrant of his screen, as well as the problem list and medication list in the other quadrants. "Your blood work all looks good, and the scans are all clear. Your blood pressure readings that your daughter downloaded are a little on the high side, so I would like to increase your blood pressure medicine by one tablet at night, and recheck it in one month – does that sound ok?"

"Well, all of that sounds good but I have this thing on my arm I want you to see. Let me put it up to this confounded camera and you can.."

"Now you know the parameters Mr. Garfield, no new problems. Only follow ups are allowed online. But I can connect you to the scheduling program and you can make an appointment, how about that?"

"Ok, I would rather see you in person anyway, I don't trust this confound thing you know."

"I know, I know," chuckled George. He loved the old patients the most. He transferred Mr. Garfield to the scheduling software, hoping he would make it through with an appointment and not get impatient with the instructions. Hopefully his daughter would help.

Four e-patients later George emerged from the office and found Becky already home drying the dishes. They took a few moments to have a cup of coffee together and discuss weekend plans before she darted into the office to start her workday. How she could get excited about civil engineering he would never know, but she was very good at it. He would never guess that someone who was such a people person would enjoy all of that time in front of a screen. It was her compassion for others that had drawn him to her in the first place. George first saw Becky at church when she gave a talk on her experiences doing mission work in Haiti and other places around the world. The pictures she showed on the screen of her team helping her set up water purifiers and building houses were a strong contrast to the professional looking woman that stood in front of the screen, but he fell in love with both of them. Her long wavy brown hair, bright green eyes and trim figure didn't hurt either. He still marveled that he had pulled together the courage to ask her out, and within just few months they were talking about marriage. George felt so lucky to have found love twice in his lifetime. But enough daydreaming, it was time for rounds at the hospital.

"Bye, Becky!" He yelled as he left, waiting just a moment for her reply before heading out.

George arrived at Mercy Hospital and checked his Device for the room numbers of his patients. He headed upstairs to oncology, dreading the encounter coming. He felt terrible about himself, but it just hurt so much that this patient was being treated successfully for the same cancer that had taken Samantha, his first wife. If she had scored just a few more prognostic indicator points she would have been able to qualify for treatment. The helplessness of that time was agonizing, only being able to give her supportive care. George's father had become incensed. He had worked in the era prior to the World Health Initiative and was angry that anyone felt they had a right to tell Samantha that the treatment would be withheld. George had only ever worked in the Initiative so his view was more fatalistic. George's dad had become so discouraged over the changes that he had retired early. Depression had set in and when he got sick he just didn't have the strength to fight it. His mom followed shortly after. George knew there was no Initiative code for a broken heart, but it was real malady nevertheless. George pasted a smile on his face and entered the room, ready to give the good news of progress that the woman and her family so desperately wanted. Then he checked on the other patients, discharging one to a rehab center and one to home.

Before heading into the office George drove through a food station, touched his Device to his selection, a double hamburger and fries, and within seconds his food was there for the taking. He ate hurriedly as he drove to the office.

George made his way through the crowded waiting room, briefcase in hand, greeting familiar faces as he did. He shared this office with five other physicians who were all quite sought after. George had done his homework prior to joining this group. He wanted to work with other physicians who had the patients' best interests at heart, but were willing to work within the framework of the World Health Initiative. This meant a quite lower salary than at other physician's groups who had drastically decreased the patient contact and who pushed the edge of the envelope in their billing practices, but for George it was worth it. Of course he had a wife with a well-paid position, so he had a little more financial flexibility. His father had paid for his medical school bills so at least he hadn't started out with debt or a military payback, and for that he was quite grateful. The vast majority of doctors graduating now had Homeland Security commitments. Still, his dream of working side by side with his father in a practice of their own would never be a reality.

George took his Device and his stethoscope from his briefcase and entered the first room. All of his rooms were identical – an exam table angled in from the corner so that he could reach both sides, a screen on one wall and the sink and cabinets on the other. It looked somewhat spartan, but it worked for him. His patient, an extremely healthy and active older woman that he knew well was seated on the edge of the exam table, obviously anxious.

"Hi, Mrs. Thompson, what's going on? You look worried," he said.

"Actually I am, Doctor," Mrs. Thompson said, "I am having these symptoms, you see."

"Symptoms? What kind of symptoms?"

"Well, some pain in my belly here," she said pointing to her upper abdomen, "and here, too," pointing to her lower abdomen.

"Anything else?" George asked.

"Also my chest – I am coughing," she replied, adding an unconvincing cough.

"Any other problems?" continued George.

"Yes my head is hurting. And sometimes I see double. And I get dizzy sometimes," she added.

George had seen this before. He took a glance at Mrs. Thompson's date of birth and confirmed his suspicions. This would take a delicate hand.

"I see you have a birthday coming up," George said gently, pointing to his Device.

Mrs. Thompson got a sheepish look on her face and stared down at her folded hands. In a few months she would be 70, and they both knew that no new therapies could be started after that age. Other patients had come to him with similar complaints, basically asking for a head-to-toe work-up in order to make sure there was nothing lurking only to be found after the treatment cutoff. Treatments that had been started could be continued, at least for now, so he could completely understand her predicament, but he couldn't go along with it. He wished it could be up to the doctor to decide with the patient, the way it used to be. Mrs. Thompson was a "young" 70-year-old– active in her church, still able to take care of herself completely. Others of his patients were "old" 70-year-olds – with multiple health problems, some with dementia or terminal diseases, and unable to get around at all. Decisions on treatment should be tailored on this basis. George understood that allowing everyone to have access to any medicine was expensive and the World Health Initiative was already close to bankrupt, but there had to be a better way.

"I tell you what Mrs. Thompson; I am going to spend extra time today looking very carefully at you from head to toe. If I find anything at all suspicious I will make sure you get the tests done and the treatment started before your birthday. How does that sound?"

Tears filled his patient's eyes and she smiled at George and took his hand, thanking him as she did. George felt a stinging in his own eyes and he turned away toward the sink to wash his hands and gather his emotions.

George finished with Mrs. Thompson and the rest of his patients, spending at least as much time in his office dictating and filling out forms on his Device as he did with the patients. He was the last to leave, shutting out the lights and locking up as he left. It had just started to rain, so he ran to the car, unlocking it and turning the lights on with his Device before he got there, and then programmed it for the trip home.

The smell of food cooking hit him as he walked into the house. He had hoped for a rousing "Daddy!" greeting, but Maya and Mark were curled up on the couch like a couple of kittens, watching the screen, so he wandered into the kitchen and gave Becky a hug.

"So how was your day?" she asked after returning his hug and adding a kiss.

"Just another day in paradise," replied George. "And you?"

"Pretty good, I feel like I am so close to a breakthrough on this energy project. I need a stroke of genius."

"You'll figure out. You are the smartest person I know."

"Flattery will get you everywhere you know," Becky laughed. "Call the kids for dinner please."

Maya and Mark complained that they were watching their show and asked if they could just please, please keep the screen on while they were eating. George knew Becky would not give in on this. She felt it was very important to have family meals, so whenever their schedules allowed it, they would gather around the kitchen table. When it was just him with the kids they knew that pizza in front of the screen was acceptable. He didn't have to worry that they were watching shows that were not appropriate since their Devices would only allow them to access shows approved for their age, so he usually watched the news or a nature show on the screen in the kitchen. But tonight was a family dinner, so Maya and Mark entertained them with stories about school and requests for a dog that they, of course, would take care of. Then there were dishes to clean, baths and bedtime stories. George and Becky poured themselves some wine, picked out a comedy to watch and then went to bed, setting their separate alarms. Just before falling asleep George realized that he had never made it to the gym.

# CHAPTER FIVE

... ◇ ...

"Cuckoo, Cuckoo, Cuckoo"

Becky awoke, startled out of her dream. She could never quite recall her dreams but they must be whoppers from the feedback she got from George. Apparently she was quite the sleep-talker. Becky arose and went to wake Maya and Mark, putting on a smile to greet them. She had read somewhere how important it was to start a child's day off well, with a smile instead of a barking command. As usual they hopped out of bed and rushed to the kitchen to greet their dad. When Becky came into the kitchen after them they were standing very still, looking at George, confusion obvious on their faces.

No breakfast was on the table. The coffee was untouched. George stood with his face toward the screen; mouth a bit agape, his Device in his hand. He turned toward Becky, his face ashen.

"Becky, we need to talk," was all he said.

Becky was alarmed. She had never seen George like this. She wasn't sure what to do now. Luckily it was not her turn to drive so she reminded George to put in the breakfast and took the kids back to get ready. As she left the kitchen she watched George as he woodenly went to the freezer to get the breakfast. She could have been watching an android. Once the kids were dressed, fed and loaded into the neighbor's car they sat down at the kitchen table across from one another. Becky held out her hands across the table, placing them over George's.

"We can handle this together, whatever it is," she said hoarsely.

"I need to tell you a story about something I agreed to when I was just a kid in college," said George. He told Becky the whole story including the promise to band together if this became a reality. Becky listened carefully and when he had finished his story she released his hands, leaned back in her chair and sighed.

"I thought you were going to tell me about a love child from your past or something. Although honestly that may have affected my life less than this might, you know what I mean?" she said with a nervous laugh.

"I know exactly what you mean," George replied, "but first let me talk to Jessica. Maybe she will think I am being silly to think that this is the mark discussed in the Bible. Maybe she could discuss it with her father-in-law – remember, he is a minister. "

"How could I forget that? He married us!" Becky exclaimed, laughing. "You are officially losing it."

George looked at her sheepishly. "I am going to reschedule my e-patients and call Jessica before I go to the hospital. We can regroup on this later tonight."

"Sounds like a military strike or something. Ok, we have a plan. Don't freak out – and you might consider praying before you call."

"Why didn't I think of that?" wondered George. He waved at Becky as she took off for an on-site meeting, sent a textmail to the scheduler informing her that there was a family emergency that required rescheduling the e-patients. He took a minute to collect his thoughts. He thought about Jessica and how their relationship had changed over the years. It seemed that lately the only times they saw each other were for big events. Weddings and funerals had become the mainstays of their contacts. Unfortunately funerals had topped weddings in their lives thus far. First Jessica lost her parents together in a car accident while George and Jessica were still in college. George's parents had grieved for Jessica's mom and dad as if they were family. Next was George's marriage to Samantha. George and Samantha had met in their third year of college after she transferred to their school and had married right after graduation. Jessica was there for Samantha during the tough times of infertility and then illness. George thought about how important his relationship with Jessica and Michael had been in those dark months after Samantha's death. Their friendship had kept him from being sucked down into the black vortex of depression. He had just started to see a clearing when Michael was killed. He was suddenly in a place where he had to be the strong one and he hadn't known if he was ready.

George had met Michael in medical school and had known immediately that he was perfect for Jessica. He was tall, dark and handsome and had that weird sense of humor that he knew Jessica would appreciate. As soon as he introduced them he knew that he was right. After dating for two years they married in a simple but beautiful ceremony performed by Michael's dad. George had been worried for Jessica that Michael's parents would not approve of an interracial marriage but his concerns were unfounded. Lebron and Sasha treated Jessica as the daughter they never had, and were completely smitten with Karen upon her arrival.

Karen was only five years old when Michael was attacked while walking home from a late night in the hospital. The senselessness of it made it so much harder to accept. He wasn't even robbed. The three young men who were convicted of the murder just described a night when they were bored and looking for excitement. Their lawyers blamed a poor upbringing and a lack of a good male figure in their lives as the reason. George had been there with Jessica every day during the trial, once having to leave the room to vomit after seeing the graphic photos of Michael's beaten body. How the jury could come to a verdict of involuntary manslaughter after seeing those photos he would never understand. Those men were out of jail before Karen even entered middle school. During the trial George confessed to Jessica that he felt guilty for even introducing her to Michael because of this horrible pain. It was the only time he could remember seeing her really angry with him. "I would never give up a moment that I had with Michael, and I would not have Karen if you hadn't introduced us. Put that thought out of your head and never let it back in," she had declared.

George had admired Jessica for how she had gone on with her life, being strong for Karen, but he realized now that she had never really gotten past the loss. As far as he knew Jessica had never dated anyone since Michael's death. Nevertheless, she had been overjoyed for George when he introduced her to Becky. Jessica had stood with Becky at the altar when Lebron pronounced George and Becky man and wife. If she found it painful she never said so. Since then he saw her rarely, keeping up with her through her social website via Becky. George said a prayer asking for wisdom, looked down at his Device and pressed a key, spoke the name "Jessica" and waited            for            her            response.

# CHAPTER SIX
··· ◇ ···

Jessica's eyes darted to the screen when she heard the ping. Despite the seriousness of the situation she allowed herself a smile. After all this time it was good to know that she and George were still on the same wavelength. She accepted the call.

"What are you smiling about? Did you see the news?" George started in before either had said hello.

"Yes, I had my Device in my hand ready to call you," she replied.

"I really never thought it would come to this," George said, running his hand through his thinning hair.

"Honestly, I never did either. Maybe we are over-reacting. Do you think that's possible?"

"Very possible, but how would we know? I go to church, but I'm no expert on end times prophesy. We won't be able to tell from the news if this is causing a stir, GTV would never air it," said George, thinking aloud. "How will we know if we are the only ones who think this is what we think it is?"

"People will start talking, that can't be controlled," said Jessica. "Maybe we should talk to Lebron. Maybe he can set us straight. Do you think I should give him a call?"

"Jessica, I don't want to go all cloak-and-dagger on you but I don't think this topic is a good idea for Device communication. This is a face-to-face discussion only. In fact, we should really watch what words we use right now."

"Ok, you're right. Did you talk to Becky yet?"

"Yeah, she thought I was going to tell her about a love child or something," said George, smiling rakishly despite himself.

Jessica laughed out loud.

"Hey, what's so funny about that? You know how the babes loved me in college!" George said laughing along. "Speaking of college, you know who else we have to contact."

"I know. I haven't had any communication with him since college – have you?"

"Yes, he called me for some medical advice a few years ago. He gave me his private number to use in case I needed anything. I doubt he was thinking of this possibility then."

George and Jessica were quiet for a moment, both contemplating the next move. There was nothing awkward about the silence, as is the case with very old friends.

Jessica spoke first. "How about this: I will call Lebron and Sasha and invite them over to my house for dinner with you and Becky. I won't tell them why, of course, but I may have to come up with something believable, or they are going to think there is something wrong with me or Karen. They only live two hours away but I can't even remember the last time they were over."  Actually she could remember, it was Karen's high school graduation three years prior. "That way we could discuss it without worrying about who might be listening. At least I hope that is true in our homes at least!  You call Josh and see what he has to say about it. He may have some information we don't have."

"That's very possible. I'd better do it now before I talk myself out of it," said George.

"Good luck with that - and George, thanks for remembering," said Jessica, suddenly feeling very emotional.

"Back at ya," said George with a smile. "Now go make your call and let me know the date and time. We'll be there."

George tapped off and spent another minute staring at his Device. He knew if he didn't call soon he would think of a million reasons why he shouldn't. Finally he pressed a button and said "Josh Davis" into the Device and waited, staring at the screen. He had almost given up when he heard a ping and there was Josh in the corner of the screen, hair a little greyer than the last time George saw him but otherwise well preserved.

"Doc!" Josh said in a jovial voice.

"Hello, Senator," said George, smiling at his old friend.

# CHAPTER SEVEN
··· ◇ ···

Jessica contemplated her conversation with George. She really wasn't sure what she had been hoping for – him to agree with her or to tell her she was completely off base. Oh well, now she had an assignment and so did George. Jessica returned her attention to the screen and logged in long enough to indicate that she was taking a personal day. She knew that would raise some eyebrows since she couldn't remember that last time she took a personal day.

Jessica thought carefully about what she wanted to tell her in-laws. Of course they would be happy to hear from her; they were very easy to get along with and had always been very supportive of her, especially after Michael's death. During the months afterward her mother-in-law had taken the place of her own mother by her side. Thankfully Jessica didn't remember too much about that time of her life, but she knew that somehow Karen had remained in school, the laundry got done and food was on the table- something she knew she could not have accomplished on her own. Jessica would be forever grateful to Sasha for that, knowing that Sasha was grieving just as much as she was at the time. Jessica thought for a second about how horrible it would be to lose your child, your only child, but the pain of even the thought was too great.

"Focus, focus," Jessica told herself as she prepared to make the call. She picked up her Device, spoke her in-laws' names and looked at the screen. After a moment she saw the strong, smiling face of Lebron on her screen. Jessica hoped he didn't hear her sharp intake of breath as she looked at him; the resemblance to Michael was indisputable. She felt herself being distracted by the thought that she would have loved to grow old with Michael. She reeled herself back, knowing there were important matters at hand.

"Well, well young lady, to what do we owe this honor?" her father-in-law boomed. When Lebron spoke you always thought his next words might be 'Ho, ho, ho!' He just had that wonderful of a voice. Sometimes he sang at church and his voice carried throughout the church without a microphone. "Did Karen win another honor? Has mom called to brag to the only people who would always want to hear such things?"

"Actually, I called to ask the two of you to dinner," Jessica said with a bit of a shaky smile.

Lebron was silent. His jovial face fell. Looking over his shoulder he called out "Sasha, you had better come over here." As he turned back to the screen Jessica saw Sasha's head peak over his shoulder.

"Oh, Jessica, it's wonderful to see you! What's going on? Lebron sounded alarmed when he called me over."

"Nothing is going on, I just want you guys to come over for dinner," Jessica said, trying to sound casual. Now Sasha's face fell and she met Lebron's eyes as he turned to look at her.

"You can tell us, sweetie. We love you and you know we will do anything in our power to help you. Are you sick? Oh, no, is it Karen?" Sasha's hand flew to her mouth. Lebron looked like he was about to cry. Jessica had never known a man as free with his emotions as her father-in-law.

"I promise you it is nothing like that. You know I would never lie to you. I just have a proposition for you. I need for you to tell me what you think about it. It is pretty involved and you have some special expertise that I need," Jessica said with a strong voice. She really needed them to believe that there was nothing being withheld. Leaving them to worry between now and the dinner was just cruel.

"What kind of expertise could a preacher and retired school teacher have for you?" asked Sasha warily.

"If I tell you now it will ruin it!" Jessica said. "Please just trust me on this one. George and Becky want to come too and you haven't seen them in years."

"Of course we will come," said Lebron. "We don't have

anything this weekend, how about Saturday? And lunch would probably be better, that way we could get back before dark. My eyes aren't what they used to be, you know, and I don't want to be a hazard on the road. Ok with you, Sasha?" Sasha looked like she was not completely buying Jessica's explanation, but she was obviously eager to come.

"We'd love to. Can I bring something?"

"No, Mom. Just bring yourselves. It will be fun to have people to prepare food for. I miss that with Karen gone. Now drive safely, and I will see you about noon on Saturday."

They said their goodbyes and then tapped off. Jessica let out a breath she didn't even know she was holding. Both Lebron and Sasha were very intuitive. She could only hope that they just thought she was nervous about her "proposition". Which, of course, she was. Talking about Karen made Jessica realize that she should call and invite Karen as well. This was turning into quite a party. Excitement mingled with anxiety as she turned back to the screen to make the call.

"What's up, Mom?" asked Karen, sounding a little out of breath. Jessica rarely called Karen, thinking it was better to wait for her to call due to the busy schedule of a college student. "I was just on the exercise bike – I am glad they never perfected smell-o-vision!"

Jessica laughed. "I just wanted to see what you were up to on Saturday. I am having Gram and Gretz over and wanted to see if, by any chance, you could come. Becky and George are coming too." Jessica smiled as she remembered Lebron trying to get baby Karen to say "Gramps", the name he had chosen for himself. But children have a way of naming the grandparents regardless of their desires, and Gretz was the name she had chosen. Oh, no, here was the same look on Karen's face that she had just seen on her grandparents'.

"I know, I know, I never get together with anyone, but I want to talk about something with everyone together. And no, I am not sick, no one is sick, it is just a lunch and discussion. Can you make it?"

"Mom, I just talked to you yesterday and you didn't say anything about this. What happened?"

The look on Karen's face made Jessica realize that she was going to have to give her daughter some explanation. Karen had been a stubborn child, which at the time was sometimes frustrating, but it translated well into her adult personality as perseverance. "Ok," Jessica said. "Something did come up – I will explain when you get here."

Karen still didn't look convinced but she said "You know what, I think I can come. I will check the bus schedule and see when I can get there. I will probably stay until Sunday and then head back. I would bring Taylor, but he has a meeting on Saturday."

Jessica was secretly relieved. She did want to meet Taylor but this really didn't seem like the right time for that. It seemed to her that the fewer people they involved in these planning stages the better. Not to mention, Jessica did not want Karen's new boyfriend to think they were all crazy. She and Karen talked for a few more minutes about the details and then said goodbye. Karen seemed quite excited to be coming home. It had been, what, three months since the semester started? It would be good to have her home even if only for a little while.

Jessica considered her next step. She really wanted to know if George had gotten through to Josh, but she didn't want to interrupt their call. If she called now, George would probably just invite her into the conversation and she really would rather he dealt with Josh. Politics had changed Josh, and not for the better. From what she could tell from GTV, he had lost his heart for the poor and downtrodden. She remembered a time when Josh had convinced George and her to go out to the homeless camp with food every Thursday. "The Three Poin-kateers" he called our little troupe. Jessica had initially been terrified, but then came to know the homeless men and women and recognized the struggles they had with mental illness, addiction, bad decisions and, sometimes, just bad luck. Now he seemed to be on the side of mandatory institutionalization of all of the homeless, presenting it as a step up in their lives, of course paid for by an increase in taxes. Anyone who had been among those people as he had been would know what a tortured life that would be for them. Had he forgotten and was really doing what he thought was best or was he just supporting the government enforcers? From the other government takeovers he supported she had to believe it was the latter. It was hard to align the two Joshes in her mind – they were so different. Jessica had lost track of Josh after college. She wondered what had drawn him to politics and to the ideas he now espoused.

"So, what shall I do now?" she asked aloud to get herself back on track. Well, even though it was still a few days away, she could plan for her lunch on Saturday. Thinking about it made acid rise into her chest, but she was just going to have to ignore that and get through it. Come on, it is her best friend, his wife, her in-laws and her daughter. These were the people who loved her most in the world – why was she so scared of them? Jessica tried to remember the last time she had anyone into the house besides Karen. Three years ago, she realized, for Karen's graduation, she had the same people over for the celebration. She tried to recapture the excited but relaxed feeling she had back then, but failed. "Oh well," she continued aloud, "just push through. You can do it." Finished with her little pity party/pep rally, she turned to her screen and contemplated a menu. Jessica realized that she should have asked Sasha if there were any special foods she should avoid. Sasha struggled with Crohn's disease, a disease yet to be cured or even fully understood, resulting in intestinal inflammation causing pain and bleeding. She had forgotten to even ask her about it. Jessica knew Sasha was on some pretty strong medications that were very expensive, and that she was very careful not to eat any dairy products, so she would just offer a variety of foods for her to choose among. Another call might open up opportunities for more questions and Jessica was feeling pretty lucky to have gotten off the phone without an inquisition.

Jessica thought of a few items including soup, salad and sandwiches, as well as some herbal tea and sparkling water. After checking her cabinets she put together a grocery list and submitted it with a click of her device. Almost immediately a light flashed on her screen and a disembodied voice cried "Fraud alert, Fraud alert, Fraud alert!" Jessica was startled and a little scared. "Wait a minute. Why I am scared? I haven't done anything wrong. I am just on edge," she thought. On the screen came a pleasant appearing young woman.

"Hello, Jessica Morrow, this is Brenda, with Government Fraud Prevention. How are you today?"

Jessica was glad she had dressed before placing the order. She realized that there was no ping, no request to accept the call. Apparently niceties like that were unnecessary when investigating fraud.

"I'm fine. I think I know what this is about. I am having a couple of friends over for lunch on Saturday, so my grocery order came at a different time and was unusual for me."

"Yes, exactly. Well I see that you match the picture on your government ID that is connected to your device, so I am so sorry to have bothered you, but certainly you understand our continued fight with fraud. We look forward to new technology that will help us with this economic threat," Brenda gave her a big white smile. She could easily have fit in with the newscasters Jessica had watched this morning.

Feeling it was important to keep her cards very close to her chest, Jessica replied, "Yes, I appreciate the issue you are dealing with, but luckily this time it's just a little lunch party with friends," mirroring the smile she saw on the screen.

"I will make a note of it. Thank you for your cooperation, and good-bye!" said Brenda from Government Fraud, and the screen went blank.

"Well that's a first for me," Jessica thought. Something about the whole interaction really unnerved her but she couldn't quite put her finger on it.

# CHAPTER EIGHT
··· ◇ ···

"So Poin, what's the occasion?" said Josh with a half-smile. Recent history told him that calls from George tended to be bad news, but his old friend didn't look sad or happy either for that matter. He looked more anxious, or maybe a little angry. Years in politics had helped Josh learn a lot about body language. He considered himself somewhat of an expert in telling what people's emotions were, or whether they were lying to him. This skill had proven invaluable in his work with other politicians as well as with reading the faces of his constituents and even entire crowds.

"Before I say anything, is this a monitored line?" George assumed that Josh's personal line was unmonitored by the government, but he had to make sure. Only government officials were allowed to have an unmonitored line which was deemed necessary for Homeland Security reasons.

Josh looked startled. "George, you are scaring me. Do you have some kind of confession to make or something?" George looked at him impatiently. "Ok, no, it isn't monitored. I promise. Now what is up with you?"

"Did you see the GTV Am Newscast this morning?" said George, coming right to the point.

"No, I didn't. Rachel had all of the screens full in the kitchen when I was having breakfast. And the Newscast wasn't one of them. What has gotten you so upset?" Now he knew that it was anxiety he was seeing. That along with the anger, and a little fear mixed in. Josh quickly thought about what had been released to the GTV for broadcast in the last few days. Yes, something was there but he couldn't quite grab onto it.

"Josh, what do you know about the device verification implant? You know, the one with the overlying *mark?*" George could hear the rise in the pitch of his voice. He hated it when he heard himself whining like that, but it was just a sign of his anxiety. He found that he was becoming angry with Josh, as if he had orchestrated this new technology, or voted for its approval. Actually maybe he had.

Josh was silent for a moment. One problem with being in tune with emotions was that it was impossible not to actually feel some of them yourself. He found that he was becoming a little anxious, too. He purposefully calmed himself and gave the idea some thought. He realized where George was going with this. The tattoo on the hand, the mark of the beast, why had he not considered it? Josh remembered their pact, seemingly lifetimes ago. Surely George was not considering following through with it? So many things had changed since then. George didn't seem to mind that Josh was not immediately answering; it actually seemed to calm him a bit.

"Have you talked with Jessica?" Josh asked.

"Yes, she was just about to call me when I called her. We are going to get together with Lebron to get his thoughts on it. What do you know about this? Are you on any committees that have been working on it?" George felt himself relax. He wasn't sure what he had expected Josh to say, but at least he seemed to be giving the idea some consideration.

"Yes, I have heard about it, and no, I wasn't on any committees studying it. Honestly it just seems the next most logical step in identity theft. It just seems like a great thing. My first thought is that it couldn't be the mark from Revelation because the government does not have any plan to force the citizens to take the implant. It is solely for their own protection."

"Seriously Josh, can't you envision a time that it would be mandatory? I can hear the rationale now – saving the government millions in fraud investigations, medical lawsuits, identification of missing persons, and the list goes on and on!" The more George thought about it the more he realized that what he was saying was true. This was going to become mandatory, and soon.

"George, I need to think some more about this, but my first reaction is that this is not the mark. The bottom line is, we just don't know. What are you proposing?"

"Hey, you are the one that proposed it. Twenty five years ago, remember? You made us promise," George heard that whine coming back into his voice.

Josh laughed. "Seriously? Go off the grid? Things have changed my old friend. I can't just pick up and leave, I have responsibilities! I can't even imagine bringing this up with Rachel. She would laugh me out of the room. We have teenagers in high school, for goodness sake. No, that is just not an option for me."

George was silent for a moment, taking in what Josh had said. His voice took on an icy edge. "You don't think I have responsibilities too?"

Josh shook his head and looked down. "I'm sorry, George, I really am. Tell me what you're thinking."

"I am not saying that Jessica and I have made any decisions; just that we are making some 'what if' plans. What about the farm? Do you still own it?"

"Yes, I took over the taxes when my mom and dad went into the Eldercare Facility. I haven't talked to them lately, but I can't imagine there would be a problem with using it. Even if you guys decide to go and I decide to stay, you would still be welcome to go there. Let me give you the address and you can visualize it on your screen on the e-Earth site." Josh brought up the address on his work screen and recited it to George, who wrote it on a sheet of paper. George had dug up a pad of paper before making this call – hard to find in his house because paper was so rarely used now- but he thought that entering data like this in his device would be unwise. He felt a little bit like a spy. He would not be visualizing this property; that was for sure.

"Ok, Josh, thanks for that. Please don't tell anyone about this, I think if it does come to us leaving the less people that know the better. And thanks for not laughing me out of the room. Do you want me to get back with you after we talk to Lebron or not? If it is an absolute no for you, maybe you really don't care what he has to say. No offense, I just don't want to bug you with this if you think it is wrong."

"No, let me know what he says. This is a good number to call, it will always be unmonitored. Say hi to Jessica, Lebron and Sasha for me, and Becky too. I do miss you guys." Josh had started out just being polite but realized as he was saying it that he really did miss them. Or maybe he just missed that time in his life; it was hard to tweeze that out. Josh and George said goodbye and signed off. The area on the screen taken up with the image of his old friend was absorbed by the other screens he had up – bills on the floor to be reviewed, financial woes, war rumors, and social sites he knew were a bad idea but couldn't seem to turn off, unless someone came in of course. There were so many things to distract him. He would think about all of this later. For now he needed to focus on what was important. His next meeting was with the president, and he had better be prepared.

# CHAPTER NINE
··· ◇ ···

"Look who we found at the bus station!" Lebron boomed, ushering in Karen and Sasha before him. There were smiles and hugs all around as Jessica welcomed her family in. It was hard to believe that just a few minutes ago she had been in such a panic that she was dreading this homecoming. She realized that the whole concept was ridiculous, but she just couldn't shake it. Jessica hoped that it would not take very long for her to adjust to having them here.

"Come on in! Here, let me have your sweaters," said Jessica. It was a bit cool out for an October in Florida, and they were all dressed accordingly. "And let me take your bag, Karen."

"Mom, don't make me feel like a guest in my own house! I know where my bedroom is – you didn't turn it into an exercise room or something while I was gone did you?"

Jessica laughed. "No, actually it is exactly as you left it – minus a few dust bunnies here and there. Go ahead on up."

Jessica turned to look at her in-laws. They were both scrutinizing her every move. "So did you have a good drive over?" Nods from both. "Doesn't Karen look great?" More nods. "Thanks for picking her up." Smiles and nods.

"Okay guys, I get it. You can hardly contain your curiosity. George and Becky will be here momentarily. We can catch up and then talk after lunch. Does that sound like a plan? Can we just be normal with each other until then?"

Sasha spoke first. "Yes, it is driving us crazy, but I believe we can wait a bit longer," she said with a pointed look at Lebron. "Now, can I help you in the kitchen?"

Jessica breathed a sigh of relief and took her up on the offer. "I hope there is something here for you. I should have asked you ahead of time what you were able to eat."

Sasha sighed, "I wish I knew. I never have really been able to pin down what the offender is, if there is one. For now I just avoid milk and soy products and that seems to help. And the medicines help too. I'm sure I won't starve!" she commented. Actually Jessica wasn't so sure of that. Sasha had the gaunt look of someone who is malnourished. She moved slowly and was obviously in pain. Jessica felt guilty about piling on stress, a known contributor to Crohn's.

Soon Karen and Lebron came in, too, laughing about something. The sound of the laughter and the presence of these people that she loved relaxed something in her that she realized had been as tight as a rubber band stretched to its maximum. As Sasha and Jessica chopped vegetables for the salad and made sandwiches, Lebron and Karen looked on. The chatter seemed so foreign, yet so comfortable. The doorbell on Jessica's Device rang, and there were George and Becky on the kitchen screen, waving as they walked up, caught on camera as they approached the door. Jessica rushed to greet them, gave them hugs and a few knowing, anxious looks before bringing them into the kitchen with the rest of the clan.

"Hey you two, long time no see!" said Lebron. Sasha and Jessica set the sandwiches and the salad out on the counter and handed out plates. Each took a place around Jessica's tiny kitchen table or perched at the counter on bar stools.

"I'm sorry I don't have much room for entertaining. It's a good thing we have a small family!"

The guests laughed and thanked Jessica for getting them all together. Before she knew it, lunch was finished. As Lebron and Karen cleaned up, Jessica made coffee and small talk. Eventually they all gravitated to the living room, taking up positions on the sofa, pulling up chairs, and, in Karen's case, plopping on the floor. Suddenly there was quiet and all eyes were on Jessica. She felt her heart rate rising and her hands were suddenly sweaty.

"So, I guess you are all wondering why I have brought you here," said Jessica in a mock serious tone, garnering smiles all around. "Well let me start by telling a story."

The next few minutes were spent telling the old college story, George adding bits and pieces and nodding his agreement with how the events had occurred. Then they fast forwarded to the morning a few days before when they both heard the newscast, their reactions, and what Josh had to say about it. "And that kind of brings us up to date I guess," concluded Jessica with a nervous little laugh. She looked at Karen who closely resembled a deer in headlights, and then at Lebron and Sasha who looked like this was old news.

"Ok enough silence, what do you think? Are George and I making a mountain out of a molehill?" Jessica found that she was hoping that Lebron would shoot the theory down with just a word.

Lebron looked at Sasha before speaking and Jessica saw her give him an almost imperceptible nod.

"Do I think you are crazy? No. I wish I did. This is something I have been preaching about in my church for years now. The signs have been there, but no one would listen. I could actually see the eye rolls and head shakes every time I started discussing eschatology. It got to where the elders of the church approached me and said that people were asking them to counsel me about this 'crazy end-times' talk. I was starting to wonder about it myself until I got a letter from the government."

"What?" George said, startled. "What would government want with you?"

"The letter said that they had information that I was talking about the One World Government and Global Banking and the parallels with prophetic books in the Bible, especially Revelation. They said that if I continued to discuss politics from the pulpit our tax-exempt status would be revoked. Of course I shared the letter with the elders who I thought would be incensed at the government for their intrusion. On the contrary, they tried to convince me that the government was right; that what I was preaching in my sermons was outside of my realm of authority. I told them that my 'realm of authority' included everything in the Bible including the prophesies, but their eye was on the dollar." Lebron looked at Sasha and she reached over and took his hand. "So they told me that I have two choices. Stop the discussion of Revelation as it relates to today's world, or retire. Now." Tears welled up in Lebron's eyes and his voice choked up as he finished his story. Tears streamed down Sasha's face as she squeezed his hand, and the rest of them looked on in shocked silence.

"I had no idea," said Becky. "I haven't heard any of this at our church, and I am there every week. Do you think they were all warned?"

"I really don't think so, I just think that many churches have settled into the 'God is love' sort of mentality. Now don't get me wrong, God is love for sure, but God is also expecting something from us – obedience and worship. I wonder how many people actually read the Bible any more, or even have one, outside of the condensed, simplistic form that is available on their Device." At that, everyone except Sasha looked around and squirmed a bit in their seats.

Jessica spoke up. "I will admit it, Lebron. I have been lax on my Bible study. I got my Bible down after I heard this and tried to read through Revelation but I was lost after chapter one."

Lebron laughed. "So you thought you would just dive right into the most intricate, symbolic, prophetic book of the Bible and just breeze through it? People have spent their whole lives studying it and many very knowledgeable scholars completely disagree on the basic timelines. But without going into all of that, what you are asking really is this – could this implantable chip and its overlying tattoo be the mark of the beast that is described in the Bible? Yes, I do believe it could be."

Jessica looked at Karen, suddenly wondering if having her come was such a good idea. Maybe this was too much for her. Jessica recognized Karen's furrowed brow and pursed lips as a sign of her deep thought. She had obviously taken it all in and was nearing her tipping point. Then it was Karen's turn to speak.

"As a history major, I can see that what is going on in the world is leading to something really big. I won't pretend to be an expert on the Bible, but I have studied it as part of my faith as well as in school as a record of history. I don't know anything about the mark of the beast, Revelation, or the end times, but I know this. The people I love the most are in this room, and if you guys are going somewhere, I am coming with you." At that point tears began flowing from all of the eyes in the room.

"'Dark and difficult times lie ahead. Soon we must all face the choice between what is right and what is easy,'" quoted George.

They all pondered that and Jessica said, "Very deep, George, is that from the Bible? Proverbs maybe?"

"I know this one," said Becky, smiling. "Albus Dumbledore from Harry Potter." They all laughed and George defended himself. "What! It was appropriate!"

Still laughing, they wandered back to the kitchen to make some plans and eat dessert.

# CHAPTER TEN
... ◇ ...

Goodbye, everyone! See you all soon!" Jessica called out to the receding forms of George, Becky and her in-laws. She watched them as they said a few parting words to each other, got into their cars and departed. Karen went up to take a shower and Jessica sat down on the couch and reviewed the plan.

They all had their jobs now, each fashioned to their strengths. Lebron promised to try to summarize the Bible prophesies related to the mark and Sasha said she would write up his summary in a way they could understand it. Sasha was also to look into getting some teaching materials for Maya and Mark. This would be an undertaking since they had all decided that there would be no use of Devices for anything in any way related to this research. They would have to use some ingenuity and old-school techniques to bring this all together. Becky was given energy production, water and sanitation as her focus. Her work in engineering gave her some unique insights into these topics. In addition, her mission work had exposed her to societies that had little or even no access to electricity. Obviously they would need to be off the grid, and her job was to figure out the way to do it. George would start gathering medical supplies and learning about natural forms of healing.

Jessica would be in charge of food, quite a daunting task. She realized that she would need to start now in order to keep from attracting attention. Her "fraud alert" experience had taught her that she would not be able to just stock up with big purchases without attracting attention, so she would have to figure out another way. Her additional jobs were to keep the communication flowing and to figure out where this farm actually was without using her Device. That could really be a challenge. Karen had been eager to have a job, but she was so busy with school that it was hard to know what to assign to her. In the end they decided that she would keep an eye on the changing winds in politics and try to keep them abreast of the changes. Also, she would keep a collection of pertinent history books and various pieces of literature on her device rather than getting rid of them, with the hopes that Becky would be able to figure out a way to use the storage on the devices while disabling the GPS.

Jessica thought back to Josh's warning about the risk of what they were considering. Even so, Jessica felt more alive right now than she had in a long time. This certainly should have set off all sorts of anxiety bells but it didn't. It just had a "rightness" about it.

"Of course, none of this may ever come to pass," she said aloud, "We are getting prepared just in case."

"Geez, mom, first you call that meeting, and now you are out here talking to yourself. What's a daughter to think?" Karen said as she came down the stairs, combing out her hair from the shower. Jessica looked embarrassed, but Karen just shook her head and laughed, "I'm just kidding, you are the sanest person I know. That is what makes this all the more bizarre, for sure."

"Karen, there is something I did want to talk to you about," Jessica said motioning to the couch, where they took their usual places. "I know this a tough topic but I need to talk to you about Taylor. I don't know how close you are and whether you would think you need to talk to him about this, but I am asking you to wait for at least a little while until we have a better handle on things. Do you think that is reasonable?"

Karen considered what her mother was proposing. She would feel bad about keeping something this important from Taylor. Also, she would want to ask his advice on things, and confide her fears. How would he feel if and when she finally did tell him, knowing that she had been hiding this because she didn't trust him? And how would she keep him from taking the mark if he didn't even know there was a controversy?

"But if we did go, what then? Would I just leave him behind without even telling him about it and giving him the chance to save himself? I don't know, Mom, he may be the one I want to spend my life with. I don't know if I could walk away without giving him the option to come too. Are you saying that you wouldn't want him to come?"

"No, I am not saying that at all. I just don't know where his loyalties lie. Isn't he at college on a Homeland Security grant? I know that they have to make certain promises, and it wouldn't be fair to him to put him in a position where he had to choose between you and the grant. Just give it a little time, let's find out more about the situation, and if you feel the time is right and you need to let him know, I will trust your judgment. How does that sound?"

Karen thought for a minute. "Reasonable," she declared. "Now let's talk about your job in this. What about food production? I know it is a farm, but it's not a working farm. We wouldn't arrive and find fields planted with vegetables and such. I know you work in agriculture but aren't you more on the pesticide and fertilizer part not the seeds? How can you obtain seeds without drawing attention to yourself?"

"Hmmm," pondered Jessica. It was going to be even harder than Karen realized. The vast majority of the plants grown in the Americas came from commercial seeds. That means that you can't just collect seeds from plants and plant them and expect them to grow. Seeds are engineered to produce plants with sterile seeds so that the farmer must buy new seeds every year. Even if a farmer has heirloom seeds, that is, seeds from old plants that produce fertile seeds, and he grows them, he can't sell the produce because it may have unintentionally cross- pollinated with one of the plants from the commercial seed companies and he could be sued. Suddenly Jared Brown popped into her head. Her boss was always trying to get her to go visit her clients. The personal aspect was really important to her boss, but she had never done any visits because it made her so anxious. Well, maybe now was the time to visit Jared Brown. She told Karen about Jared and his family, about his recent invitation to visit, and asked her opinion.

"What a great idea!" Karen exclaimed. "Now the same thing goes for him you know. It sounds like you know him, but you really don't know where his head is at politically or religiously. You would have to tread very carefully when asking him questions."

"You are right, sweetie. It will be hard because I get such a good feeling about him and his family, but I will be careful about what I divulge. I will textmail corporate on Monday and ask if I can make that trip."

Jessica felt a familiar tightness developing in her chest and throat.

"OK, I think I have had about all can take on this subject. Tell me about what's going on with you and college and friends and all that. I feel like a stalker sometimes when I am checking out your social network site, but I feel like I know these kids."

Karen laughed and filled Jessica in on the goings on at the University of Florida. It seemed like Karen had a fun, smart, grounded group of friends. How would she be able to leave them and settle in with two senior citizens, three middle-aged people and two little kids? Was she thinking this through? And what if she decided not to go, how could Jessica leave her behind?

# CHAPTER ELEVEN
··· ◇ ···

Lebron and Sasha drove home in silence, each thinking about the responsibilities that they had been assigned. Lebron thought about the prophesies and scriptures that he wanted to share. He also thought about the world events that backed up these prophesies, some having already come to pass and some still in the future. There was so much controversy among Bible scholars as to the meaning of the scriptures relating to the end-time events, who was he to say his view was right? Possibly all that mattered was that a person should be ready to meet his Maker at any time – whether by death or by Second Coming. And if events of the time, such as this mark, seem to an individual to be that which is prophesied, he must pray about it and ask for guidance about what to do. It was this tact that Lebron decided to take. When he got home he would get on his knees and ask for guidance concerning what to relay to his friends and family. He would ask for wisdom and the strength to follow through with what he felt God was calling him to do. He also needed wisdom to know what to tell his church, and who, if anyone, he should tell about his plans. He was terrified and excited all at once. Lebron thought about Karen, and how different a prospect this was for her than for him. He was at the end of his life, while hers was just beginning. How much more difficult this idea must be for her. In addition, her dependence on technology was much more ingrained than it was for him. She had never known a time when there was not constant access to the internet and other technologies. The change for her would be so much greater. But then again, how awful if she decided to stay behind and take the mark; it would break his heart. He also worried about Sasha. Her disease was kept at bay with expensive, intravenous drugs. He hated the thought of what might happen to her if she was not able to get them.

Next to him Sasha was lost in her own thoughts and plans. She would need to look back in her old lessons for what Maya and Mark would be learning in the next few years. So much of that would be on the internet, but if she accessed it that way it might send up some red flags. She would have to look back and see if she had any notes on paper or old textbooks she could bring. She would have liked to have ordered new books for them, but that would cause a fraud alert since her teaching license was no longer active. This would take some finesse and a constant assessment of danger.

Sasha gazed out the window. She knew what was going on in her husband's mind. The furrowed brow, so much like Karen's, told her that he was trying to figure out what he was going to pass on to the group. Then the worried look and a few furtive glances in her direction clued her in that he was thinking about her and what might transpire if she stopped her meds. She knew she should also be worried but for some reason she was not. She had a peaceful feeling when she thought about it.

"Lebron, I know you are worried about me and that the Crohn's might become really bad if I stop taking my medicines," Sasha stated.

Lebron glanced over at her. After so many years of marriage he shouldn't have been surprised that Sasha knew what he was thinking. "Are you worried about that too?" he asked.

"Well, I know that it would be logical for me to be worried but I'm not. And I don't think you should be either. I really get the sense that I will be alright but even if I'm not, what would that change? I won't ask you to stay behind and where you go I go too. There really isn't a choice for me anyway," she concluded.

Lebron thought for a moment. "Well, when you put it that way I guess you are right. I just can't stand the thought of you suffering. That is what I worry about."

"Ok, then that is what we will ask of George. Of course he would never be able to bring the Crohn's disease medicines, but he may be able to bring some medicines to alleviate the pain. Would that make you feel better?"

Lebron considered it for a moment. "Yes, I believe it would. At our next gathering we can ask him about it." He reached across the car's console and took Sasha's hand in his and, drawing it to his face, kissed the back of her hand. "But now and always we can ask the greatest healer to be with us, guide us and protect us, help us as we make these decisions and give us peace."

"Amen," said Sasha.

# CHAPTER TWELVE
··· ◇ ···

George and Becky got into the car at Jessica's townhouse and sat quietly for a minute. George felt a need to compose himself before turning the car on for the short drive home. He still felt an adrenaline surge from the group's discussion. They were all surprised at the news of Lebron's difficulties with his church regarding this issue. George wondered how he would have reacted if his pastor had begun discussing these topics so frankly if he hadn't already been primed by Josh. Honestly, he may have had the same reaction – and been concerned about the government cutting off the tax-free status. How would Becky's mission team be able to function with funds so tight already? He shouldn't be so hard on the members of Lebron's congregation even if they were wrong. After a few deep breaths George looked over at Becky who was looking straight ahead. He wondered if she had even noticed that the car wasn't moving.

George thought about his assignment. Obviously, he was in charge of the medical end of things, but he wasn't completely sure how he was going to pull it off. He couldn't steal from his partners. Maybe he could total up the cost of the things he ordered and took with him and leave the money in the partnership account. He wouldn't need money if they left anyway, and if they never left he could just use the supplies in the practice. As for medicines, that would be trickier. There were a few medicines given to him by the companies as samples that would be a possibility. Other medicines would need to be prescribed to someone, and to do so under false pretenses would be insurance fraud. He wanted to research sources of medicines in nature, especially in the area of North Carolina where they were going. George thought that this could be done without causing any alarms since he was a doctor and would naturally have an interest in such things. He would ask Becky if she had any information about medicines used in third world countries by natural healers. Plus there were a lot of medicines that were now over the counter that he could get, and he would ask the others in the group to pick up some too, so he wouldn't appear to be stockpiling. George worried about Sasha and her dependence on prescription meds that he could not get for her. He would see what he could get in the way of pain medicines to help her through the rough times. On the other hand, he had patients with Crohn's who had experienced great improvements by getting all of the processed food out of their diets, and they certainly wouldn't have access to processed foods. Then, of course, their biggest worry –Maya and Mark. What would they be doing to their children by taking them away from their peers and their education? Sasha had been a great teacher but that was years ago and how would she obtain any of the materials she would need? George knew that Maya and Mark would have a tremendous adjustment to make but his limited experience with pediatric patients during medical school had shown him that kids are incredibly resilient, it was their parents who suffered the most with change and loss.

Next to him Becky was feeling very anxious. Of all of them, she should be the most at ease with the idea of striking out into the semi-wilderness; she had done it several times now in the mission field. But not, however, since she had become a parent. Oh, how that changed everything. Her faith was strong though, and she knew that if Lebron had been on this same track there must be some validity to it. She was anxious to read his explanation of the mark. Meanwhile, she had a lot of work to do. Her first job was to figure out a power source. There were several options for power, many of which she had used in her mission work, but she would have to take into consideration the very limited packing space they would have. Solar arrays could be rolled up like a blanket and packed into a very small space. Unfortunately, they would be very obvious to the GPS drones that updated the e-Earth maps for the government. If there was a river nearby they might be able to use that, but the equipment might be difficult to pack. She would have to research that. Also, she was in charge of clean water. This shouldn't be too difficult, as there were several commercial filters available to buy. The problem with both the array and the filter was that she would have to come up with some good reason to buy them. Maybe she could sign up for another mission trip in order to fly under the government radar, but she felt dishonest doing that knowing that she didn't intend to go. Or maybe she could buy two of each and list the reason as a donation for a mission trip and donate one and keep one. That sounded like a better option. It was a good thing they weren't going to need money because this was going to drain their savings. The last thing she needed to figure out was whether or not the Devices could be used once the GPS was disabled. Her gut feeling was no, and she would have to be very careful not to cause any alarms while she was trying to figure it out. Of course, once the GPS was disabled the alarms would definitely go off. It would probably make sense to leave most of the Devices at their homes to delay detection. If they could bring one with books and texts on it for education purposes that would be ideal.

Becky suddenly realized that they were in the driveway at their home and the car was off. She hadn't even remembered pulling out of Jessica's driveway. It was going to be hard to concentrate on her everyday life with difficult tasks ahead. She turned to look at George, who was looking at her with worry creasing his face. She reached over and laid her hand on his cheek. "I know you feel responsible for this, George, but you shouldn't. You may very well have saved me from an eternity in hell, how can I thank you for that?"

George laughed. "We'd better go inside before the babysitter wonders what we are up to out here."

# CHAPTER THIRTEEN
... ◇ ...

Josh was lost in thought as he drove to church. Rachel and the kids shared the car with him but each was absorbed in their own Device. Rachel was textmailing so fast that her fingers seemed to blur like a character in a cartoon, and the kids were listening to music. He felt completely alone. He thought about the conversation with George and wondered if anything had come of it. Josh thought again about how Rachel would react if he brought up the idea of going off of the grid. Although they were here in church every Sunday, he doubted that she would embrace the kind of sacrifice for faith they were talking about.

They arrived at church and stepped out of the car. Rachel smiled and called out greetings to the other church members. As they walked into the church, Josh noted Ben and Hannah's clothes. They were dressed like all of the other teenagers in the service, with strategically placed holes in their clothes to showcase their tattoos, hair spilling out of their hats, and heavy makeup. On the girls it was bad enough, but Josh could never get used to the boys wearing makeup. He was all for being comfortable and letting kids show their individuality in school, but it just seemed like church was a place to dress a little more respectfully. Rachel disagreed. She felt that as long as they were there, that was all that mattered. The service began, as always, with announcements. The number of service projects and special events seemed endless. At one point, the ministers asked Rachel to come up and discuss one of the projects that she was heading up, the Winterfest. Josh made a mental note to ask her about that later. He wondered what he could do to help. He also wondered why it was called a Winterfest and not a Christmas celebration. As she sat back down he put his arm around her protectively and gave her a squeeze. She turned and smiled at him. Then the band began to play and the screen changed from a picture of a cross to the words of the song.

Josh thought about how different these services were from the Catholic masses of his youth. The church he had attended had been more modern than his grandfather's church, which held the masses in Latin even to this day, but still had a high level of respect and a solemn tone to the worship time. When he was in college, Josh had become disillusioned with the Catholic Church amid the scandals of priests preying on young boys and the church's attempt to cover it up. He also had a problem with praying to statues of Mary and the saints which he thought of as idols, and with the power of the Pope to make changes in the belief structure. When Josh met Rachel she introduced him to her non-denominational Protestant church where he felt much more at home. It definitely caused a problem for his parents, though. He hoped that the tears his mother shed at his wedding were those of happiness but he had always been afraid to ask.

Since that time, though, the casual nature and the tolerance for all views as acceptable seemed to be more and more the norm. The emphasis on reaching out to all was commendable, but at some point there has to be a stand taken, or why even call it a church? The most disturbing thing he had heard lately was the minister leading the group prayer to the "God of our understanding". Josh remembered this term from the Al-Anon meetings he had gone to in the wake of his sister's death. He found it very appropriate there among people of variety of faiths but questioned it in a Christian setting. Even so, the youth group was good, and there were a lot of things that Rachel was involved in so he had decided not to make waves. Josh knew there were some "churches" now that had been created by people who enjoyed the social aspects of the church but did not believe in God. Josh figured he should satisfied that at least belief in God was acceptable here.

Josh took his arm from around Rachel and settled back to listen to the sermon. As the minister began to speak Josh realized that they were more than half-way through the service and had yet to hear any passages read from the Bible. The thought was that services should be uplifting and entertaining so more people would come. Then once they were there they could be "plugged in" to a small group Bible study. Josh tried to remember if there was any discussion of Bible studies in the announcements, but couldn't recall any. Josh glanced at the program which had auto-loaded onto his Device when they had entered the church. Under the church's name and the date was the church's motto:

*If You Believe It, We Believe It Too*

Focusing his attention back to the front he listened to the minister as he talked about the love of God and finding the presence of God in nature. Josh wondered if he was the only one who found that a bit pagan. Behind the minister was a screen showing images from nature, one after another, each one more spectacular than the last. Josh looked over at his kids, both with a relaxed posture and passive smiles on their faces. Josh was thinking about how happy he was that they were enjoying the sermon when he saw the tell-tale foot tap. He leaned back a little bit and saw that they both were wearing wireless ear buds, small enough to escape casual notice. Of course this was enjoyable-they were listening to music and looking at pretty pictures on the screen! He made a mental note to discuss this with them later. The minister was discussing that we should show the love of God in our interactions with our neighbors ending with "do unto others as they have done unto you".

*Well, that is the problem with paraphrasing right there,* Josh thought. If he had read it directly from the Bible he would have said "Do unto others as you would have them do unto you." Amazing how just a word change or two makes all the difference.

After another rousing and uplifting song, they were off to the fellowship hall where the kids broke off to join their friends and Rachel darted behind the counter for her turn to help with the coffee and doughnuts. Josh braced himself for those that saw this as their opportunity to bend the ear of their appointed government servant, and he was never wrong. As the group thinned, Josh gave the nod to Rachel who forwarded it to each of the kids. They made their way back to the car, waving at friends and promising to see them next week. As they got in the car, Josh asked Ben and Hannah what they thought of the sermon.

"You told us we had to go, you didn't say we had to listen!" Ben exclaimed. Rachel gave Josh a warning look. He knew the old argument – as long as they are there, that is what matters. Really, though? Is that all?

Josh listened to the conversation between Rachel, Hannah and Ben with increasing agitation. It seemed that everyone that they had come in contact with that day had something to be ridiculed about, whether it was their appearance, something they said, or something they were doing. Finally he couldn't hold it in anymore.

"Well if anyone had been listening to the sermon they might have heard that Jesus said we should do unto others as we would have them do unto us. Would you want people talking about you this way?"

There was silence for a minute. Josh thought that perhaps they were thinking about how badly they had behaved. He realized he was wrong when Ben said "Geez, Dad, freak out much?" and all three of them began to laugh. Then, shaking their heads, they all plugged into their devices and Josh was alone again.

# CHAPTER FOURTEEN
... ◇ ...

Karen had a lot of time to think on her three-hour bus ride back to school. The events of the past few days were overwhelming. She thought about Taylor and having to watch what she said to him. They had become so close in the past six months that keeping this from him made her feel terribly guilty.

Karen looked out of the window of the bus into the darkness and smiled as they pulled up to her stop. Illuminated by a street light was Taylor, stretched out on a bench, sound asleep, his long legs dangling off one end. He had insisted on meeting her bus to walk her back to her dorm, citing the recent muggings of female students as his reason. She assured him that she would call security to walk her but he insisted. She had joked with him about bringing along his coat in case there was a mud puddle she might have to cross, but in truth she was very appreciative of his protectiveness. Her mother would say he had been 'brought up right'.

Karen got off of the bus, perched on the bench and put her hand on his shoulder. As she kissed his cheek Taylor jerked upright, a momentary look of confusion on his face as he looked at her and at his surroundings. Then a half-smile crept over his face. That smile was what had drawn her to him. It spoke of a sense of humor that she needed in a boyfriend, or any kind of friend for that matter.

"Come on Sleeping Beauty, I thought you were supposed to be the prince not me," she said jokingly, tousling his blonde hair. Taylor gave her a confused look. Karen remembered that Taylor's parents had never allowed him to read or watch any fairy tales. They thought all of the stories were much too violent – witches, evil stepmothers, poisoned apples and such. Karen had asked her mom about that one time. She said that although the prevailing parenting concept was to protect children from such stories, she had once read a quote from G.K. Chesterton that had made a lot of sense to her. "Fairy tales do not tell children the dragons exist. Children already know that dragons exist. Fairy tales tell children the dragons can be killed." Evil had already touched Karen's life by the time children's stories were being told. There was no denying its existence.

"Never mind, thanks for meeting my bus. I've missed you," Karen said.

"I've missed you too," said Taylor, taking her hand and helping her up from the bench. "So what was the mysterious emergency?"

Karen was dreading this moment. She understood her mother's reluctance to share their plans, but she knew Taylor, and knew she could trust him. In the end she decided to go with what her mom said and just wait until they had a better idea of their options.

"Luckily it was nothing. You know how I told you she has problems with anxiety? Well, she said she just felt a need to see me in person and make sure I was okay. You must think that is kind of weird, huh?"

"Not really. She is there all alone. I bet she can get some pretty ugly scenarios going on in her head. I'm glad you were able to go, I just wish I could have gone with you."

Now she really felt like a heel. How would she be able to keep this from him? Oh well, if it became too awkward she would just tell him after making him pinky-swear, yes, literally pinky-swear, not to tell anyone.

"So how was your weekend?" Karen asked, taking his hand in hers as they walked back to her residence hall. Taylor told her about his meeting on Saturday morning with Homeland Security and about the good time he had hanging out with his fraternity brothers Saturday night. He had been up early this morning putting in the study hours required for his engineering major.

"No wonder you were asleep on that bench, you must be exhausted!" Karen exclaimed. "Now off to bed with you!" she said, having reached the door to her hall.

Taylor pulled her close and kissed her. "But I will be so lonely," he whispered in her ear.

Karen hugged him tightly and whispered back, "Not gonna happen," laughing as she broke away.

"Well, you would wonder about me if I didn't keep trying, right? Call me tomorrow and maybe we can meet up for some chow, okay? I'm glad you're back, I really am."

"I'll call you when I get out of class tomorrow. And thanks again for walking me to my hall, Prince Charming," giving him a peck on the cheek. Taylor smiled. He didn't have to have heard any fairy tales to know that being called Prince Charming is a good thing.

# CHAPTER FIFTEEN
··· ◇ ···

Jessica stared at her Device. She knew the plan was for her to visit Jared and his family and that it would be very interesting for her as well as educational for the group, but rational thought and anxiety often don't share the same stage.

"Just take it one step at a time," she counseled herself. "Lao-tsu said 'the journey of a thousand miles begins with a single step'. Just request authorization for the trip. Just that one thing, then deal with the next step."

Jessica sent the textmail to her boss asking for permission to visit Jared. She didn't want to attract attention by blabbering on and on, so she simply stated that the client had requested a visit, which he had, and that she would like to comply. While Jessica was awaiting his reply she reviewed the products that Jared had used in the past and compiled a list of products to discuss with him for use in the future. She included the fertilizers that she had recently researched as well as a fungicide that was new on the market. Even though she had her own reasons for visiting Jared, Jessica didn't want to feel like she was cheating her company, which she felt had been more than fair and generous to her during her whole career. An hour after sending the message the visit was approved.

*Absolutely!* responded Grady, her boss. *Just forward any expenses directly to me and I will approve them. I don't know what brought this on, but I like it!*

Truthfully, she doubted that he would like it one bit if he knew what brought this on. Step one accomplished, onto the next step.

*Jared, I thought about your invitation to visit and have decided to finally take you up on it. Is the offer still open? Do you have any plans that I need to*

70

*work around? My schedule is pretty open.* Now wasn't that an understatement. Jessica was just about to change sites and do some other work when Jared's response pinged back. *Well of course the offer is still open! In fact this week would be great, next week we start harvesting again, and then we will be taking the crop to market. I would be happy to pick you up at the bus or train station, or at the airport, just let me know!*

So there it was. Jessica expected a surge of panic that didn't come. Something about this just seemed easy and right. *Thanks so much Jared. I will let you know where and when. Also, can you give me the name of the nearest hotel?*

*Hotel! Don't be silly, you can stay here. Besides, there are no hotels for miles.*

Now the familiar panic started in. What if she was trapped there and Jared and his wife ended up being wackos. Jessica had seen enough slasher movies to know that it was always the person you would least expect who ended up being the crazy guy with the machete. 'No hotels for miles' played right into her terrible fantasy. Probably no people for miles, too. "Nobody to hear you scream," she said aloud. Hearing her own voice made her realize how melodramatic and silly she sounded. *That is so kind of you,* she textmailed back. *I will get back to you before the day's end.* And that, as they say, was that.

Jessica started to research her travel plans when she realized that this trip was not only an opportunity for agricultural research, but also for travel research. Having just made this plan to visit her client, naturally she would want to download maps of the area with the types of crops that are grown. She would just make sure to download ones that also had roads on them, and include the area between there and here. If questioned she could say that she was comparing the agriculture needs of the two areas. Jessica jumped up from her desk and went into her bedroom to get the paper George had given her with the farm's coordinates she had hidden in her sock drawer. Returning to her office, she realized that she couldn't enter the coordinates like she normally would or there would be a history of it on her Device. The map that she downloaded would have to also have coordinates on it. Eventually she would need to copy the map onto paper herself, including the roads from Florida. Jessica had no idea if Josh's family farm was anywhere near Jared's, but it shouldn't be too hard to figure out. Jessica spent the next few hours looking at crops grown in the area around Jared's farm, familiarizing herself with the problems requiring her help with products. In addition, she broadened her research to all of North Carolina, finally uploading a map of the state with the roads, coordinates, and primary agriculture. Then she extended it to include coordinates and the route from Florida. Jessica held her breath as she finished her download. If there was going to be an alert she would know within the next few minutes. First one, then two minutes passed. No alert. Even though she would be able to explain, it would still be better not to have the alert in her history.

"Whew, what a relief!" she thought. Then she realized how awful it was that she was so afraid of her own government. She was actually afraid of what they might do to her if she downloaded a map with no good reason! Seriously, how had it come to this? She thought of a quote from David Hume. "It is seldom that liberty of any kind is lost all at once." It had happened slowly, she realized, and on her watch. There were those who had warned that we were choosing security over liberty, but the threat of terrorism was so real and so scary that it seemed worth it. Now, she had her doubts.

As for her upcoming trip, Jessica found that there was a small airport about thirty minutes from the Brown's farm and a flight available in two days. Before she had a chance to change her mind, Jessica notated the flight, forwarded it to Grady for approval, and leaned back in her chair. A ping and a few textmails later her plans were finalized. From his textmails, Jared actually seemed to be looking forward to her visit. He promised fresh vegetables but warned of loud children afoot. Sounded like heaven to Jessica. She punched out for the day and headed for the kitchen. "Punched out". The phrase caught her attention for the first time. Where did that come from? Who was getting punched? And why? She would have to ask Lebron and Sasha the next time they were together.

As Jessica got out her frozen dinner to cook in the microwave her kitchen screen lit up. The corner pinged and displayed

Karen's face. "What great timing!" Jessica said when she accepted the call. "I just finished in the office and had a very productive day."

"Oh, really?" said Karen, "How so?"

"I made an appointment to visit the farmer in North Carolina that I was telling you about. My boss approved it and I leave in two days! Isn't that great?"

"That is so great! Now don't forget to.."

"Yes, to be very, very careful. I know." Jessica tried to telepath her thoughts to her daughter. She didn't want anything that Karen said to be later seen as foreknowledge if she decided to stay. She also didn't want any of their conversation to be seen as threatening.

Karen looked a little confused for a second and then Jessica could tell they were on the same page.

"I spent some time today looking at maps of North Carolina and the agricultural base to familiarize myself with the problems the farmers in that area face. It was really quite enlightening." She knew Karen would know what she was talking about. "So tell me about your day!" Jessica said, steering out of shark-infested waters. Karen took the lead and they settled into comfortable, familiar conversation.

# CHAPTER SIXTEEN
···◇···

Jessica stood in the security line at the small airport near her home. She carried her travel items in a backpack to prevent racking up extra company charges for checked baggage. It wasn't like she needed formalwear for her trip to a farm, but when packing she found herself bewildered about what to bring. Jessica realized that she had not been on a trip, even for business, since Michael was killed. She had helped Karen pack for trips many times but had not packed for herself. It was no surprise that she was feeling anxious, partly because she was traveling and partly because she wasn't exactly sure how she was going to handle the discussion with Jared. She knew he could help her with her questions about getting some crops started for their little tribe, but she wasn't sure how much information she could entrust to him. Jessica walked down a corridor lined with ferns. Although they appeared ornamental, she knew that they would have suddenly turned white if she had an explosive device in her bag. After putting her backpack on the conveyor belt for examination, Jessica approached the agent at the screening booth.

"How are you doing this morning?" the agent asked, smiling with the lower half of her face. Her eyes were laser-focused on Jessica, watching her expressions and movement, belying the casual question. Agent 19, as her badge identified her, was clearly well trained. Her uniform was crisp and her dark hair was pulled back in a tight bun. Jessica was nervous and it showed. She felt one side of her face twitch and she could feel perspiration forming on her upper lip. Agent 19 held out her Device without taking her eyes off of Jessica and mutely Jessica tapped it with her own.

"I see you are not much of a traveler," noted Agent 19, glancing at her Device.

"No, I am really not," agreed Jessica. "I get nervous leaving my house actually." She could actually feel the color draining from her face and heard a roaring sound in her ears.

"According to your Device your anxiety readings are quite high and have triggered an alert. I need you to step into the security booth, please," said Agent 19, gesturing to the closed booth a few feet away. As Jessica moved toward it her head started to clear. She couldn't blame the agent for being suspicious, she was sure she looked terribly guilty. Of course she wasn't a terrorist, but she actually was conducting covert operations to avoid the government. Jessica suddenly realized how ridiculous she was being. She was starting to sound like one of the adventure books she read before bed. This agent didn't care if Jessica was trying to avoid taking the mark, she just wanted to make sure that Jessica wasn't going to blow up the plane! Jessica sat down on the bench in the security booth, closed her eyes for just a few seconds and lifted up a quick prayer for peace. She heard the door lock after the agent closed the door behind her.

"Are you ok?" she asked, her eyes softening.

"Yes, I think I just let my anxiety get the best of me," Jessica replied smiling up at her wanly.

"You know, flying is very safe. We take all of these precautions just to make sure of that."

"I know, and I really do appreciate it. I understand that my travel anxiety could certainly be seen as a red flag." Since random searches had been eliminated after they had been found to be fruitless, Jessica knew that the agent had her reasons for this special measure.

Agent 19 smiled at her, and this time her eyes joined in. "Ok, well let's get you on your way. Just step in here, count to 3, and step out." When the scan was complete, Jessica stepped out and within a few seconds the light over the exit door turned green and there was a sound of the exit door lock opening. Agent 19 walked out behind her, gave her a little wave and reminded her to get her backpack from the security station. Jessica continued on to the gate, exhausted by the experience and she hadn't even boarded the plane yet. No wonder she didn't travel, she mused. At her gate Jessica reviewed some work materials on her device. She found her thoughts drifting back to Agent 19. Jessica wondered if she was a career Security agent or was just fulfilling her commitment from college. She had a tough job, but Jessica could tell that she was a nice person. It was good to know there were still some left. Jessica wondered if Agent 19 had a family, and if she planned to take the mark. She wished that she could talk freely about this with people and find out what their thoughts were but she knew that it wasn't safe. She hoped that Agent 19 hadn't put anything in her record that would make her look suspicious later, more than just a routine flagging for anxiety. She doubted it, but there wasn't anything to be done about it now anyway.

Jessica's Device pinged that it was time for her seat to board. She walked up to another agent and they tapped their Devices together in an odd greeting, and she was waved on to board. After stowing her backpack and settling into her window seat, Jessica realized that although she was still anxious she was eager to meet the Brown clan. She hoped they liked her. A large man sat down in the seat next to her. He made eye contact with Jessica and gave her a pleasant smile and a nod. Jessica felt startled by this and found herself hoping that he wouldn't speak to her. After so many years of having most of her conversations on line, she had to admit that spontaneous conversation was really difficult for her. Luckily, the man popped his earbuds in and closed his eyes, listening to who-knows-what. Maybe he had the same issue. According to the talk shows she watched, it was a growing problem. Jessica finally relaxed and the next thing she knew the plane landed with a slight bounce.

Jessica gathered her things and disembarked into the tiniest airport she had ever seen. It was easy to pick out Jared even though Jessica realized that she had never seen him on-screen, looking the part of a country farmer in khaki work pants, a t-shirt and heavy work boots. In addition he held a sign made of cardboard that said "Jessica". She waved and rushed over, feeling guilty that he was wasting precious daylight farming hours waiting for her. Jared smiled and reached out his hand to shake hers. As she took it she noticed that his middle and ring fingers were amputated past the first knuckle.

"Yep, farming is dangerous work!" he laughed, following her gaze.

"I am sorry, I didn't mean.."

"No worries! Come on, let me carry that backpack and we'll head out to the truck," Jared said in a loud voice that rivaled Lebron's in timbre. "Let's go, Mary's waiting dinner on us."

Jessica was confused for a minute since it was only noon, then she remembered that in the south, lunch was dinner and the evening meal was supper. Even though Florida is clearly more southern than North Carolina geographically, it really isn't in the south, culturally.

Jared put her backpack in the back seat of his truck and politely opened the passenger door for her. He had clearly been brought up right, she thought. As they traveled the half-hour or so, Jessica watched the congestion of the city give way to the fields mostly planted with soybeans. Jessica found the raw earth smells that wafted into the open windows of the truck quite intense. Even the sunlight seemed brighter than at home. Luckily Jared kept the conversation going since Jessica was becoming overwhelmed with the barrage to her senses. Jared gave her a running commentary of the types of crops grown on the fields they passed as well as information about each of the farmers by name, their troubles with their crops as well as business problems caused by constant intrusion by the government regulations. Each of these farmers had eventually hired support staff to handle the regulations, which was costly. Jessica felt for them. She knew the profit margins were slight, and realized that the only way to pay for these extra staff and fees was to raise prices. No wonder it took more than half of her take-home pay just to pay for food for herself and for Karen's meal plan at school. Jared told her that some of the farmers augmented their income with agritourism. It had initially surprised him that people from the city would pay money to come and work on a farm, but he realized there is something just bred into us that gives us satisfaction from tilling the land. Jared told her with pride that the land they were driving through now was his, passed down through four generations on his mother's side. The crops looked healthy, and she found a little bit of his pride to be contagious, since her products had helped him with his success. He explained that while some of his neighbors grew only one or two "money crops" he farmed as the Bible recommended.

"It says in Ecclesiastes 11:2 'Divide your portion to seven, or even to eight, for you do not know what misfortune may occur on the earth.'" He quoted.

As they pulled up to the farmhouse, two large dogs bounded toward the truck. Jared laughed at her alarmed look.

"Come on girls, say hey to Jessica," he called out to the dogs. He went around to her side of the truck and opened the door, apparently recognizing her discomfort with exposing her meaty flesh to the dogs. "They are boxers, working dogs. They keep the raccoons and rodents out of the fields. They won't hurt you, I promise." He called them over and introduced them as Maggie and Molly. "Yeah, I should have named them something else – I am always afraid I am going to call Mary by one of their names – they sound too close! I don't imagine that would go over well do you?" Jared laughed as Mary came out the side door to great them.

"You must be Jessica. Welcome!" said Mary. "Let me show you to your room. Jared, would you mind getting some lettuce for me from the garden? And pick some tomatoes if you see any good ones. We are having salad with chicken for dinner."

Jessica felt herself salivating as she passed through the kitchen. Between the smell of chicken cooking in the oven and the discussion of fresh salad greens, she realized that she was starving. Mary led her through an obstacle course of toys scattered on the ground, past a hip-high bookcase filled with children's books, spines looking well worn, through an area that seemed reserved for crafts with crayons and coloring books as well as paints and brushes and pictures in varying stages of completion. There were colored handprints smudged on the wall and a flat of seeds sprouting in a windowsill, dirt spilling out of the sides onto the floor. Jessica was fascinated.

"I am sorry about the mess," said Mary. "I would like to tell you that it is usually much neater than this but I would be lying. The kids are in school right now, but I have found that there are a lot of things that aren't taught now, so when they get home we pick up the slack."

Mary led Jessica up the back stairs to the guest bedroom. Here the atmosphere abruptly changed to what you might expect from an upscale bed and breakfast. A fluffy queen-size bed was covered with an antique-appearing quilt and lace covered pillow shams. In the corner an overstuffed chair with a floor lamp invited her to curl up and read. The window streamed light through the sheer white curtains. A claw-foot tub with a shower curtain on circular rod was visible through the door of the attached bathroom.

"This is beautiful!" Jessica said.

"As you can tell, this is a 'no kids allowed' area. Sometimes I come up here just to enjoy some peace and quiet. The kids know that if I am in here they had best not disturb me," Mary laughed. "Make yourself at home, relax, and freshen up if you would like. I will be putting dinner on the table in about thirty minutes, so you have some time."

"Thank you so much for letting me stay here," Jessica said. She felt strangely emotional, like she was coming home after a long time away.

"We love having guests," replied Mary. "So many people have lost touch with God's earth; it is great to be able to show it to them." She smiled and slipped out.

Jessica looked out of the window and saw fields as far as the eye could see. Under the window was an arbor with bunches of grapes hanging from it and beyond that was a patch of plants that looked like blueberries, but it was hard to say from this distance. How wonderful it must be to just walk out of your door and have food growing there! Jessica took a few minutes to unpack and went into the bathroom to "freshen up". As she washed her hands she suddenly felt a rising panic. What had she been thinking? This was all too much for her. Suddenly she was shaking and crying.

"Honey, are you ok?" asked Mary through the door. "Can I come in?"

Jessica opened the door, feeling ashamed that she was burdening this wonderful family with her neuroses.

"I'm sorry, I don't know what has come over me," she said.

"You know, Jessica, this is not uncommon to visitors here. Even though people from the city are used to a lot of technological stimulation, they aren't used to all the sights and smells of the country. Please don't apologize. Come with me, I know something that will help" said Mary.

Jessica followed Mary down the stairs and through the kitchen. Mary picked up two cups of hot tea that were on the counter and motioned to Jessica to open the back door. Outside there was a small lake surrounded by reeds waving in the breeze. Mary sat on a concrete bench facing the lake and Jessica sat beside her, taking the cup of tea that Mary offered.

"I find that looking at water is quite a stress reliever. I don't really know why, but I know it is true. I think if people took some time every day to look out over water, or at trees in the breeze, or maybe a campfire, they would find their anxieties a lot easier to handle. I also find prayer helpful. Of course the more children you have the more prayers you need!" she laughed. "I am going to go get dinner ready, take your time coming in."

Jessica looked out over the water and sipped on the herbal tea. She had to agree with Mary, the water seemed to take away her anxiety. She took some deep breaths and felt the tension leaving her shoulders. After a few minutes she felt ready to return.

Mary was at the kitchen sink, washing the fresh vegetables that Jared presumably had brought in, and Jared was at the stove, tending to something in a large, cast iron skillet. Something that smelled very good.

"Have a seat Jessica, this is just about ready. After dinner we can go for a tour of the farm on the four-wheeler. We will want to get out of the way when the kids get off the bus, that's for sure."

Jessica sat at the kitchen table already set with plates and silverware for three. Mary and Jared brought bowls of food and put them on the wooden turntable in the center of the table, each with its own serving utensil.

"I hope you don't mind family style," said Mary with a smile, "Please help yourself."

Mary and Jared sat down and bowed their heads and Jared blessed the food and thanked God for Jessica's visit. It was great to be in a home that was so unashamedly Christian, so rare in these times. Discussing faith was tantamount to admitting stupidity in most circles it seemed. Even those who attended church became uncomfortable when discussing real matters of faith. Not these folks she would bet.

"This is marvelous," Jessica said between mouthfuls. "These vegetables have so much flavor compared with what I am used to getting at the store. And the texture is completely different too. What is this that you made Jared?"

"It's a hoe cake, kind of a flat bread made of cornmeal. My dad used to make it, and he passed his cast-iron skillet down to me when he died. Do you like it? I made a lot so the kids can have a snack when they get home."

"I love it," said Jessica, trying not to eat the whole plateful. "What is the secret to staying slim with all of this good food so plentiful?"

Jared laughed. "I would say hard physical labor and no junk food. If you look at this table you won't see any unpronounceable additives, preservatives, high-fructose corn syrup, or refined sugar. It just isn't necessary for fresh food. Not to say I wouldn't mind a bit of that lemon cheesecake tonight though, Mary. Let's not get too crazy!" Mary gave him a smile.

The screech of bus brakes interrupted their discussion. Mary got up and went to the door. A big yellow school bus pulled right up to their driveway and dumped out nine kids, all appearing to be about the same age.

"Before you even say it, no, they are not all ours!" Mary said. "I watch some of these kids for their parents until they get home from work." Mary waved at the bus driver and she waved back. The kids came into the house like a stampeding herd, heading for the kitchen. "Whoa, slow down troops. What do you do first?"

"Wash hands," they said in unison, and headed off to the bathroom.

"I think this is our cue to escape," said Jared in a stage

whisper. He kissed Mary's forehead and grabbed some keys from a hook on the wall and two jackets from the closet, handing one to Jessica. She followed him out to what looked like a rugged golf cart and they took off for the fields. The dogs ran happily beside them. The quiet electric cart allowed her to hear all of the birds chirping. Even the insects buzzing about intrigued her. They came upon a field that was flourishing with soybeans.

"This is the area where I used the Malhindrone. You can see how well it works." Jared said. "Tell me about the other products you have coming out." The afternoon slipped away amidst discussions of fertilizers, crops and insects. Jared stopped a few times to check on some things, repair a gate that wasn't closing properly, check on a calf, and feed the chickens, gathering a few eggs in the process. Jared explained that because the chickens had free range to peck around instead of being crowded in the industrial henhouses, they didn't have a problem with Salmonella, so she could have a fried egg in the morning if she would like to. Jessica couldn't remember the last time she had a fried egg, since the contamination of eggs had become close to universal in the past decade or so. Jessica sat in the cart and enjoyed the sights, sounds and smells holding the eggs gingerly as they headed back to the farmhouse. As they neared the house they passed a woman and two kids walking along the path. Jessica recognized the kids from the troupe from the bus. Jared called out to them and they waved.

The screen door slammed behind them as they entered the house through the side door. Jessica realized that the way the house had appeared before was tidy compared to the scene now. The crowd of kids had whittled down to four, and Mary walked among them picking up scattered debris and reorganizing the supplies and books. Jessica watched and chatted with Mary as Jared excused himself to get washed up for supper. She noticed that each of the kids had a duty. Even four-year-old Courtney, the youngest, was putting all of the crayons back into the box that housed them. In very little time the house was back in order. Jessica followed Mary into the kitchen, asking if she could do anything to help.

"Well, it's nothing fancy, just the chicken from supper and

some vegetables. I have green beans canned in the summer. If you would like to get them, they are in the pantry right through that door," pointing at a door in the kitchen Jessica had not previously noticed. "Two jars ought to be enough for this clan. Then if you wouldn't mind chopping those tomatoes for the salad that would be a great help." Jessica opened the door and gazed in amazement. There were shelves from the ceiling to the floor in this small room, about the size of a large walk-in closet. On one side stacked four deep were large mason jars with various types of food, all looking perfectly fresh. There were pickles, okra, green beans, and beets to name a few. On the other side were dried beans, flour, cornmeal, rice, coffee and other supplies. Jessica grabbed two jars of green beans and returned to the kitchen and started chopping tomatoes. She found herself enjoying the simple food preparation.

"Wow, that is an impressive food storage you have there," Jessica exclaimed. "It looks like you could live for six months out of your pantry."

"We will have to when it gets cold; there aren't too many crops we can grow in the winter. In the back is a freezer for meat and other vegetables and fruits that are better frozen than canned. Amanda," Mary said to her ten-year-old daughter, "Ellen's mom brought us some bread, can you slice it up for dinner?" Amanda nodded and got the bread knife from the drawer. Mary noticed Jessica's look of alarm as Amanda began to cut and laughed as she poured the beans into the pot on the stove. "Don't worry; she knows how to use that knife without hurting herself. She has been helping in the kitchen since she was Courtney's age."

"I'm sorry, that was rude, "Jessica said. "I have never seen kids so involved in their chores. You have done a great job with that."

"It is kind of a necessity on a farm. Those vegetables don't get into those jars by themselves, and Jared and I can't do it alone. Of course we have our neighbors, too. I have a degree in Early Childhood Education and I am able to stay home so I watch the neighbor kids until their parents get off of work. In return they bring us produce from their farms, hand-made items or baked goods, like that bread there. And the cheesecake comes from Margie, who works in a bakery in town. We take care of each other."

"Sounds like a perfect system to me," Jessica said sincerely. She looked around for a trash can to put the trimmings from the tomatoes in. Amanda saw her and pointed out the covered crockery canister on the counter. Puzzled, Jessica lifted the lid and saw other vegetable scraps and eggshells in the canister.

"That's for compost," explained Mary. "It is a miracle really – we put the vegetable scraps and eggshells in pile, turn it every now and again, and it becomes rich black dirt. Have Jared show you the pile in the morning."

Jared came in and the kids all stopped what they were doing and ran over for a hug. He toppled onto his back comically and the kids scrambled over him like Lilliputians on Gulliver. Jessica watched wistfully remembering how happy Karen was when Michael would come in from work.

"Supper's ready!" called Mary. Jessica turned to see her setting large bowls of food on the turntable (Mary called it a Lazy Susan, but that seemed offensive), Amanda right behind with the bread. Jessica was delighted to see some other vegetables in steaming hot bowls as well. Jared herded the kids to the table, pulling out a chair for her in the meantime. As they settled into their seats, everyone became quiet and Mary asked Jonah, the oldest at 12, to say the grace. They joined hands and listened quietly as Jonah thanked God for this feast and for his family and friends. Jessica was embarrassed to find tears in her eyes and dabbed them quickly with her napkin.

Dinner was a loud affair with everyone seeming to compete to tell their story or at least their version of the same story. Jessica was amazed at how easily they accepted her into their bunch. She was equally amazed at how well she was tolerating all the chaos. That water gazing was a miracle. When dinner was finished and the dishes were washed, dried and put away, Mary shooed the kids up to their rooms for showers and homework. Mary assured them that she and Jared would be up shortly to read a story and say goodnight, kissing six-year-old Luke on the top of his closely cropped hair before he went.

"Tea?" asked Mary as Jared sat back down at the kitchen table. Jessica accepted and sat down with them. Apparently the kitchen table was the nerve center of this house. Just then, Jessica had a startling revelation.

"Where are your screens?" Jessica asked. "I just realized that haven't seen a single one!"

"We don't have any," Mary said. "We did at one time, but we realized that the kids were getting dependent on them for entertainment. We have devices, and the small screens on those provide for some things, mostly educational, but this way works for us." The way she said it made Jessica realize that she was a bit defensive of this decision. She must have gotten a lot of heat about it.

"I think that is a great idea," said Jessica quickly. "Our society is way too dependent on the technology we have created." Mary was visibly relieved. Jessica paused for a moment and then said, "Actually I have been doing a lot of thinking lately about how my family could live outside of the influence of the government." Oh, no had she said too much? Jessica had been so adamant with Karen about not telling Taylor and here she was telling a family she had just met. "Thank you again for the wonderful meal," she said, quickly changing the subject. "Of course, I am supposed to be here to find out how you are using our products, so tell me, were those vegetables grown with the help of Dacon chemicals?

"Actually, the vegetables we eat at the house are from a different part of the property, grown organically," Jared said. Mary shot him a quick glance and an almost imperceptible head shake. Jessica watched the interaction with keen observation. She was always amazed by how couples who had been together a long time could have entire conversations without saying a word. Jared replied to her look with one of his own, one of understanding; Mary countered with a pleading look, Jared volleyed with a reassuring one. Then from Mary, came a look of resignation and a nod. Jared turned his attention back to Jessica.

"We have an entire field planted with heirloom seeds of all

kinds of varieties. Kind of a Noah's Ark of the seed world. It is surrounded by a wind break of trees, but even so sometimes the engineered, and therefore copyrighted, seeds get in and I have to keep an eye out for them and pluck them out. It is a lot of work, but it is a cooperative effort with our neighbors. We have been keeping this field up for years, before the possession of heirloom seeds was made illegal."

Jessica realized why Mary had been worried. Jared was taking a risk by telling her this. Jessica now knew she could trust them with her plans.

"I won't tell anyone, I promise. In fact, I have something to tell you that I need you to keep secret too."

Much later, Jessica reviewed the evening's events while taking a bath in the claw foot tub. They had talked long into the night with only a brief break for Jared and Mary to get the kids into bed. Jared had told her that they had seen this mark coming for a long time, as had their neighbors. They would hold out as long as they could and then cut themselves off and live off of the land. Once the mark was required, there would be no more buying of seed or fertilizer or selling of crops. They weren't willing to leave their farm, but they had thought of a number of ways to make themselves less of a target. Even so, the community knew that there would come a time of persecution, but they would not take the mark. Jessica told Jared and Mary about her plans, and found them to be quite supportive as well as being a wealth of knowledge. Jessica's head swam with all of the information she had acquired. She toweled off and prepared for bed. Tomorrow would be a hectic day. Jared had promised her a tour of the secret garden on the way to the airport. Jessica hoped that they would start off the day with some of those eggs that she and Jared had brought from the chicken house and who knows, maybe one of those neighbors raises pigs and there would be bacon!

# CHAPTER SEVENTEEN
... ◇ ...

Josh waited. This president did not seem to find punctuality very important. He looked down at the conference room table. It was so highly polished that he could see his reflection. He looked around the table at the dozen members of the president's cabinet, a mixture of ages, races and genders, and all here to brief the president on their various committees. They all had their Devices out and were reading or typing madly. Josh closed his eyes and rehearsed his report in his mind. As the head of the World Health Initiative, his main concern was sustainability. He was going to have to ask for another increase in the budget, and he knew that the other cabinet members would go berserk. He really didn't blame them, but there was only so much that could be accomplished with strategic uses of medical treatments and lowering the payments to doctors and hospitals. Now he was going to have to ask for money to give to the medicals schools so they could offer incentives to get enough students to fill their classes. When he and George were applying for medical school there were many more applicants than there were spaces and a high grade point average and high MCAT scores were required for acceptance. George wanted to follow in his dad's footsteps and Josh thought the idea of being a doctor sounded interesting and prestigious. The reality of late nights, stressful work environments and mediocre pay made him consider politics instead. Little did he know that he would encounter the same conditions in government work. But he could use his medical knowledge to help improve the system, he had reasoned, and he could fulfill his Homeland Security obligation quickly. Politics came naturally for Josh. People listened to him for some reason. Josh thought it might be because he recognized their needs. He had once read that children of alcoholic parents had an unusual ability to quickly evaluate the mood and meaning of a situation, a skill formed as a child from the need to be able to look at their parents and read their status to know when to get out of the way. He could definitely relate to that. As a child Josh had known almost the instant he entered the house that his parents were drinking. He had felt unable to help his mother and his older sister when his dad had become abusive. His dad never hit them, at least Josh didn't think he did, but the things he said would sting like a whip. Strangely, he never directed his attacks at Josh, but it was still painful. His mother coped by drinking too, which escalated the problem. His sister had become depressed and Josh knew she had begun cutting herself months before she died in a car accident. There was never any proof but he didn't believe that she just lost control of the car and ran into a pole. She never hit the brakes.

Josh shifted back to the problem at hand and was trying to figure out how to present his case without begging when he heard someone enter the room. Josh opened his eyes and saw the president enter with an aide in tow. The president was speaking softly to the aide on her right. The aide nodded his head and left the room.

The cabinet rose and a dozen voices murmured "Good morning, Madam President," not quite in unison. President Sontara took her place at the end of the table and smiled at them.

"I'm sorry I am late," she said, tucking her white hair behind her ears as she looked at her Device. She made no excuse; she never did. Something about her smile seemed to completely erase the tone of irritation that permeated the room just a minute before. Her calm presence was contagious, something that was quite beneficial for her position. Josh felt drawn in by that as well, and, he had to admit, by her stunning appearance. Although she looked her age, 68, with well-groomed white hair, President Sontara seemed raceless, or perhaps more accurately, race inclusive. Josh could look at her and see every race imaginable, which added to her attractiveness. Josh remembered George's father once saying that the most beautiful people were those of melting pot families, who had a variety of races in their bloodline. Josh didn't really understand it at the time but now he had to agree. President Sontara's appearance had also aided in her ability to interact with other regions, since they could all accept her as one of their own. As soon as the president and the cabinet were settled in their chairs President Sontara started the meeting. They turned their attention to the screens on all four walls which currently listed the agenda. "We have one hour and thirty minutes for this meeting, so let's get to agenda item number one, a presentation from Homeland Security. Senator Thomas you may begin."

Senator Thomas, a burly ex-marine, stood up to begin his presentation. Although he retired from the service many years ago the senator's perfectly creased suit and meticulous appearance made it look like he had just come from inspection. He stood at attention and pressed a button on his device, changing the screens as well as their devices to show his report entitled "Identity Chip –Reception by the Public". After the discussion with George, Josh's attention was riveted.

"As I am sure you all know, GTV was recently briefed on the eminent availability of the identity chip. According to our Community Security sources, there has been talk of this being what is called in the Bible "the mark of the beast". There are some who are talking about refusing the chip if it becomes required. Of course that inevitability has not been discussed with GTV yet."

"But they will need the chip for any commerce," stated the President, her face revealing confusion. "I am not a Bible scholar, what is their concern about this mark?"

"Apparently there is discussion that anyone taking the mark is doomed to burn in Hell," replied the Senator, looking somewhat embarrassed at having to relay this ridiculous information. There was a smattering of soft laughter. "I know it sounds like mystical thinking, but we still need to come up with a consensus on how to deal with it."

"Do you have any ideas on the matter?" asked President Sontara, her hands folded and her full attention on Senator Thomas.

"Yes, I do have a few ideas I am working on, but I would like to get some feasibility studies done before I present them. I think I can have them ready by the next meeting in two weeks."

"Very well, Senator Thomas, you do that. Now moving on to agenda item two, Senator Davis of the WHI. Senator? Senator Davis? Are you alright?"

# CHAPTER EIGHTEEN
··· ◇ ···

When Jessica returned home she found a letter in the s-mail. Sasha's beautiful handwriting on the envelope, almost like calligraphy font, gave away the sender. Jessica carefully opened the envelope and found a letter typed on what looked like an antique typewriter, some of the letters smeared. She remembered the typewriter that Lebron had in his study – an old Corona. He kept it as a reminder of his college days when he used to bang out papers on it. He was a terrible typist, he had confided, recalling that his papers were stiff with white-out. Jessica smiled as she thought about Sasha wrestling with the old typewriter so that they didn't leave an electronic trail. Of course there would be a record that this letter had been sent, but at least there was no way to know what was in it. Jessica settled down on the couch to read the letter.

Dear Friends,

I take very seriously this task of relaying to you my take on what prophesies in the Bible mean to us today and how they might relate to the events that we have discussed. Please keep in mind that there are people who devote their entire lives to this study and there is disagreement among them as to the meaning of the prophetic scriptures. We were never meant to know the day and time of Christ's return by studying the scriptures, we are to use the study of scriptures to learn how to lead a better life, a life more pleasing to God.

Revelation is the book everyone thinks of when they think of end time events, but fully one-quarter of the Bible is written prophesy, much of which has already come to pass. In the Book of Daniel you can read about King Nebuchadnezzar's dream of a great statue with a head of fine gold, a chest and arms of silver, a belly and thighs of bronze, legs of iron, and feet partly of iron and partly of clay. Daniel was given the interpretation of the dream by God. He was told that the first part of the statue, the gold, was the king's own kingdom. Then the next after the king's would rise up another kingdom, inferior to the king's. This was Medo-Persia, which conquered Babylon in the fifth century B.C. This happened within Daniels lifetime, but well after the dream. The third part of the statue, the Bronze, was Greece, which conquered Medo-Persia 300 years after Daniel. Remember though, that Greece included what we know of as the Middle East, including the former countries of Egypt, Jordan, Israel, Syria, Turkey, Iraq and Iran. Next came the strong iron kingdom of Rome. The final portion of the king's statue dream recently came to pass with the formation of the ten regions in the Federation of Regions as signified by the ten toes, partly iron, but partly clay, both strong and fragile. We all know that some of the Regions are stronger than others. At the end of the dream a stone that was cut without hands from a mountain destroys the whole statue. Then the stone becomes a great mountain and fills the whole Earth. God's kingdom.

Later Daniel has a dream that is very much like this one of King Nebuchadnezzar's. He too had these kingdoms listed, but his dream had more detail about the ten final earthly kingdoms, which were horns rather than toes. In his dream one individual rises up from the horns and is described as a little horn. What individual has risen up out of the Federation of Regions? I know it is almost blasphemous to say considering he is credited with so much good, but Supreme Principal Levine certainly fits this description, including the signing of the Middle-East Peace Treaty. A later dream describes this individual to be pompous, arrogant and cruel, and he will compare himself to God and cause an abomination that causes desolation. That has not happened, but at some point Supreme Principal Levine may set himself up to be worshiped as God. He is described as plucking out three other horns, or causing three regions to fall which I think could be the Mideast domination over the African, Chinese and Russian regions since the Middle-East war. Just as in the king's dream, this one ends with God's takeover of the world when One like the Son of Man comes on the clouds to rule the Earth. Fast-forward to Mark 14:61-62 when Jesus is arrested and stands before the high priest who asks him if he is the Christ, the Son of God. "I am," said Jesus. "And you will see the Son of Man sitting at the right hand of the Mighty One and coming on the clouds of heaven".

I hope I haven't lost you - we haven't

even touched on the Book of Revelation. I will skip over the details of the first part of the book except to say that the enormous loss of life that was caused by the civil wars, the droughts and subsequent famines, the meteor strike with the resultant earthquake and tsunamis were all foretold. The war in the Middle East with the use of nuclear weapons and massive armies- all foretold. So what about the mark of the beast - the reason we are having this discussion? In Revelation 13 a beast is described. It has ten horns (sound familiar now?) and seven heads and is given its authority by a dragon, representing the devil. Then another beast rises up and gives authority to the beast and has all the people worship it. This beast forces everyone to receive a mark on his right hand or on his forehead, so that no one could buy or sell unless he has the mark, which is the name of the beast or the number of his name, which is 666. Now I don't know what the 666 is about, there are a lot of guesses, but the mark seem pretty clear to me. I always thought it would be trickier to spot but here it is. There are clear warnings about the consequences of taking the mark – Revelation 14:8 says "A third angel followed them and said in a loud voice: 'if anyone worships the beast and his image and receives his mark on the forehead or on the hand, he, too, will drink of the wine of God's fury, which has been poured full strength into the cup of his wrath.'"

Scary stuff. But there is good news.

Now this too is very controversial. Some say that the saints, the Christians that is, are taken up to heaven before all of this. Well, I certainly hope not because we are still here! But right after this mark of the beast discussion there is a harvest of the Earth by one "like a son of man", which is how Jesus is described. A message is relayed to him from God by an angel that the time to reap has come and Jesus swings down his sickle and harvests. I believe that this is the rapture, or the time when the saints are brought to heaven to be with God. There is yet another group that are then harvested and thrown into the great wine-press of God's wrath. I am sure I don't have to tell you how that works out for them. What follows after this is the seven bowls of God's great wrath. I have seen some horrible things in my life that have been brought upon us by people, but when God passes his judgment on the world there will be no time that is comparable. I believe we won't be here, so I prefer not to think about it.

So there you have it, my precious ones. Know that this summary just scratches the surface of what there is in the Bible about these times we are in and I hope you are motivated to do some reading on your own. Be very careful who you discuss this with because the times are very dangerous for Christians. The persecution will be awful with beheadings being foretold. But there is more good news! Although the beast tries to fight back, Jesus prevails and reigns and eventually there is a new heaven and a new

```
Earth  where  there  is  no  more  death  or
mourning  or  pain.  Jesus  makes  everything
new.
              Halleluiah!
```

Jessica set the letter on her lap and closed her eyes. It was hard to believe that this could really be happening. She could actually be living in a time prophesied about over 2,500 years ago. The thought was staggering. She thought she understood what Lebron was trying to get across but she would have to read it a few more times before passing it on to George and Becky. As she pondered these things she felt a peaceful feeling settling over her like warm blanket. Jessica knew in her heart that God was with her and felt that he was telling her to trust him. She also knew in her heart that she could.

# CHAPTER NINETEEN
... ◇ ...

George and Becky walked up the winding path to their church, holding each other's hands as well Maya's and Mark's. They were walking more slowly than normal and were quiet, but Maya and Mark held up their end of the conversation for them. The constant chatter was a welcome break from the consuming thoughts that had plagued Becky's mind. The group meeting seemed like months ago, but actually only three weeks had passed. Since that time Becky had ordered a solar generator, a water purifier, and solar paint. It had been nerve-racking to order these items without a clear need, such as an upcoming trip. She had decided on a story about donating the items to a previous mission site, but no fraud alert sounded. Apparently she had ordered enough similar items over the years to be able to fly under the radar. Next she planned to order a self-contained toilet, a super battery, and a solar oven. Keeping the total bill down by ordering over time was another strategy Becky was using to keep from drawing attention to her project. She was still researching the possibility of disabling the device's GPS while retaining the information gathering capabilities. The possibility seemed so close, but she just didn't have time to devote to it outside of her busy work and home schedule. And of course she couldn't ask anyone for help. There really wasn't anyone she trusted that much.

Becky glanced over at George and could tell he was going through his list as well. Each day when he came home from work he emptied his briefcase into a box that they kept under the bed. So far he had collected mostly first aid items. Bandages, suture kits and skin glue, samples of antibiotics and other medicines in children and adult strengths were nestled in the box. They had also ordered over-the-counter medicines and antiseptics from the pharmacy in small enough quantities to keep from attracting attention and stored them in there as well. George felt there was so much more they needed for him to feel comfortable. A few nights ago George had confided in her that he was very anxious about his abilities to be a doctor without his Device and all the machines in his office. "How will I treat anyone when I can't even do any tests on them to find out what is wrong? Maybe the old doctors can listen with a stethoscope or tap on a belly and be able to figure out the problem, but I wasn't trained for that. What if one of us gets sick and I can't help them, how can I live with that? What use will I be?"

Seeing him so insecure broke Becky's heart. She consoled him by saying that she knew that he had good common sense and that his medical knowledge was so much more than just blips on a screen. Of course she had her own anxieties as well. None of them knew what they were going to find at the farm. It would be one thing if it was just the two of them, but risking the safety of their kids was what kept her awake at night. Sometimes she would look over at George in the middle of the night and see him staring at the ceiling, jaw clenched with worry. They would remind each other that this was just a drill, the situation may never arise that required them to take action. In her heart Becky doubted her ability to follow through, even if she was sure that this was the real thing.

Maya and Mark dropped Becky and George's hands and ran toward their Sunday school class, calling out to their friends. Becky smiled at the teacher and George reminded the two to be on their best behavior.

"Oh to have the carefree life of a seven-year-old child, only worrying about whether or not you were going to be invited to a friend's birthday party," said Becky.

As they turned to go to the church service they were startled to see Jessica standing in their path.

"Jessica! What are you doing here?" asked George, "I mean, of course you are welcome, but I don't think I have ever seen you here," he said, backpedaling.

"I know it is a surprise, but I needed to talk to you and didn't know how else to contact you without being heard by prying ears. Lebron sent me the letter that he promised, and I wanted to pass it on to you. I also wanted to find out about your progress. Do we have a couple of minutes before the service starts?"

"Sure we do," said Becky, "Let's sit over here in the memorial garden where it's quiet." They sat on the concrete benches and caught each other up with quiet voices. Jessica told them about her trip and about a package from Jared. She had received a strange textmail on her return. *You left your hair dryer at our house. I sent it in the package mail.* A very strange textmail considering she didn't own a hair dryer. A few days later a package came with handmade envelopes of heirloom seeds of various kinds with instructions on planting and caring for them. She had felt tears sting her eyes at the thought that he had trusted her that much that he would send them to her and risk discovery.

Once they had exchanged the needed information and George had slipped the letter into his pocket they made their way toward the church.

"I have never been to this church. I feel really safe here," said Jessica, surprised by the revelation. Jessica attended an e-church, rationalizing that it was the same message and that she didn't have to get dressed or waste money on transport. Some of her e-friends attended the same church. Now she wondered if there was something important about being around fellow Christians in person.

"Well we should feel safe here," said George, "That's why they call it a sanctuary." George wanted to believe what he had said, but as he looked around at the people in the pews, he just wasn't sure.

# CHAPTER TWENTY
· · · ◇ · · ·

Taylor and Karen walked hand in hand on the way to the library. The air had a cool, crisp feel, a welcome break from the humidity of the summer, but not quite cold. Having grown up in Florida, Karen didn't really expect changes in the seasons but Taylor had grown up in Colorado. The lack of fall colors made him a little sad. He knew that he would appreciate not having to dig out of the snow in a couple of weeks, but for now the pictures on his mom's social network showing the brilliant hues of the late October leaves made him a little homesick.

"Maybe someday we could visit Colorado during the leaf changing. Or we could even take a long weekend up to the mountains in North Carolina and just do some leaf-peeping. I would really like that," Karen said.

"Hmmm. What would your mom say about us going up to the mountains alone? How would that look?" Taylor said, smiling his most charming half smile.

"Well, we wouldn't necessarily be alone for one thing, we would probably bring along some friends. Maybe Jake and Sarah would like to come. I don't know if I could trust myself alone with you," Karen said, blushing and squeezing his hand. "My mom wouldn't be upset, she trusts my decisions. I wish you could meet her. Maybe sometime soon we can go down for the weekend. Would you like that?"

"Wow, two trips offered at once. So many decisions!" Taylor said, laughing. When Karen gave him a slightly worried look he added, "In a good way that is! I am not trying to put you off – I would like to do both of those things. We should look at the university schedule and see when we could plan them."

Karen smiled. Taylor loved that smile. When Karen smiled something strange happened in his chest that bordered on painful, almost like a balloon had been blown up and was crowding out the rest of his organs. Or maybe like there was a light bulb that had been turned on and was a little too hot. He wondered if that's what love feels like.

"Ok, we'll do that," said Karen. They had arrived at the library. Karen had some research to do in the old books section and Taylor was heading back to his dorm to change for Lacrosse practice. Taylor had played Lacrosse throughout high school and even though he probably could have played as a walk-on, he really didn't want the commitment of a college level sport. Club lacrosse was the perfect compromise.

"I will give you a call after practice. Maybe you will be ready for a study break by then. OK?"

"That sounds great. Have a good time at practice. Get all your frustrations out!" Karen said, giving him her best lascivious look.

"Yeah, that could take all afternoon. And I mean that as a compliment, of course," returning her look with one of his own. He leaned down and gave her a quick peck on the lips. "There's more where that came from. See ya later."

Karen smiled and opened the large, wooden double doors of the library and stepped inside.

Taylor thought back to the first time he had seen Karen, coming out of these very doors. He was first struck by her beauty of course, but not the typical beauty of the college-age girl. There were no eye-catching peek-a-boos in her clothes, no strange colors in her hair, no outrageous heels on her shoes. Somehow she managed to look stylish without all of that. There was something else about her, something about the way she moved, or maybe it was the expression on her face, that made him feel like she was different. Special. Feeling like a complete stalker, he had surreptitiously taken a photo of her on his device and identified her, then lurked her social networking site. After a few failed attempts, he managed to stand in line behind her at the food station and "accidentally" bump her tray, creating an opportunity to apologize and introduce himself. Once they started dating he told her that whole story, feeling the need to come clean.

She had just laughed and actually seemed flattered rather than creeped out, as he had been afraid she would be. He had been right about her being special. He found that he could spend all evening with her and not get tired of the conversation like he had with other girlfriends. Her discussions did not center on spoiled celebrities' antics or those of their own friends. Karen talked about current events, her faith, new things she was learning in school, stories about her family, and ideas she had been pondering. She made him think like that too, and not rely on the shallow banter of his other peers. They had long discussions about God that made him really assess what he believed without feeling pressured. Being with Karen made him a better person.

Taylor touched his Device to the pad on his dorm room and slowly opened the door, just in case his roommate had forgotten the old sock-over-the-doorknob sign that there was a girl in the room. There had been no socks over the knob for him since before Karen. That was another thing that made her vastly different from the other girls he had gone out with in college. They were all too eager to put that sock over the doorknob, sometimes the first night they met. Karen had let him know right away that she was not that kind of girl. At first he had been unsure if he could handle that, but he found that he felt closer to her without sex than he had with the other girls that he had been "intimate" with. The affection she showed him was real, not just drunken going through the motions. Not that he would reject her if she gave him the thumbs up. Not for a minute.

Taylor glanced in. The room was empty of people but was a mess. Clothes were piled in each corner and the place had a locker-room odor that was unpleasant. His mom would be aghast. He thought about his parents and felt another pang of home-sickness. His mom lived in Colorado with her new husband, a really nice guy who had always treated Taylor like his own son. His mom and Stan had two kids together, one seven and one ten years old. He hated leaving them to come to college. He knew they would change so much while he was gone and he wished he could be a part of it. His dad lived here in Florida, so he was able to apply to UF as a resident. Having always lived in Colorado, Taylor felt that it would be a good idea to try living in another place. His dad had been able to visit him on campus a couple of times when he was traveling for business. That was nice, but his dad was really a stranger to him. Taylor didn't feel comfortable staying at his dad's house since he didn't know his dad's wife at all. The times he had seen the two of them they seemed lukewarm with each other. They had never had any kids together, but her two teenage sons lived with them. Taylor had met them once, at his dad's wedding. One time Taylor asked his mom what had happened with his dad to make them divorce. He had braced himself for a story of infidelity or abuse or addiction of some sort. But it was nothing like that. She told him that over the years they had just lost the spark that they had known early in their relationship. They had grown apart while pursuing their own interests. They had both felt like they wanted to find someone new to feel that with again. In some ways this knowledge was worse than anything he had imagined. Maybe if they had taken some time to get to know each other again they could have rekindled that spark. They had just given up.

Taylor grabbed his Lacrosse stuff and headed to the field. This weather would be perfect for practice, and they had a game coming up in two days so they really needed it. When Taylor was younger he thought he wanted to be a professional lacrosse player. As he grew older he realized that it wasn't in the cards for him, and he considered other options. He entered college as pre-med, but after being involved with Homeland Security he was sure he didn't want to do anything that was controlled by a government division like the World Health Initiative. Of course these days it was hard to find anything that the government was not involved in. Karen had asked him what he could really enjoy doing. He had replied that he really loved reading, being outdoors and working with his hands. They had laughed at all the crazy jobs that could include them all. When Taylor had been accepted to college his mom and step-dad sat him down and discussed the financial aspects of a college education. There was no money for him to go on his own, so he signed up for Homeland Security. His state school tuition would be paid for and he would even receive money for room and board, but he would have to attend Community Security meetings and then commit to two years working for Homeland Security for every year of scholarship. It wasn't ideal, but it was the only way college was going to happen. Taylor really hated the Community Security meetings. They were very secretive, some with lectures about identifying security threats and some one-on-one meetings with higher level agents asking questions about what was being said around campus. Luckily, Taylor pretty much kept to himself and never had anything to contribute.

Taylor arrived at the field just as a few of his other teammates arrived. As he put on his cleats his thoughts drifted back to Karen, thinking about calling her for dinner later, whether she would want to go to the game this weekend, how she looked in that pink sweater she was wearing when she went into the library. He found that his thoughts often drifted back to her. He knew he need to focus on the practice or he was going to get clobbered, but he also knew from recent practices that he could be in the middle of the field and start thinking about something she had said and lose focus like a four-year-old kid picking daisies on the soccer field. He laughed at himself, feeling ridiculous. But then again, maybe that was what love felt like.

# CHAPTER TWENTY-ONE
··· ◇ ···

Jessica sat at her kitchen table reviewing her to-do list. The sun was barely up and her alarm had not even sounded yet. "Why is it that on the weekend I wake up early on my own and on the weekdays it takes an alarm to drag me out of bed?" she said to herself. She knew people who could sleep until noon on the weekends but she was not one of them. Her routine on Saturdays was to watch The Initial Edition, the live GTV news that was replayed the rest of the day on demand. Sometimes there were little misspeaks that were edited out later which she found somewhat amusing, a little chink in the perfection armor of these newscasters. While this was in the background she reviewed her list. One of today's projects was to copy the map from her device since she would not be able to take the device with her. She hoped that Becky would be able to take hers, minus the GPS, but they couldn't count on that.

Jessica copied the map carefully onto a piece of paper left over from her Christmas cards last year. As she drew the map she noted that it looked kind of like a tree in the winter, with the trunk as I-95 and the branches as the smaller roads. The combination of the map and the leftover Christmas paper gave her an idea. What if she made the map into a Christmas card? That way she could print it and give it to multiple people and not worry about calling attention to herself. After all, she always sent Christmas cards around this time. Jessica went at the project with a new eye and actually enjoyed the artistry of it. She finished and sat back to admire her work. There were a few inconspicuous arrows and road numbers that were disguised by tree branches, but she didn't think anyone who wasn't looking for them would notice. She decided that it would be best to just reproduce them by hand rather than at a print shop so that there would be no record. She wanted to do more now but her hand kept cramping. Writing with a pencil was quite rare for her these days.

Instead she went on to her next project while keeping her eye on the news. So far no gaffe, which, she had to admit, was a little disappointing.

The group had agreed at their initial meeting to start getting together backpacks for each person containing survival supplies and a few personal items and clothes. The travel plans had not been completely worked out, but they knew that packing room would be limited. Jessica would also need to pack her agriculture supplies – the precious seeds as well as the dried and canned foods she had been collecting. George would bring medical supplies, Becky power related supplies, Lebron hunting and fishing supplies and Sasha teaching materials. Karen would bring any books she could collect. Each of them would, of course, bring their Government issued disaster packs. This was one government program that Karen had wholeheartedly supported. Due to the multitude of recent disasters, including the meteor strike, earthquakes and hurricanes and the difficulty and expense of getting aid to people in the middle of them, the government began giving a disaster pack to anyone who wanted one. In it was a water filtration device, two days of MREs (meals ready to eat – the same as the armed security got) a solar powered light and heater, hygiene supplies, and a change of clothes- scrubs, like doctors wore. It all fit in a small waterproof case about the size of a shoebox. Everyone was instructed to keep their pack with them in case of emergency; most people kept them in their cars. Even Maya and Mark each had one with age-appropriate items. This went into the bottom of the backpack. Now came the difficult decision of what else to bring. Some necessities – warm clothes and other hygiene items of course, but what about memories? Jessica decided to bring a solar powered digital frame and a photocell of pictures dating back to her childhood. She thought about her mom's closet full of albums that Jessica had converted to digital after her parents' death. That had been quite a project, but she couldn't bear to just throw them out and she certainly didn't have room for them here. Now she was glad to be able to have them all in the thumbnail-sized photocell. That and one printed photo of Karen, Michael and herself would be all the personal items she would need. Jessica thought about her last real conversation with Karen, when she was at home. They had agreed that she would go to her grandparents by bus and head out with them if they felt the need to go. Jessica had stressed that this was a huge decision and that she would understand if Karen decided not to go, or at least not go until later. Jessica would send her a Christmas card map just in case she decided to wait.

Jessica was just finishing her packing when the screen caught her attention. Annette was showing Stephen her newly placed chip and tattoo. She held out her hand like she was showing off an engagement ring. Stephen smiled but seemed uncomfortable. Apparently as anchors on GTV they were in the first round of people to be offered the identity chip.

"So Stephen, I don't see your identity chip tattoo. Were you out sick that day?" Annette said teasingly.

"No," Stephen said slowly. "I opted out." At this point Jessica's attention was glued to the screen.

Annette looked confused. "You mean, you'll get it with the next group?"

"No, actually, I mean I am not going to get it at all."

Jessica could hear commotion in the background of the studio. Stephen continued, but now in a rushed, stressed voice. "I believe that this is the mark of the beast that was prophesied in the book of Revelation in the Bible." Stephen turned to the camera which, for the moment, was on him alone. "All of you need to read Revelation for yourselves. Stand up for what you believe in. Don't take this mark, even it means persecution." At this point the camera swung away from Stephen in a nauseating spin and landed on Annette. She was staring at Stephen while the commotion increased as Stephen was obviously being removed from the anchor chair. Annette sat rod-straight in her seat with her hands pressed palms down on the anchor desk. She turned toward the camera with her mouth open, speechless. The camera swung back to Stephen's seat which was now occupied by a white-haired man Jessica had never seen. She guessed he was a news producer.

"Excuse us for a moment as we sort out some technical difficulties," he said with a shaky smile. "Now don't touch that dial, we will be right back with more news." Then they cut to a commercial.

Jessica stared at the TV. Don't touch that dial? What was that supposed to mean? She thought about the broadcast. Jessica was glad she was up early enough to see The Initial Edition since she was certain that none of that would make the final news cut. She thought about the bravery of Stephen. He had said his piece knowing that he would lose his job – or worse.

"Goodbye, Stephen," she said aloud. Then she took out the paper and the map she had drawn. She suddenly felt a need to get these done and mailed. After what she had just seen, a cramped hand seemed like a poor excuse.

# CHAPTER TWENTY-TWO
··· ◇ ···

*Déjà vu.* That's what Josh was thinking as he found himself at the gleaming table with his fellow cabinet members again, waiting for the president. It was probably his imagination, but he felt that the other members' gazes were falling on him longer than would be considered normal. Not that he would blame them, the last time they gathered here he sounded like he was having a stroke, trying to speak after the presentation by Homeland Security. Luckily he was not presenting today so he didn't have that to worry about. After the last meeting he had contemplated sitting down with Rachel and the kids and talking to them about the mark and about the possibility of fleeing Washington for North Carolina. By the time the train pulled up at his home station Josh had decided that he didn't have enough facts to present it to them at this point. He was afraid they would just laugh at him.

Everyone stood as President Sontara entered, looking self-assured and well- groomed. She took her seat at the head of the table and began the meeting.

"Welcome everyone. Let the record show that this meeting of the cabinet has been called to order at 10:26. We have one hour for this meeting. First on the agenda as old business is a follow up from Homeland Security. Senator Thomas?"

Josh turned to face the speaker. It was difficult to put a finger on the emotion emanating from the Senator, but Josh would say it was a combination of anxiety and giddy anticipation. He clearly had a proposal that he thought was exciting.

"Thank you, Madam President. As I am sure you all recall, at the last meeting we discussed that there is a group of Americans that believe that the identity chip is the 'mark of the beast' prophesied in the Bible. I don't know how many of you are up at crack of dawn on Saturdays, but I would like to play a segment from The Live Edition of GTV two days ago." Senator Thomas tapped his device and the screens changed from the agenda to a recording of the familiar anchors of GTV. When the newscast went to commercial the Senator touched his Device and the screen went blank. Some of the cabinet reacted and some didn't, revealing the early Saturday risers. The President did not react.

"Obviously this was edited from the later editions," the Senator stated with a dismissive gesture. "Since that time Community Security agents and communications screeners have noted an increase in the chatter about the mark and related anti-government sentiment. There is clearly a segment of the population who intend to boycott the identity chip."

"You spoke last time about some concepts that you were developing, have you had a chance to come up with some more specifics?" President Sontara asked.

"As a matter of fact, my team has come up with a proposal. I feel that it provides a delicate balance between government control and personal freedom. Since commerce without the identity chip will eventually be impossible, our proposal is to segregate the refusers into camps where they will be free to trade among themselves. We do have precedent for this idea. Think of the Native Americans on reservations, the Japanese internment camps in World War II, the Homeless camps, disaster camps, and the Eldercare facilities. Senate Bill 3081 – the Enemy Belligerent, Interrogation, Detention and Prosecution Act of 2010 applies here as well. It allows for detention of people who are considered to be 'unprivileged enemy belligerents' - those engaged in hostilities against the United States and its partners, in this case the World Government- without criminal charges or trial for the duration of these hostilities. It was meant for terrorists but we believe it applies here."

"That sounds very reasonable. If you can textmail me some details we can begin this right away. Where would these communities be placed?" President Sontara asked.

"We know from the community sources that many of the refusers are landowners. Since they will be unable to pay taxes without a functioning Device, their land will be assumed by the government. Some of the parcels can be united into communities while some can be set aside for government use and some can be sold to help finance this endeavor."

"What if they refuse to go?" she asked.

"Well, of course, that is something we will have to decide, but we have the option that we have used in the homeless camps," replied Senator Thomas, looking uncomfortable, to his credit.

Josh felt sick. He had voted for the homeless camps, thinking that getting the homeless together and providing nutritious food, shelter and medical care was amazing progress. He had not really factored in that homeless people didn't want to be controlled any more than people with a roof over their heads did. When homeless people started getting belligerent and trying to leave the camps, it was decided that it was in their best interest as well as the rest of the citizens to force them to stay. The method that was used was a chemical frontal lobotomy. Similar to the lobotomies of the last century where the frontal lobe was removed surgically, a chemical was injected that targeted the frontal area of the brain, disconnecting it from the rest of the brain. Since the frontal area is the area that controls emotions, after the procedure the patient was perfectly docile and cooperative. And now they were talking about using it on the "refusers".

Suddenly Revelation 20:4 came into Josh's head. 'And I saw the souls of those who had been beheaded because of their testimony of Jesus and because of the word of God, and those who had not worshiped the beast or his image, and had not received his mark on their forehead and on their hand. They came to life and reigned with Christ for a thousand years.' Chemical beheading was what Senator Thomas was proposing.

"We have some work to do on how and when these camps would be set up. We need to have a plan ready to go into operation quickly so that if there is an uprising we can squelch it quickly by detaining those who are refusing. Soon we will have to present the mandatory nature of the chip, and present the camps as a rational alternative."

"Well, I applaud you for the ideas you have brought to the

table and will look forward to hearing more about this at our next meeting. Does anyone have any questions?" asked President Sontara, turning the rest of the cabinet.

Josh tried to keep his face neutral. At this point he didn't know how these people would feel about his sympathy with the refusers. He thought about brave men of the past. John F. Kennedy said, "A nation that is afraid to let its people judge the truth and falsehood in an open market is a nation that is afraid of its people". Martin Luther King said, "He who accepts evil without protesting against it is really cooperating with it." He considered protesting, he really did. But they had already moved on to the next agenda item.

# CHAPTER TWENTY-THREE
### ··· ◇ ···

Sasha looked over the jumble of clothes, supplies, and memories laid out on the guest bed. Narrowing down what to take with them was a nightmare for her. A packrat by nature, Sasha couldn't imagine leaving any of these things behind, but the truth was that their tiny car had room for less than half of it. It was times like this that she longed for the car of her youth, an SUV. Memories of such cars were spoken about with disdain, as if they were evil, not just inefficient. This small car was certainly big enough for them normally, but not for all of this stuff. Also, they needed to leave room for Karen, even though they were not sure how that was going to work. Somehow she would get here and then the three of them would head toward the farm, meeting up with George's family and Jessica. Since they didn't know what the actual scenario was going to be they had to keep it flexible. Sasha picked up Jessica's Christmas card from the nightstand. How clever of her to imbed the map in the picture on the front. They could keep it with them and not be worried about anyone knowing their plans.

At this point Sasha thought of the exodus as "when" and not "if". It didn't take a Daniel to read this handwriting on the wall, especially after Stephen's outburst on The Initial Edition. Sasha felt somewhat vindicated for Lebron's sake. How could the church elders see that and not realize what he was saying was true? Lebron said she was taking the wrong attitude – she was being vengeful, and that was not their place. How she wished she could have Lebron's faith.

Actually she used to have a faith like his, but Michael's death had changed that. Well-meaning friends would say "it was God's will" or "God wanted Michael with him" or "we can't know God's plan" only strengthening her anger towards God. Whereas Lebron had turned toward God to give him strength to make it through, Sasha had turned away from Him in anger. In the years since

Michael's death Sasha's anger had dulled, but she never regained that closeness to God she felt before. She missed that presence, that sense of peace, but couldn't bring herself to let go of the resentment of being wronged by God. Sasha had continued to serve in the church, studied the Bible, visited the sick and arranged for meals for the new moms. The exterior hadn't changed but the interior was dead. She wondered how many people in the church were like that. Lebron knew her state of mind of course, and she knew he was praying for her every day. Sasha loved Lebron so very much and felt guilty that she couldn't share this important spiritual connection, but she just couldn't. She couldn't trust God with her heart again.

Sasha tried again to thin her piles. She knew she couldn't take much out of her medicine pile. She ordered a three-month supply of all of her medicines last week, a risky maneuver because she wouldn't be able to order again for three more months and if they didn't leave for two more months she wouldn't have very much saved up. Then again, they could leave tomorrow. It was all a gamble. At some point she would run out of medicine that was for sure. It had been 45 years since she had been off of medicine, when she was pregnant with Michael. She had become so ill after he was born it was recommended that she not go through another pregnancy. She had mourned the children she would never have, but had thoroughly enjoyed Michael. After his birth Sasha began a string of medications, each one working for a while, and then losing its effectiveness. The most recent medicine had been quite effective for the last five years, allowing her a nearly normal life. What would happen when this medicine ran out?

Sasha made some radical cuts and was able to fit her disaster pack, medicines, clothes and personal items into one bag. Lebron's clothes, some over-the-counter medicines that George had asked them to pack, and a few photos went into a second bag, and teaching supplies into a third bag. Food went into a fourth, and Lebron was packing some hunting and fishing supplies in the car. Of course even if they had permits for guns Lebron wouldn't have wanted one, so hunting was going to have to be by bow and arrow, trapping and fishing. Now that he was officially retired, buying these types of supplies was not a problem – hunting and fishing was well within the expected activities of the retiree. Sasha hoped that Karen didn't have a big backpack; there just wasn't any extra room. Actually it wasn't so much the space but the weight. She and Lebron had figured out that to get to the farm on a full gas tank and electric charge they could only have 200 pounds of cargo in addition to their own body weights. Sasha had joked that it felt like they were packing for a mission to Mars. Of course there would be no opportunity to refuel without their Devices, so she hoped their calculations were accurate. Sasha weighed the bags and added them together. One hundred and forty pounds. That left sixty for the hunting supplies and Karen's bag – that should be plenty.

Sasha put the bags into the closet, glad that she had that chore done. She left the guest room, shut off the light and walked down the hall. At the door to their bedroom she paused then entered, removed an item from her nightstand and took it into the guest room.

"Just enough space," she said aloud as she slipped the worn Bible into her belongings.

# CHAPTER TWENTY-FOUR
··· ◇ ···

"Dr. Greene, do you have time for me to ask a couple of questions?" Karen asked as she knocked softly on her professor's door. It was Thursday afternoon and office hours had just begun. "They are not related to what you are teaching in class right now, just some things I have been thinking about." Karen really liked this professor. She was very approachable and reminded Karen of her mother. She looked quite a bit like her and was probably about the same age.

"Well, I certainly encourage outside thought! Sure, come on in and close the door behind you," said Dr. Greene, beckoning with one hand while pushing aside her screen with the other. "What's on your mind?"

"I have been thinking about what I just heard on the news. They said that they have decided to segregate the refusers into camps and have them trade among themselves. I know they are presenting it as a win-win solution for those who don't want to take the mark, but can they enforce that? Is it legal? Who can make that kind of decision? The military? The president? Is there any historical precedent for this? What do you think about this?" Karen shot the questions out like bullets, and the professor reacted by looking shell-shocked. She was silent for just a moment, and then glanced at her Device. Quietly she opened a drawer, pulled out piece of paper and made a quick notation on it.

"These are all very interesting questions, but I am sure you agree that it would not be considered unless it was legal, right?" she said, passing Karen the slip of paper and putting her index finger to her lips.

*Meet me in Library North at 5 pm.*

Karen glanced up from the note to see her professor pointing at her Device. Karen realized that she was putting her professor in a bad position and responded quickly. "Yeah, you're right. It must in the best interests of the people. Also, I have a question about the answer to number four on the last test. Can you help me with that?" Karen scrambled to come up with a question as the professor relaxed, looking visibly relieved.

Karen waited out in front of Library North. She felt like a spy and had mixed feelings about that. It was exciting, sure, but anxiety provoking too. She had never been one to watch scary movies or even edge-of-your seat thrillers, and here she was living it out. As Dr. Greene approached, Karen was about to greet her when she was again shushed by the professor. They entered the library and Karen followed Dr. Greene toward the study rooms. The professor set her Device by the door to the study room where she could see it from the window and pointed at it, obviously suggesting Karen do the same. When Karen set hers down Dr. Greene laid her sweater over them and then entered the study room. Karen followed and closed the door behind her.

"I am sorry to be so secretive, Karen, but I didn't want to get either of us in trouble with Homeland Security. I don't know if you know this, but all teachers' Devices are set to record while they are working. This was started to protect students after the increase in inappropriate contact in the second decade, but now it is also used to make sure that students are being taught accepted government curriculum. It should be off now but there is no way for me to tell. I don't think it should register a problem if there is no sound recorded in a library. Anyway, back to your question. Yes, there is historical precedent for internment camps such as this. After the bombing of Pearl Harbor in World War II more than 100,000 people of Japanese descent were put placed into a total of 10 camps. This was organized by the War Relocation Authority, or WRA. These were people who had never shown any anti-American sentiment, and most were citizens. Many had been born in the United States. Their possessions and real estate were sold off, and they were put into these camps that were run in part by the government and in part by the prisoners."

"How is it that I don't know this? I just took an American

History course where we discussed World War II and I never heard this, I am sure I would remember," said Karen, flabbergasted.

"Your materials are from online study guides. All internet sources have been sanitized in order to keep people from developing a distrust of the government. There was a rising anti-government sentiment when the World Government was being banded together, with riots and home-grown terrorists. It was a desperate time and it called for desperate measures. But, as is often the case, there were unintended consequences. One of which is that most people don't know the true story of American history, the one with mistakes. Under President Reagan the government formally apologized for this terrible act and gave token restitutions in The Civil Liberties act of 1988. People make mistakes. Governments make mistakes. But if students like you never learn about them, we are destined to make the same mistakes over and over. Edmund Burke said "Those who don't know history are destined to repeat it." I am afraid we are about to do so. Now Karen, I have to go, but you might learn a lot here in the library. I know it is old school – literally- to learn from books but they are here for you. And watch what you say, chatter is being analyzed and the walls have ears. But I am glad to know that there are young people like you out there that are thinking."

Before Karen could say another word Professor Greene had slipped out, picking up her sweater and Device. Karen came out after her and picked up her own Device. It seemed heavy in her hand. What had seemed just a few weeks ago to be an amazing piece of technology now seemed like a terrible burden. Karen slipped her Device into the Device pocket of her jeans and headed into the history section of the library.

Two hours later Karen was startled by the pinging of her Device. She forgot she had set it on emergency-only mode when she went for her meeting with the professor. She glanced at it and realized that she was twenty minutes late for a dinner date with Taylor. She textmailed him that she was in the library and that she would meet him at the dining hall in 15 minutes. Hurriedly she put away the books that she had strewn all over the table in the stacks and headed toward the dining hall. Karen had researched the information that Dr. Greene had given her and found that it was completely accurate. She wanted to look up the information on the internet to see if it was there but she was afraid of the digital fingerprint it would leave.

Karen entered the busy dining hall and scanned for Taylor's curly blonde mop of hair. She picked him out easily and went over to the table where he sat alone.

"I am so sorry, I got caught up in some research in the stacks in the library and the time got away from me. Did you already eat?"

"Yes, but I can sit with you. I have a Homeland Security meeting but not for a couple of hours. Go ahead and get a tray, I'll save the seat."

Karen got some pizza, an all-time college staple. She sat down with Taylor and ate ravenously, not realizing until she started how hungry she was.

"So what class has you doing research in the stacks? Isn't it hard to find any information that way?" asked Taylor.

"Well it isn't for a class; it is just some stuff that I am interested in." *The walls have ears.* "Anyway, what have you been up to?" she said, and they went on to a less controversial discussion.

Later, as they walked back to the dorm, Taylor took Karen's hand. "There's something I want you to know," he said, suddenly nervous.

"What is it?" she said, turning toward him and taking his other hand as well.

"I love you," he said, looking her in the eye as he said it.

"No one has ever said that to me outside of my family," Karen said. "I love you, too, Taylor." Just then it started to rain. They ran over to a nearby gazebo to take shelter. The rain come down harder and harder until they could barely see the dorm just ahead. Taylor wrapped his arms around Karen and kissed her. Karen felt so safe there with Taylor. He had been honest about his feelings for her; she just didn't feel she could keep these plans from him any longer.

"Taylor, there is a reason I have been doing this extra studying in the stacks. There is something I need to tell you."

As she began to speak, Taylor's heart sank. He thought about his meeting coming up soon. He had seen people whose Devices had registered anxiety when they entered the room being taken off to have a "private session". He would like to think he could keep a secret, but he had never had such a secret to keep, or had anyone so skilled try to pry it out of him.

# CHAPTER TWENTY-FIVE
$\cdots \diamond \cdots$

Jessica awoke in a panic. There was an alarm sounding that she didn't recognize, fast and persistent, coming from her Device. It dawned on her that this must be the sound of the emergency tone, the one she set at night and, until this moment, had never actually heard. Jessica fumbled with the Device and accepted the call.

"Mom you've got to go!" Karen said as soon as the call was accepted. "Right now!" In the small screen on the device Jessica could see that Karen was crying.

Jessica shook her head to try to clear the fog that remained from sleep. She checked the time on the device. 1:00 AM. "What?" she said, still trying to process what was going on.

"Mom! Concentrate! You have to go, now. They know!"

Suddenly Jessica understood. She had been outed as a refuser somehow. "Ok I get it, Karen. We will do as we planned. You stay there, finish school, just as we planned."

Now it was Karen's turn to be confused. "What?" she said.

"Just as we planned. I've got to go. I love you sweetie, forever, remember that always," said Jessica, tearing up.

"I love you too, Mom! I am so sorry!" Karen sobbed, and then she was gone.

Jessica jumped out of bed. What now? Leave in the middle of the night? Could she wait until the morning? No. How would she get to George and Becky's house without using her Device? She couldn't leave breadcrumbs to their house by taking a transport. She would have to walk the nine miles. After dressing quickly in dark clothes and exercise shoes Jessica went downstairs with her backpacks and Device. She entered the kitchen and the lights came on and the coffee started brewing as Jessica packed a few more food items in the bag. She set the Device on the counter. She put one backpack on her back and one facing front. Jessica realized that she would not be able to lock her door with having her Device with her, but what did it matter? She had committed to this now. She doubted she would ever be back. One last look around the room and she slipped out the front door.

Two hours later the doorbell on the Device rang, unheard by anyone. Then came a knock on the door. The door opened and two uniformed men called out Jessica's name. Seeing the Device on the counter, they scanned the house for heat signatures and found none. One of the men entered some information into his Device and they left, locking the door by changing the code to the universal code for refusers. As of that moment the residence and the property inside were available for government use.

Across the street a couple was awakened by the knocking on Jessica's door. They watched as the uniformed men entered the house, and wondered what crime had been committed that would warrant such a search. They knew that a woman lived there alone just from seeing her come and go for the five years they had lived there, but they had never spoken to her. They didn't even know her name.

# CHAPTER TWENTY-SIX

### ··· ◇ ···

Karen hung up her Device, tears streaming down her face. 'Just as we planned' her mother had said. The plan was to get to her grandparents' house and then go from there. They had also discussed the possibility that Karen could stay behind, but for Karen that was never really an option. Now she turned around to face Taylor, angrier than she had ever been in her life.

"Two hours? You could only keep my secret for two hours?" She stared at Taylor, who was sitting at Karen's desk chair, head in his hands, eyes puffy from crying. Just a few minutes ago he was pounding at her door, calling her name, spilling out the fact that he had told Homeland Security that her mother was a refuser.

"I am so sorry," he cried, "I am so weak. They knew as soon as I came into the meeting that I was hiding something. They can tell, just like the agents at the airport. They took me aside to a different room, two of them, and kept asking me questions. I am so sorry I told them. I would give anything to take it back, please believe me!" Despite her anger she couldn't help but feel a little bit sorry for him. She knew how intimidating those airport agents could be.

"Did you tell them about me? What about my grandparents? George and Becky and the kids?" she asked angrily, arms across her chest.

"No, once I had told them about your mom they seemed satisfied and let me go."

Karen nodded. She grabbed the backpack she had stashed in her closet and put her toiletries in front zipper area. Then she pulled down another backpack and started adding some books and papers that she had stacked neatly in a corner of her desk, causing her to brush up against Taylor's arm. The contact felt like an electric shock. Suddenly a thought came to her.

"They will know won't they? They will know that you came and told me as soon as they go to my mom's house. What will happen to you?"

"Does that really matter now?"

"I want to know." Karen replied, softening.

"Well, I will be dishonorably discharged from Homeland Security, so I will lose my scholarship," said Taylor.

"And?"

"And I will probably go to jail but I don't know for sure. It doesn't matter to me. I deserve whatever punishment I get. Just let me help you get out of here."

Karen stared at Taylor. She believed that he was sorry but was that enough? "What if you came with us?" she asked.

"I can't believe you would even consider that," said Taylor, visibly shaken. "But yes, I would come. I believe what you are doing is right."

"We would have to go right now. You wouldn't be able to contact your family or your friends. You would just walk away. Could you do that? Not even say goodbye to your family?" Karen asked.

Taylor thought for a moment. "In the Bible a man asks Jesus if he can go back to say good-bye to his family before he follows him and Jesus replies, 'No one who puts his hand to the plow and looks back is fit for service in the kingdom of God,'" quoted Taylor.

There was a momentary silence as Karen and Taylor looked at each other.

"That's from Luke," Karen said. "How did you know that?"

"I don't know," replied Taylor, bewildered. "It just came into my head."

Karen sighed and bowed her head in resignation.

"Grab your backpack," Karen said. "We have to go now. Apparently God wants you to come with us."

# CHAPTER TWENTY-SEVEN
· · · ◇ · · ·

Lebron awoke to the sound of the emergency alarm on his device. It was a sound he certainly recognized after years as a minister. Most of his least favorite duties came at night. Life threatening accidents and illnesses, sudden deaths, runaway children, they had all been announced with this tone. A Pavlov response sent his blood pressure sky-rocketing. But then he remembered that he had retired. He realized that it must be an emergency of his own, and his blood pressure shot up even higher. He tried to answer the device but he realized that there was no one there. It was the doorbell that had set off the emergency alarm.

"Sasha, there is someone here," he said, shaking Sasha awake. After years as a pastor's wife she had become desensitized to the alarm tone, but now she awoke.

"Who could it be?" she said, frightened.

"I don't know. I'll check the cameras. Touching the Device he accessed the security feed and got three views of the front door.

"It's Karen, and a young man!" he said excitedly. He and Sasha rushed down to the door, grabbing their robes and hurriedly donning them.

Lebron flung the door open wide. "Karen! Come in! What's wrong?" Lebron said, pulling her into a hug.

Karen turned toward the cab that had taken them from the bus station. The driver had insisted on waiting until they got in to make sure someone answered at this late hour. She waved him on, mouthing "Thank you!". He smiled and drove on. Karen took Taylor's hand and they stepped into her grandparent's house.

Lebron sat them down at the kitchen table as Sasha made coffee. As Karen talked, Taylor stared at the table, finding it difficult to meet the eyes of Karen's grandparents. As Karen came to the end of the story, Sasha sat down at the table with them, bringing the coffee.

"It doesn't sound like we have much time. We'll get dressed and grab our bags and be right down - get something to eat. It will be a long drive," Sasha said. She and Lebron hurried upstairs, leaving Taylor and Karen alone again.

"Well, that went better than I expected," offered Taylor.

"I'm not sure they understand that we are planning for you to come too," Karen said, smiling. "I kind of left that part out." During the bus drive down she had thawed as she realized that this evacuation was inevitable, and Taylor's indiscretion had just pushed the timing. She rummaged around in the fridge, poured some cereal into bowls for them and popped bagels into the toaster for her grandparents to take to go. Just as they finished eating their cereal and wrapping up the bagels Lebron and Sasha came down laden with suitcases.

"Ok let's go," said Lebron to the two as he headed for the garage.

Taylor stood off to the side as they packed their bags into the car. Sasha turned to him and asked, "But Taylor, what are your plans?"

Taylor and Karen exchanged glances. Then Karen explained that she wanted Taylor to come also. "There should be room in the car," she said, "I can put stuff on my lap, or under my feet."

Lebron looked at Sasha, and they came to a decision without a word. "It isn't the room, Karen, it's the weight," explained Sasha. "We won't make it there with the extra weight." She took out her personal bag from the trunk and opened it. After removing her emergency pack she set the bag against the wall in the garage and put the emergency pack in the trunk.

"Are you sure, honey?" asked Lebron softly, "I know how much that stuff means to you."

"Stuff. That's all it is. Compared to this boy's life it is worthless. Yes, I'm sure."

Lebron smiled at her and removed the bags from the car one by one. Karen set aside both of her bags, and Taylor put down his lacrosse bag, unable to speak past the lump in his throat. Lebron brought down the scale and after careful weighing, leaving some room for error, they had kept three emergency packs, Sasha's medicine and some food for the trip. The map/Christmas card was safe in the glove box.

"God will provide," Lebron said. He led a quick prayer for guidance and safety, pulled the car out of the garage, came in and shut the garage door. A Device was needed to start the car, but luckily not to keep it going. Leaving the car outside running, the four travelers came through the house and paused to leave their Devices on the kitchen table. Silently they filed out, never looking back.

# CHAPTER TWENTY-EIGHT
··· ◇ ···

"Finally," Jessica whispered to herself as George and Becky's house came into view. She had been walking for two hours with two heavy backpacks and was exhausted. The normally brightly-lit streets were dark. Early in her journey Jessica had realized that since the street lights came on with presence of a Device, she would have to make her way without them or her GPS locator. Luckily she had a good sense of direction and found the house with only one wrong turn. The lack of light actually worked in her favor since someone walking along carrying two backpacks in the middle of the night was sure to look suspicious. She darted in and out of the shadows, hiding whenever the streetlights came on since she knew that meant someone was near. Jessica stood at the door, realizing that without a Device the doorbell would not ring, and the cameras would not be activated. She knocked on the door. No one came.

"Come on George, wake up," she said under her breath and knocked a little louder, but not loud enough to wake the neighbors, she hoped. She didn't know what time it was without her Device, but she figured if she walked about three miles per hour it should be about four a.m.

"Who is it?" hissed George from the other side of the door. "Identify yourself or I will call the police right now!"

Jessica suppressed a giggle. Sometimes when she was under a lot of stress the most inappropriate emotions surfaced. "George – it's me, Jessica!" she said, just loudly enough to be heard through the door. "Let me in, quickly!"

George opened the door and Jessica slipped in. She shut the door quietly behind her then turned to face George. The sight of George in his boxers with his hair standing on end, brandishing a t-ball bat was more than she could handle. Jessica started laughing and couldn't quite get a grip on herself, slowly sinking to the floor. George looked down at her, confused. Becky came into the kitchen and took in the scene. She kneeled down on the floor, gently removed the backpacks from Jessica's body and set them on the floor. By this time the laughter had turned into sobs. Becky sat with her on the floor, pulling her into a protective embrace as Jessica recounted the events of the night. When she finished there was silence as they all considered their next move.

"Do you think Karen went to Lebron and Sasha's?" asked George.

"I don't know," replied Jessica, "I gave her the option to stay, but I am guessing that she has gone." Hoping, really.

"How can we know?" pondered Becky, rising from the floor. "If we call her or her grandparents they will have us as contacts, and you don't have a Device so you can't call. I guess we just have to assume she told them. If not, they will figure out eventually that you aren't there. Then they can decide what they want to do."

George was watching Becky. He had a feeling she wasn't completely getting this.

"Becky, we have to get ready to go," said George, giving her a gentle hug. "We have to go now."

"What?" said Becky pulling away from him, "No, we're not ready! I don't have all of the supplies I ordered, the kids aren't packed and I haven't figured out how to disable the GPS tracker on my device. No, we're not ready. We have a plan; we're going to travel at night, and in the spring… "

George knew that for an engineer like Becky the idea of having her plan disrupted was devastating. "I know, Becky, but the fact is, in only a matter of hours they could be here asking about Jessica. Besides, if Karen did go to her grandparents she is probably there by now and will have left a trail, so they will have to leave right away and we have to meet them up there. They need us," he added gently. He lifted her chin, looked at her eyes and saw her disbelief turn into understanding.

"You're right. We need to get this show on the road," she said, with new resolve. "Jessica, why don't you take a shower and then come down and make us some breakfast. George, how about you start packing up the items in the closet, and I will get the kids packed up." As she stormed out of the room on a mission, George turned to Jessica.

"I know this isn't how we planned it, but it is what it is," he said. "We'll manage."

An hour later the car was packed and stomachs were full. Maya and Mark were excited at the idea of an impromptu vacation. They had never known either of their parents to be so spontaneous, and the fact that they weren't told the destination made it even more of an adventure. Becky had allowed them each one toy to take, tearing up as they decided, knowing that it was the only toy they would have. Maya chose a stuffed dog that she snuggled at night, but Mark had a little more trouble deciding. Most of his playtime was spent with Device related games and toys. The two looked at Becky with disbelief when she told them that they would not be bringing their Devices. Since there had never been a time in their lives that they hadn't had a Device the idea of not having one was foreign. Mark settled on a toy dump truck that he hadn't played with for years. Becky took their bags to the car and loaded them in with the supplies and their other personal bags. Luckily their car had a large gas tank, hybrid technology and solar paint, so according to Becky's calculations there would be no problem getting there even with all of the weight. Becky pulled the car out of the garage, closed the garage door and went back into the house. She found George in the office, constructing a letter to his partners.

"I know it is dangerous to lay it out like this but I really feel like I need to tell them what's going on. I also transferred some money into the partnership account to cover supplies I ordered for us and to cover the overhead while they are looking for another partner. Hopefully the government won't notice it and take back the transaction once we are marked as refusers," George said. Becky was standing behind him. "Are you ready?" he asked.

"I'm scared, George," Becky said, tears threatening to

overflow from her eyes. "What have we done? This is a huge step, are we really sure it is necessary?"

George took her hands in his and kissed them. "It is a huge step. It is a leap of faith. And yes, I do think it is necessary. Search your heart, you know it to be true," he said, smiling at her.

"You have a Star Wars quote for everything, you nerd," Becky said, "Of course I would feel better if that quote came from Yoda instead of Darth Vader."

George drew her into his arms and kissed the top of her head. "We are going to be just fine. I feel at peace with this, don't you?"

Becky searched her heart. Yes, she did feel at peace with this. "Let's go," she said, wiping away the tears. "We have a lot of driving to do."

# CHAPTER TWENTY-NINE
$\cdots \diamondsuit \cdots$

Lebron drove. There was no question about who would drive and who would navigate. It was a given in their relationship. Lebron drove. Sasha looked straight ahead, afraid of accidentally catching the eye of someone passing, fearful that they would somehow read in her expression that they were fleeing. Taylor and Karen dozed in the back seat, exhausted both physically and emotionally from the previous night. Lebron and Sasha spoke in tense whispered voices as they discussed their worries. Sasha was concerned that even without their Devices the car would be tagged somehow and traced. Lebron couldn't completely discount her fears but felt relatively confident that with the past decade of dependence on Devices and the need to have the approved Device to start a car, the likelihood that Government Auto also placed a tracker was low. Up until now that would have been a waste of government funds. He suspected that the cars coming off the line might be equipped, assuming there were others like them who were abandoning their Devices.

Lebron was worried that they would not be able to find the farm with their limited map. Since modern travel was assisted by GPS on Devices, the need for detailed road signs had become obsolete. Many of the old road signs remained, but not all of them. Lebron remembered going on trips with his family when he was a kid. While his dad drove, his mom would consult the map, telling his dad the name of the next turn off and the approximate distance. This was an imperfect system, and sometimes they would have to pull over at a gas station to ask for directions. Well, they certainly couldn't do that now. Not only would the gas station attendants have no idea about direction, being Device-dependent themselves, such questions would raise all kinds of red flags about why they weren't using their Devices. The miracle of turn-by-turn navigation on the Devices was their enemy now. There were so many things that could go wrong, yet Lebron still had a sense of peace about this decision. He could tell by Sasha's stiff posture that she was struggling with her doubts. The weakening of her faith because of the loss of Michael was a constant source of pain for Lebron. He prayed about it daily and felt certain Sasha would eventually regain her once close relationship with God. He hoped it would happen soon, but he knew from other aspects of his life as well as the lives of the saints in the Bible that his time seldom matched up with God's time. He would just continue to be patient and wait it out.

Another concern Lebron and Sasha had discussed was their value to the clan. They worried about being a burden on the rest of the group at a time when they all needed to be useful. Then again, they had lived their youths during a time of less dependence on technology, so perhaps there were some memories they could dredge up that would be helpful. Lebron felt the current concept that old people were worthless was wrong, and they would just have to prove it.

Lebron looked over at Sasha studying their Christmas card map. She felt his eyes upon her and turned to give him a wan smile, but it was a smile nonetheless. They turned to look at the road ahead and were startled to see a perfect rainbow, starting on the left side of the highway and ending on the right. It looked as though they could drive right through it. Lebron glanced at Sasha's expression of amazement and reached over to take her hand. There were only so many experiences like this that she would be able to chalk up to coincidence.

# Chapter Thirty
· · · ◇ · · ·

George drove in silence, occasionally checking the back seat for signs of life. Maya and Mark had initially been quite animated, excitedly asking questions and bouncing in their seats. Even through this extremely loud discussion, each twin raising their voices in decibels and octaves to be better heard, Jessica slept soundly, sometimes adding a soft snore to the din. After about an hour, the kids wore themselves out with excitement and fell asleep, Mark resting his head on Maya's shoulder and Maya resting hers on her stuffed dog, Fluffy.

Becky studied the Christmas card map as though something new was about to present itself. George watched the road carefully, glad that the police no longer patrolled the roads for speeders. They could tell how fast a car was going by how long it took the Device to travel between toll booths and if a driver was speeding a ticket came up on his Device within minutes. Accidents were reported by the Device as well, signaling police and ambulance responses. Technically George could drive as fast as he wanted to but he didn't want to attract attention.

"Do you think Karen went to her grandparents right away? Do you think they are on their way? Do you think they will get there first?" Becky whispered George, all questions that she asked him an hour before. George recognized her need to be reassured.

"I'll bet that we will get there within a few hours of each other. I suspect that the time it took Karen to pack up and get on a bus, then get to her grandparents and take off from there was pretty comparable to the time it took Jessica to walk to our house and then for us to get on our way. Actually I hope we get there first since we have the things that we need right away in the way of power generating and such," George said. He looked over at Becky's look of alarm and backpedalled, "Of course they will be ok if they get there first – they have their three day emergency packs with heaters and food to keep them warm and fed."

"What if we can't find it? I think I am having a panic attack. I feel like I can't breathe."

"Becky, you're anxious. I am anxious too. If Jessica was awake she would be just as anxious. It is completely rational to feel anxious about the unknown. You told me one time that 'Fear not' or some version of it is one of the most common phrases in the Bible. Why don't you close your eyes and pray for guidance and peace. Once we are there and safe you will relax. Trust me," George said. "We'll find it, don't worry. We may take a wrong turn here or there with no navigation, but we will find it, I am certain of that." George was using his most authoritative doctor voice, hoping to instill faith in his directional abilities. During the drive he had glanced regularly over at Becky, sometimes catching her with a look of peace and a slight smile, only to be replaced in a few minutes by furrowed brows and nail biting. George had to admit to the same rapid mood swings himself. One moment he felt like they were on their way to a freeing adventure, the next he was awash in doubt.

Jessica awoke with a start. She had been dreaming about their arrival to the farmhouse. Karen and her grandparents were there, and in her dream, there was a rusty key under the front mat that let them into the house. The house looked much like Jared and Mary's, with a large kitchen, solid wood cabinets and a big farm table with lots of chairs around it. When they went upstairs there were beds all made up, dusty but sturdy and comfortable. The living areas were sparse but functional. It seemed like a reasonable dream to Jessica.

"Where are we?" asked Jessica.

"Not too far now," replied George. Of course he couldn't tell her exactly, which frustrated him. He was used to knowing his arrival time to the minute. George watched the exit signs, hoping that the one he was looking for would actually be marked. He spotted it up ahead and signaled to turn off. Becky switched to efficient engineer mode, keeping a close eye on the map and the road while simultaneously watching for evidence that they were being followed. By this time everyone was awake and hungry. Maya and Mark suggested a fast food stop, but Jessica doled out the sandwiches and juice boxes without commenting on the fact that there would be no fast food. Ever again.

After minimal rest stops taken in shifts since they couldn't turn off the car, the roads became narrower and the houses farther apart. Maya and Mark became more and more enrapt with the countryside. There had never seen open areas like this in their lives, and they were fascinated with the cows and horses roaming freely out on the pastures. George slowed as they approached the bridge which signaled that Josh's farm was down the next driveway. They were so eager to get there that the excitement in the car was electric.

George pulled slowly into the driveway. The weeds were high, obscuring the view of the house, but they were matted down, like someone had passed through before them. Becky and Jessica exchanged nervous glances. George inched the car up to the side of driveway and they all erupted into cheers. There, at the head of the driveway, was Lebron and Sasha's car.

# CHAPTER THIRTY-ONE
··· ◇ ···

Josh rode the train home. He stared unseeing at his Device, using it as a prop so that his thoughts would not be interrupted by other passengers asking questions or giving their comments on the recent news about the identity chip. Over the last few days since GTV had aired the intent of the government to universalize the chip and to segregate the refusers, these trips home had become one long discussion with constituents. Josh had always prided himself in being available to the people that had elected him, but his own views on this matter were so muddled that he had a hard time defending the decisions of the government. In the past people seemed to be pretty happy with how things were going, they had everything they really needed provided by the government. Edward R. Murrow, a journalist in the 20th century during the time of the McCarthy hearings said "A nation of sheep will beget a government of wolves". Josh felt like a wolf. He hid behind his device, hoping that he would look like he was reviewing important matters. Maybe he should skip the train for a while and just drive his car. The extra expense of the gas might just be worth it.

Right now his thoughts were on his family. He wondered if this was the time to discuss his concerns with them. He also wondered how it could be that he was so fearful of this discussion. How had it come about that he was afraid to have an honest discussion with his wife and his children? Why was he so afraid of their ridicule? He felt as though he had somehow lost his place as the head of the family by letting the kids have too much power in the mix, which seemed to be the current parenting trend. Certainly a far cry from "children should be seen and not heard" of his great-grandparents, which he also thought was a bit extreme, but perhaps the pendulum had swung a little bit too far the other way.

Josh got off at his stop and made his way toward his car. As he started it up he realized that neither Rachel nor the kids had even asked him about the identity chip. Maybe they thought that it was the last thing he wanted to talk about when he got home from work. Still, he would have thought they would want his insight into such a big event of the day. As Josh pulled into the driveway he could see his family in the kitchen through the front window. They looked relaxed and happy, the three of them sitting at the table, smiling and talking with wide sweeping hand gestures.

"Must be the Italian in Rachel coming through," Josh thought with a chuckle. Yes, today was the day to have this discussion- they were already around the table like they were preparing for it.

"Hi, guys!" said Josh as he came in.

"Hi, Dad," said Hannah and Ben.

"Hi, Honey," said Rachel, rising to greet him with a hug and kiss. "We were just talking about going out to the Bistro for some dinner, does that sound good?"

"Sure," said Josh, not wanting to spoil the good mood but also not wanting to lose his nerve, "But first there is something I wanted to talk to you about." Josh took off his coat and pulled up a chair. "It's about the identity chip."

"Oh hey, Dad, you don't even have to discuss it. We got them today at school. See? We were just talking about it," said Hannah holding up her hand to show him the tattoo.

"And I got mine today at the mall," interjected Rachel.

Josh was stunned. "But we never even discussed it," he stammered, "Didn't the kids have to have a parent's permission to get the chip placed?" Actually, he already knew the answer. They had to have a parent's permission not to have the chip placed.

"Honey, I don't know why you are so upset," Rachel said placing her hand over his, the freshly placed tattoo facing up at him, "You of all people knew this was coming and you never said anything about a concern. Did you have one?"

"Yeah, Dad, you weren't planning to be a refuser were you?" asked Ben, confused.

"It wouldn't look too good if a Senator refused, would it?" asked Hannah.

Josh quickly regrouped, trying to hide the emotion he was feeling. He realized that it would be of no use to voice his concerns now. He had waited too long.

"I just wanted to discuss it with you before you did it, that's all. Just discuss the pros and cons and all that, but it is certainly a moot point now. So who's up for the Bistro?" Josh said as he put his coat back on and grabbed his keys. He turned his back to the rest of the family as they chattered and put on their coats. Darkness settled over his heart and his face contorted in grief as he thought about the eternal consequences of this for him and his family. Scripture from Revelation 14 came into his head uninvited.

"If anyone worships the beast and his image and receives his mark on the forehead or on the hand, he too, will drink of the wine of God's fury, which has been poured out with burning sulfur in the presence of the holy angels and of the Lamb. And the smoke of their torment rises forever and ever. There is no rest day or night for those who worship the beast and his image or for anyone who receives the mark of his name."

He had put off the discussion. And now it was too late.

# CHAPTER THIRTY-TWO
### ··· ◇ ···

George, Becky and Jessica piled out of their car and made their way toward Lebron and Sasha's car.

Jessica's number one priority was Karen. Would she be with them? Jessica felt certain that Michael's parents wouldn't leave without Karen unless she had told them to go without her. As they approached the car she saw that someone had cut the vines and tucked the car in so it would not be seen from the road. This was curious to Jessica since she really couldn't see Lebron or Karen being strong enough to do that, and certainly not Sasha. She looked toward the house, barely visible among the masses of vines. Large trees competed for space with the back porch, the roots lifting the foundation and tipping it so that it looked like something from a Dr. Seuss book. All of the lower windows were obscured by bushes, and the upper windows were covered with dirt. From Jessica's vantage point she could see one window was cracked, but none appeared opened. She could only hope for the same on the other sides.

"Lebron! Sasha! Karen!" called Jessica, forgetting about the danger of being discovered. By now Maya and Mark and had joined the group and were looking with astonishment toward the dilapidated building.

Jessica led the way around the house, pushing aside branches and vines and calling out the whole time. George and Becky followed closely behind with the kids tucked in between them.

"So when we find the others can we go to the hotel?" Maya asked. "This place is pretty creepy and I think I just felt a bug on me."

George and Becky stole a glance at each other. Maybe they should have discussed this a little more on the way here, but honestly they just didn't know what they would find. As Becky was opening her mouth to reply they heard a whistle.

Jessica stopped and laughed. It was the whistle that Jessica and Karen had used since she was a child to find each other when they got separated at stores, parks or wherever. The sound of the familiar whistle brought tears to her eyes, choking her up so much that she had a hard time returning it, but she did. A return whistle was her reward and in just a moment she saw Karen and her grandparents making their way back through the underbrush following a young man who Jessica recognized from Karen's social site as Taylor. Karen slipped past him and rushed into her mother's arms.

"You're here! We were so worried!" cried Becky as she came upon the little troupe. Soon everyone was hugging, Jessica was crying and Maya and Mark were looking confused.

"Why do you think they are going so crazy?" Maya asked Mark.

"No idea," he replied.

"I guess I have some introductions to make," said Karen, wiping away a tear with a grimy hand and managing to smear dirt across her cheek. Now that they were all together safely she didn't feel quite as guilty about her role in this unscheduled exodus. Karen introduced Taylor to the rest of the group. She got the raised eyebrow look from her mom which begged for more information, but at the moment it seemed more imperative to make a plan for the night. Karen was getting chilled and she knew the temperature would be dropping soon with the setting sun. She returned the look with a quick head shake and hand gesture which she knew her mother would know meant 'later'.

"Have you had a chance to look around?" asked George.

"We had made our way around to the front thanks to Taylor's skill with the machete," replied Sasha. "The other sides of the house are pretty much like you see here. The front of the house is a little less wooded, and the front door is hanging on one hinge. We were just about to peek inside when we heard you calling."

Becky looked at Maya and Mark, who were holding hands and looking at the house with wide eyes.

"This looks like a Halloween house," said Maya in a shaky voice. "What kind of vacation are we on?"

"Come on Maya," said Mark. "How cool is this? Who do we know has ever had an adventure? I can't wait to tell Justin about it!"

Becky smiled at her excited boy and her fearful girl. She could identify with both of those emotions herself. She felt a pang of guilt at Mark's comment about Justin. She doubted he would ever see Justin again. Becky wondered how they were going to explain their new situation to their kids.

"Let's go back around to the front," said George, trying to sound enthusiastic and unafraid.

Becky looked at Sasha. She looked pale and exhausted. "Sasha, would you mind staying back with the kids? I'd like to check it out without worrying about what they are up to."

"You know I don't mind," said Sasha. "Actually, I would prefer it that way."

Mark protested weakly, Maya not at all. Sasha waved them towards the car as the rest made their way through the brush.

The house was large and well made. From what they could tell the wooden siding was intact, although the majority of the paint was peeling or completely gone. The first floor windows, barely visible due to vines, were cracked and one window was open halfway.

"This doesn't match up with my fantasy at all," said Jessica. They all laughed nervously. Jessica could tell that it was not what they expected either.

Once they turned the corner to face the front of the house, the vegetation receded a bit. There was moss and ivy covering the front, spilling out over the upper floor balcony and partially obscuring the front door, which was hanging ajar.

"That can't be good," commented George. "Seriously, anyone who wants to wait out here while we investigate should feel free to do so."

George and Karen looked pointedly at Jessica.

"What?" Jessica exclaimed. "Do you think I am a scaredy-cat?"

"Mom," said Karen gently, "there might be mice."

"Mice?" said Jessica, squeaking like the little vermin she despised. When every kid went through the rodent phase – hamsters, gerbils, guinea pigs – Jessica had stayed strong. No rodents in her house. The thought of them made her skin crawl.

"There could even be rats," George said softly, trying not to embarrass Jessica. He knew of her fear and also of her pride in being able to handle any situation. "Why don't you stay out here and keep watch. We shouldn't all be inside in case something happens."

Jessica nodded and held the door as the others entered. She gave the flashlight that she had taken from her emergency pack to Karen as she passed.

"Be careful in there," Jessica said.

"Yes, Mom," Karen said teasingly. "I'll be fine."

Jessica sat on the porch and looked around. No, not like she had imagined at all, but they were here, they were safe, and they would make the best of it.

Inside, the house was quite dark. Between the overgrowth and the dirty windows, almost all of the light was obscured. Karen turned on her flashlight and the group stood still, taking it all in. It was hard to tell what damage was from animals and what was from humans. They went into the front room and found a single piece of furniture, a couch, torn to shreds. Undoubtedly there had been other pieces of furniture, all carted away by looters over the years. Some nails on the wall suggested that artwork had walked off as well. Another room across from it had a similar story. The floors were hard wood and were in pretty good shape, though there were a few loose boards. One tripped Taylor as he wandered without watching his footing, landing him on his hands and knees.

"Are you OK, Taylor?" asked George. "Everyone please watch where you are going. I don't trust my medical skills out here."

The group moved slowly through the house, noting a downstairs bedroom –sans bed- before entering the kitchen. A fireplace dominated the south wall, and a few rusted cast iron pans and a pot lay discarded inside. A large, solid wood table sat in front of the fireplace, the surface marred by what appeared to be cigarette burns. Three chairs were jumbled in the corner, all broken into pieces. Gaping holes denoted where the appliances had once been. A few of the cabinets had been torn from the wall and the rest were missing their doors. For the most part the cabinets were empty save a few mismatched plates and cups. While they watched, a mouse peaked its head out of a teacup, squeaking angrily. Other noises from the cabinet led them to the conclusion that there was a whole family in there. Karen and George smiled at each other. Jessica would have freaked. An old black phone sat on the counter and was plugged into the wall by a cord. Instinctively Lebron picked it up to listen for a dial tone. Silence.

Quiet settled over the group as they surveyed their new home. Wordlessly they moved toward the stairs. George went first, testing each stair gingerly before bearing his whole weight on it and motioning them to follow. As he cleared the last stair the sound of wings flapping filled the air and they all instinctively ducked. Above their head flew two pigeons, disappearing into the kitchen as they watched.

The group gathered at the top of the stairs, wordlessly taking in all that they could see from that vantage point. Vandals had written obscenities over the walls and there was a foul smell coming from the bathroom. There were four bedrooms upstairs, each with mattresses on the floor. It appeared that the antique beds had been smashed and used as firewood, some of which remained incompletely burned in each fireplace. A layer of dust over the whole floor indicated that no one had been using the place for quite some time. They split up, checked out each bedroom, and carefully inspected the ceilings, windows and floorboards.

"What a shame," said Becky, her quiet voice sounding unusually loud in the silence. "Antique furniture being used as firewood just seems so disrespectful to the craftsmen who made them."

"It's like a really dark version of Goldilocks and the Three Bears," Karen commented. Taylor gave her a funny look. "I'll tell you that one later," Karen said, smiling and giving him a hug.

"This is quite a fixer-upper," remarked Lebron. "And certainly not livable for the time being."

"Well, the floors seem solid and the windows are remarkably intact. It will definitely take some work but I don't see anything insurmountable here, what do you guys think?" asked George. They all responded in half-hearted agreement.

"Let's go back down and tell my mom what we found," said Karen, "You know she is dying of curiosity."

They stepped outside and found Jessica pacing in the small front clearing. "Well?" she asked. "Is it inhabitable?"

"Eventually it will be," Lebron stated. "But for tonight, no. Let's go back to Sasha and the kids and figure out a temporary plan."

George and Taylor led the way back to the cars, with Karen and Jessica following closely behind and Lebron bringing up the rear. Karen was amazed at how well he was holding up. She had always thought that men of his age were pretty feeble.

"So were there, you know..," Jessica whispered.

"Yep," Karen replied. "But not very many."

George peeked into the car and laughed. Sasha had the seats flattened and an emergency blanket over them, making the car into fort. Maya and Mark were giggling as Sasha was acting out some story with wide sweeping arm movements and exaggerated facial expressions. When Sasha saw all of them watching her through the windows she stopped, embarrassed.

"No! We want to hear the rest!" cried Maya. Mark echoed the sentiment.

"Later, you two," Sasha said, "I want to hear the report, don't you?"

George took out another emergency blanket and spread it out in the area between the two cars. The adults gathered around in a circle with Maya and Mark listening from the car. Lebron filled Sasha in on the status of the inside of the house. The darkening of her face made Jessica realize that Sasha must have had a similar fantasy about what the place would look like. Jessica suggested that they get out their emergency packs and figure out what they wanted for dinner. Each dinner packet had in it a small bottle of water that heated up once a cylinder inside was crushed. The water was then poured into the packet which created a full meal. They assembled on the

145

emergency blanket with their food and collapsible cups that came with the packs. Becky poured water that she had brought to hold them over until she could find a water source. Two of the heat sources from the packs were set in the center. It looked like a weird combination of camping and romantic dining. Lebron said grace and they began to eat.

"So, Karen, what happened that made you call your mom and get this party started?" asked George.

Karen looked at Taylor. "Let me explain," he said, glancing across the blanket at her. Karen had told the story to her grandparents, but this was his responsibility. His shame. Up until now Karen's mom, George and Becky had been so accepting of his presence. How easily that could change once they knew he was the one responsible. Taylor took a deep breath and told them about the secret shared with him by Karen and his betrayal to Homeland Security. He wanted them to know how sorry he was and how he would do anything in his power to make it up to them. Once his story was finished the adults looked around the circle at each other. Lebron bridged the awkward silence by stating that we have all done things that we regret but they had to give the boy credit for coming to Karen immediately at his own peril. He also reminded everyone that now that the intention for the mark to become mandatory for commerce had been released, this move was inevitable. Maybe a kick in the pants was just what they had all needed.

Maya and Mark listened from inside the van. They were bewildered by all of the grown-up discussion. Normally when adults were having discussions Maya and Mark were parked in front of a screen. They weren't used to listening in.

"Did you understand what they were talking about, Mark?" asked Maya.

"Not really, but it sounded pretty exciting, like a spy movie or something. Maybe Mom and Dad will explain it later," said Mark. Gram (as they had always called Sasha) had been telling them a story about a family that was escaped from government soldiers by going into the woods to live on their own. She had made it sound so fun and exciting. After Taylor's confession Mark had realized that they

146

were the family in the story. He was pretty sure that Maya hadn't put it together yet.

"Well," said Lebron. "Clearly we are not going to be sleeping in the house tonight, so we need to figure out alternate sleep arrangements before it gets dark." The sun was disappearing over the trees and the temperature was dropping fast. They evaluated the space the cars provided once seats were repositioned and such and with much discussion, positions were decided. Shortly thereafter the exhaustion of the day and the anticipation of a rough day to follow got the best of them and they headed for their spots. Taylor curled up in the back seat of Sasha and Lebron's car as they reclined in the front seats, leaving him little room to move. Lebron tried to convince Taylor that he and Sasha could sleep sitting up, but Taylor didn't buy it. A compromise was struck, with Lebron and Sasha semi-reclined. In George and Becky's car they were able to fit themselves and the kids in the back with the seats down, with Jessica and Karen up front. As everyone took their places, Karen motioned to her mother and they stepped away from the car.

"I just wanted to tell you that I am really sorry that things worked out this way. You were right- I should never have told Taylor about this. I should have thought about his Homeland Security connection and how difficult it would be for him to keep the secret. Anyway, I'm sorry."

"I believe I said that you should use your judgment, I didn't tell you not to tell him. You never said how he ended up with you on the trip. How did that happen?"

Karen told Jessica about the confrontation and Taylor's recitation of the scripture from Luke. Karen smiled.

"Do you love him?" she asked.

"I do, Mom. I really do."

"Well, maybe you did use good judgment. Maybe Taylor is supposed to be here with us."

Back in the van, Becky and George were already asleep with Maya and Mark sandwiched between them. Maya stared at the ceiling. Turning her head, she whispered in Mark's ear.

"We're the family in the story aren't we?"

"Yes, Maya, I think we are," he replied in a whisper. Mark had no idea what was going through her head.

"I thought so. I wonder how the story will end," she said, her voice starting to waver.

"I don't know, but I can tell you this, it is going to be an adventure story!"

# CHAPTER THIRTY-THREE
··· ◇ ···

Cock-a-doodle-doo!

Jessica reached for her bedside table to grab her Device. Her normal morning confusion was intensified by the fact that there was no Device and no bedside table. She opened her eyes and looked around, trying to get her bearings. She was asleep in the front seat of George's car and Karen was asleep next to her, peacefully curled up with her hands folded under her face like an angel. She had slept in this position since she was a baby. Michael had always thought she was returning to her position in the womb when she slept. No matter where Jessica awoke, thoughts of Michael greeted her in the morning.

Cock-a-doodle-doo!

Now Jessica was really confused. The events of the day before passed quickly through her brain. The call from Karen, leaving her home and Device, the trip, getting to the house, the confession from Taylor and then falling into a deep sleep here in this car all came back to her in a rush. Could that really have been only yesterday? And if she had left her Device at home why was she still hearing it? Suddenly it dawned on her that there was a reason why a rooster crowing was a wake-up tone, they have been waking farmers for ages, and here she was on a farm! She smiled at the realization that she had never really put that together. More importantly, clearly there was a rooster nearby, so maybe there were some hens. Jessica slipped out of the car quietly, trying not to wake George's clan and Karen. She had no idea what time it was but the sun was just rising, and she was sure Karen could use a little more sleep. Jessica was still dressed in the clothes she traveled in, having fallen asleep without bothering to strip down. She tip-toed around to the back stoop and was startled to find Lebron and Sasha already there.

"Good-morning, Sunshine!" said Lebron, "I hope we didn't

wake you, I have been trying to talk quietly but you know how hard that is for me!"

Jessica told them the funny tale of mistaking the rooster crowing for her Device, admitting she had never really put together the reason for the rooster alarm tone. They laughed quietly and speculated on the possibility of nearby chickens. None of them had any idea what other farms were nearby, or even what the boundaries were to this farm.

"Well, certainly fresh eggs would be a wonderful find," said Jessica. "With the exception of Taylor we all have our three-day packs, and we do have some other canned and dried foods, but we really don't have much. I had in mind spring, not fall as our leaving time, with the thought that we would plant right away and have at least some crops started while we lived off of our supplies plus our foraging. Now I just don't know…" she trailed off, obviously anxious.

"I know, it is natural to be anxious. Jessica. Do you believe in your heart that what we are doing is right in God's eyes?" he asked.

"Yes, I really do," she replied without hesitation.

Lebron opened the Bible that he had in front of him, leafed quickly to a passage and began to read aloud in an uncharacteristically soft voice.

"This is from Matthew 6, verse 25 – Jesus is speaking to the disciples: 'Therefore I tell you, do not worry about your life, what you will eat or drink; or about your body, what you will wear. Is not life more important than food and the body more important than clothes? Look at the birds of the air; they do not sow or reap or store away in barns, and yet your heavenly Father feeds them. Are you not much more valuable than they? Who of you by worrying can add a single hour to his life?' " Lebron gently closed the book. "Of course this doesn't mean that we should just sit here and wait for manna from heaven, but it does mean that God will provide for us," he added.

Jessica glanced over at Sasha. She looked unconvinced. A rustling noise from behind Jessica startled her. She turned around quickly and saw George and Becky with Maya and Mark skipping along behind. Karen dragged behind them, an emergency blanket wrapped around her, with Taylor taking up the rear.

"The sun is up and so are we!" said Mark in a sing-song voice. Maya giggled.

"Yep, yep, we are all up," said Karen, plopping down on the slanted stoop and resting her head on her grandmother's shoulder.

"What time is it?" asked Becky.

"I don't know, and I don't know how we are ever going to find out!" said George. "All of us have used our Devices for telling time, and without those how are we going to know?" George's voice sounded a bit desperate.

"Truly, George," said Lebron calmly, "Why does it matter? We will probably end up going to bed with the sun and waking up with it, and besides knowing when to meet, why else do we need to know the time?"

George thought for a minute. He had been a slave to time his whole life. It was hard to admit that something that had been such an integral part of his life really didn't matter.

"I guess you're right," he said, sounding unconvinced.

"What do you have there, Becky?" asked Sasha, pointing to a five-gallon bucket that Becky was toting.

"This, friends, is our toilet for now," Becky stated. "We will line it with one of these plastic bags and when you have done your business you put another one on top and it's ready for the next customer. When it gets full we tie up the bag and bury it. Pretty ingenious, right?" she said in a voice that was a little too chipper for the content of her speech, giving away her nervousness with presenting this distasteful information. Before retiring to the cars last night they had slipped into the woods, but that solution wouldn't last long. Hopefully the septic system was functional but that would have to be tested.

Taylor looked at the setup thoughtfully. Then he slipped away from the group and returned a few minutes later with a toilet seat. "I noticed that the downstairs toilet seat was off. We can use this until we get the inside up and running." He set the seat atop of the bucket and transformed it into a normal appearing toilet.

"Thanks," Becky mouthed.

"I'll try it out," said Sasha, taking the bucket with the toilet paper, the bags, and the hand sanitizer.

"I'll go with you and we can pick out a private spot," said Lebron, and they took off into the woods.

Once they returned and everyone had taken their turns at the latrine they gathered for breakfast. Powdered milk was mixed with a tube of water and poured over cereal for a relatively normal meal. Sasha, who had sworn off of dairy products years before, left hers dry and gave the kids the milk to drink.

After breakfast they split up chores and went their separate ways. Becky suggested that she, Jessica and Mark go and look for water. Jessica jumped at that, favoring it over the mice infested house. She wasn't sure if she would ever be able to sleep in there.

"The water source would not be far from the house," Becky said, more to herself than to anyone else. "Most likely it would be near the back door." She looked around the stoop, but didn't see a pump.

"This is heavy," complained Mark, struggling under the weight of the one gallon jug of water. "Why do we have to take water to find water?"

Becky looked at her son. He was pitifully out of shape with doughy arms and legs, a protuberant belly, and a round face. His shirt was wet with sweat from just this small amount of exercise. She didn't understand it. He had PE two days a week for 30 minutes and was on a soccer team that practiced two days a week for an hour and had games on Saturdays during the season. Apparently that just wasn't enough exercise for a seven-year-old boy. Also, she had to admit, his diet wasn't always that great. They were busy parents and often brought home take-out dinners. No more than other families, she had rationalized. But now watching Mark struggle under the load of one gallon of water made her realize that the time in front of the screens had taken its toll. Of course, Maya had the same level of fitness.

"When we find the pump, we'll need to prime it. Wells that have stood unused for years need to be primed with water," she explained. She watched as Jessica hacked away at the underbrush with the machete.

"I think I see it!" she exclaimed. As she broke through the last of the thicket between them and the pump, they stepped into a clearing, with the pump in the center. Jessica and Becky looked at each other with a combination of fear and wonder as they entered the small clearing.

"Hey, this thing looks like the faucet in your bathroom!" Mark said and, dropping the jug of water, ran over to it.

Becky laughed, realizing that the faucet he was talking about did indeed look like this pump, but of course, very few people of the generation that was currently living had ever seen a pump like this.

"Actually, the faucet was fashioned to look like this pump. It works by lifting the handle and pumping it down," she said.

"Like this?" said Mark, grabbing the handle and pushing it down.

"Yes, but remember, I told you that we need to prime.." Becky stood speechless as clear water poured from the pump. Mark laughed and put his hands under the stream.

"It's cold!" he exclaimed. "Can I drink it?"

"No, we don't know if it is contaminated," Becky said distractedly. She was trying to figure out why the water was running and why there was a clearing around it.

"Look, Becky," said Jessica, pointing to a path leading out of the clearing. "Let's check it out."

"Yeah, let's check it out!" said Mark jumping up and down. "Let's explore!"

Mark ran down the path, but suddenly stopped short, reached out and grabbed something out of the air. He looked closely at it, then came to show Jessica and his mother.

"Look at this bug," he said excitedly, "I've never seen one like it. It has armor on it that is shiny like metal."

Becky snatched it from his hand, dropped it and crushed it with her shoe.

"Poisonous," she said to Mark. He looked disappointed but turned to continue down the path.

"Drone," she whispered to Jessica. The women exchanged worried glances. Becky had known that it was a possibility that they would be spotted by a World Government drone. Since the second decade they had multiplied almost as fast as the insects they were designed to mimic. She just didn't think it would be so soon. Becky and Jessica knew without discussing it that they would keep this find to themselves.

The path from the pump to the street spanned about five feet, with dense briars at least five feet high on each side. It was no surprise that they hadn't noticed the path from the house even though it was only about twenty feet away. The path ended at the road, with a curtain of vines blocking the entrance from easy view. Parting the curtain, Jessica peeked out and looked around, seeing nothing out of place. She returned the curtain to its original place and turned to face the other two.

"You know what this means don't you?" she asked.

"We are not alone," Becky said gravely.

"That's great!" exclaimed Mark. "I hope they have a little boy!"


Back at the house the rest of the crew had decided to take one area at a time. Sasha, Karen and Maya concentrated on the kitchen.

"Look at these old pans, Maya," said Sasha, stooping to look at the cast iron pots and pans that lay in the fireplace. "I know the looters didn't take them because they look so old and rusty, but actually these pans are really special. They hold heat really well and they last forever. It will take a lot of work to get them nice enough to use though." Sasha sighed.

"What will clean them?" asked Maya.

"Well, several things. Let's look around."

Karen, Maya and Sasha looked under the sink; first opening the door then backing off like a SWAT team searching a building. When nothing crawled or flew out they knelt down and peered in.

Apparently the looters hadn't bothered with the cleaning supplies, for which they were grateful. In the mix of abrasive cleansers, soaps and detergents were wire brushes and steel wool.

"This is going to be a big job," said Sasha.

"I want to do it!" said Maya, grinning.

Sasha smiled. She had never known a child to be so excited about a chore. Sasha didn't really know how George and Becky had raised their children, but she did know that chores for the children had pretty much gone the way of the dinosaur in the current society. Children were so busy with activities and homework they didn't have time to do anything else. She had always felt that was wrong, that children got a sense of satisfaction and accomplishment out of doing household tasks. In addition, they got a sense of what is needed to run a household. The eager look on Maya's face told her she was right.

"Ok, Sweetie, you go for it. Take this pan out to the stoop and start scrubbing. I will come out and check on your progress in a few minutes."

Maya struggled with the heavy pan but managed to get it out to the stoop and start her task. Inside, Sasha scrubbed down the table with supplies she had found. Karen started going through the cabinets one-by-one, taking out the contents and setting them on the table to be cleaned. When she got to the mice in the teacup Karen put a bowl over them and slid them out onto a plate, taking them outside past Maya like a meal under a cloche. Maya squealed when Karen told her what she had hidden under the bowl, but was curious to see the little rodent family. Together they walked out into the woods to set them free, backing away when the bowl was removed. The little mouse mama did not seem at all happy about the relocation, making no move to escape, so Maya and Karen returned to the house, leaving the plate, bowl and teacup behind.

"Remind me to go back and get those things," said Karen.

"OK," said Maya, glancing over her shoulder to see what the mice were doing. "They're so cute!"

"My mom would completely disagree," Karen laughed. They came upon the stoop where the abandoned fry pan lay. Karen was amazed at Maya's progress and complimented her on her work. Maya glowed with the praise and set to work finishing the project.

Karen rejoined Sasha in the kitchen and began setting all of the usable items on the table so that she could clean the cabinets.

"Why do you think they built such a big house?" Karen asked Sasha.

"Back when this house was built it was not uncommon to have two or even three generations living under the same roof," Sasha explained. "Back then people often lived with their adult children once they retired from working and needed help taking care of themselves. Then a number of government programs came into existence like Social Security, Medicare and Retirement homes, so people came to rely less on their families than they did before. Similarly, programs such as Welfare, Food Stamps, Homeland Security college grants and higher minimum wage requirements lessened the younger generation's dependence on their parents while they got on their feet. While all of these programs were good safety nets to lessen poverty, it did cause people to feel less responsible for each other."

"Well I guess one benefit of this mess we are in is that I will be able to spend time with you guys and with Mom, something I probably never would have been able to do otherwise," Karen said, smiling. "I think I am going to like helping to care for you when the time comes, Gram, but for now, can teach me how to cook real food? The only things I ever cooked at school came out of a microwave."

"I would happy to," said Sasha, returning the smile weakly. Fatigue was starting to set in and she knew if she didn't listen to her body she would be sick tomorrow. Even though she hadn't completed her task to her satisfaction, she had to quit.

"I think it is time for a break. Let's go outside," said Karen. She saw the fatigue on her grandmother's face and took the cleaning products from her hands. On the stoop, Maya was just finishing her task and the pan looked brand new. Maya had scrubbed it inside and out. Now it would just need to be wiped out and re-seasoned, and it would be good to use. Sasha was just thinking about what kind of fat they could use for that process when Becky, Jessica and Mark came toward them. Mark looked exhausted, but excited to tell the story of the well and the pathway to the street. Sasha had mixed feelings about the news. On one hand it would be nice to have neighbors to help look out for each other, but it also increased their risk of being turned in as refusers. "Well, that is in God's hands," she thought, surprising herself that God had come into her mind after so many years of pushing him out.

**********

  In other areas of the house the men were at work. They had decided that they should stay together and just go room to room, assessing and cleaning. No one said what they really thought – they were afraid to be alone. Methodically they cleaned out the two front rooms and the downstairs bedroom, using a broom and dustpan they had found in a small closet downstairs. As Sasha had found in the kitchen, marauders were apparently not too interested in cleaning supplies. In the closet they had also found a vacuum cleaner, worthless without power of course, some cleaning products and rags, as well as a few coats and a couple of boxes of clothes which they left to peruse later. In the library, as they had come to call one of the front rooms, they found that the couch was infested with mice. George and Taylor took the couch out to the front porch and left it, hoping the little vermin would leave on their own. They also took the braided rug outside and beat it with the broom. Lebron swept the wood floor, cleaned the cobwebs out of the corners of the room and used a cleaning solution he found in the closet to wash the windows. Taylor took the books out and wiped them down with a cloth, noting some familiar titles – Huck Finn, To Kill a Mockingbird and others - as well as many he didn't recognize. The idea of reading a paper book intrigued him. He had never seen the value of toting around a book, preferring a lightweight tablet. Now as he turned over a book in his hands he could see that the touch and even the smell of the book were appealing. Flipping through the pages he saw that someone had put some notes in the margin, which added to the appeal. He couldn't wait until they took a break from the cleanup so he could come back and explore these books. George, Lebron and Taylor looked around the library and complimented each other on a job well done, and then moved on to the living room.

George removed the sheet covering the couch in this room and was surprised to find it without evidence of mice inhabitation and appearing quite clean. They all plopped down on it at once, causing a cloud of dust to rise and provoking a coughing fit in each of them. Laughing, they got up and finished the room. After this was done and they had again congratulated each other on the results, they went to search the area behind the house. They found a barn whose exterior walls still had a little bit of red paint on them, and whose metal roof which was just as much rust as metal. Next to it was a large shed. The three men stood at the door and peered in. There was enough light coming in through the holes in the roof that they could see that it was full of old farm tools. They went in and looked the tools over carefully, doing their best to avoid spiders and always on the lookout for snakes. Lebron had visited the farm of a friend's grandparents when he was a kid and recognized many of the tools, explaining their uses as they went through them. They needed some attention but would be good as new with a little work. Lebron could tell that Taylor was intrigued by the tools but he was quiet the whole time, nodding when appropriate, but not speaking much.

"Cat got your tongue, son?" bellowed Lebron. When Taylor looked confused he explained. "I don't think I have heard you string five words together since we met you. Are you always this quiet?"

Taylor paused. He knew Lebron was sincere but he felt like an outsider around this family. And besides that he was the one who had exposed them. What he really wanted was to be as invisible as possible.

"I'm just trying to see where I fit in at this point I guess," he said tentatively.

"Taylor, you fit right in the middle of us," said George. "I get the feeling that you are still feeling guilty about this situation, am I right?" George was a bit afraid of bringing up this topic but knew they had to clear the air.

"Well, yeah, I don't know how I can expect you to forgive me."

"We all forgive you, Taylor. Now you need to forgive yourself. Sometimes that is the trickiest part."

They walked back to the house and found the rest of the family on the stoop listening to Mark tell the story of the well.

It was a beautiful day with just a touch of chill in the shade while quite warm in the sun. The whole crew spread their blankets in the clearing by the pump and pulled out a sparse meal from their packs. Jessica had put together a pack of sorts for Taylor from the supplies she had brought, not wanting him or Karen to go hungry sharing Karen's pack. Discussion centered on their morning accomplishments and what treasures they had found. There was a lot of chatter and Jessica was enjoying the camaraderie, but as she looked at the meals and calculated their dwindling supply, she felt a bit of panic. She had taken on the responsibility of the food and she felt like she had let the group down. Tomorrow she would look around for the wild sources of food that she had researched. Glancing up, she noticed Lebron staring at her. He tapped his Bible and raised his eyebrows at her. Now how had known she was worrying about that?

At the end of the pathway leading to the pump the vines parted slightly. The picnickers were just clearing up their lunch and getting ready to return to work. Sasha announced her plan to sit under a tree and read To Kill a Mockingbird. She explained that someone else would have to clean the toilet and check the septic system since she had a weak stomach. Laughter filled the clearing. The vines closed quietly.

# CHAPTER THIRTY-FOUR
··· ◇ ···

Josh gazed out of his office window at the snowflakes drifting slowly down from the sky, some alighting on the trees across the street at the park. A Florida boy from birth, he still was amazed at every snowfall. The quietness of it, the beauty and the individuality of the snowflakes all filled him with wonder. Watching the snow gave him the same sense of peace that he used to get when he would look out over the lake as a kid.

"I could use a little peace," he said to himself. Since the night that his family had revealed their chips, or marks as he had come to think of them, he had barely slept. His wife kept asking him if he was sick, his staff gave him curious stares, and he noticed that other senators were going out of their way to avoid him. Josh knew that he would be required to get his mark soon, and he still didn't know what he was going to do. Part of him wanted to insist that his family go with him to the farm, and part of him just wanted to go with the flow and take what came to him. He felt terribly guilty about not talking to his family well before the chips became available. He had been afraid they would laugh at him. What a coward he had been. His self-flagellation was interrupted by a knock on the door.

"Senator, do you have a moment?" asked one of his long-time aides.

"Sure, William, what have you got?"

William entered, carrying a tablet under his arm, and shut the door carefully behind him. "I got this from Homeland Security and wanted to advise you of it," he said, handing over the tablet.

Josh studied William as he took the tablet. His aide was clearly nervous. A slight sweaty sheen covered his brow and his shirt looked damp at the collar and the armpits. He gave off the acrid odor of someone who is anxious. Josh looked at the tablet and saw why. A drone was honed in on Josh's property in North Carolina. The infrared detectors had noted nine unauthorized humans. Josh stared at the tablet. Nine. Karen and George's family made six, then probably Lebron and Sasha which would make eight. Plus one more, maybe a friend of theirs. Would they have gone without contacting him? Yes, he thought, they would have if they had felt it was necessary. He would like to look up whether they had been labeled refusers, but he didn't want that trail. Years ago, before any of this identity chip mess, a report had come to him from the infrared census that there was an unauthorized person living on his land. William had brought him this information also and Josh had asked him not to act on it. Josh felt that if someone needed a place to stay and he was not using the property there was no harm in letting them stay. Of course now the rules were different. Nine people squatting on a property were most likely refusers. To ask him to ignore it was more than just overlooking squatters; it was a matter of not reporting probable refusers, a criminal offense. No wonder William was so nervous.

"There's more, sir," William said, taking the tablet from Josh and swiping to the next page. He tapped it and handed it back to Josh.

Josh watched in fascination as a boyish version of George's face appeared on the screen, coming close to the camera and then receding. There was some video of the ground and a quick shot of a woman's face. The video ended abruptly. Josh struggled to keep his voice dispassionate.

"Listen, William, I really don't want to cause these people trouble. I realize that they might be refusers, but I have sympathy for them. I would like you to put in your report that you passed this information to me and I told you I would take care of it. That way you can document that you brought it to me and if there is ever a problem it is all me, alright?"

William breathed a sigh of relief. "Yes, sir," he said, taking back the tablet and quickly leaving the room.

Josh turned back to the window. Now he knew for sure that his friends had followed through. The irony that he was the one who had called for this course of action was not lost on him. He ran through his mind all the reasons why he needed to stay here from his kids' education to his role in government to his wife's happiness. It all sounded very unselfish but in reality it was ultimately self-serving. Josh knew he was putting his comfort, his happiness and his family above his God. He looked at the snowflakes again, each as individual as fingerprints. Who could look at them and possibly not believe in the presence of a creator? Josh closed his eyes and put his head in his hands. For the first time in quite a while, he prayed.

# CHAPTER THIRTY-FIVE
··· ◇ ···

By the afternoon of their third day in the house it was relatively clean, the mice and birds had been ousted, and makeshift beds had been made up on the floors in the bedrooms using the emergency blankets and various materials scavenged from the house and the cars. The beds would not be very comfortable, but they would do for the time being. The last of the emergency rations had been consumed for dinner and they were all hanging out in the living room, each immersed in their own thoughts and worries.

"I'm bored," said Mark.

"Yeah, what did they used to do in the old days before screens? Just sit around and stare at each other?" asked Maya.

"Well, that was a little bit before my time even," said Lebron, "but I know they told a lot of stories."

"Tell a story, tell a story!" cried Maya and Mark.

"I don't know any stories," Lebron said. "And I don't have a very good imagination. Someone else tell one."

"You do know stories. There is a book you know well that has a lot of good stories in it," Sasha smiled. Lebron smiled back and glanced at the Bible he held in his hand.

"Tell one about a princess," said Maya.

"Well I do know one about a young queen,"

"Tell it!"

"Alright. Once upon a time long ago in Persia, there was a foolish king named Xerxes. Our story starts with Xerxes giving a party. Not just any party, but a seven day long blowout with lots of food, wine, and fancy decorations. All the important people were there. On the seventh day, Xerxes called for his servants to bring to him the lovely Queen Vashti. Well, Queen Vashti was having her own party in a different area and, for whatever reason, refused to come."

"I bet her party was better and she just didn't want to go his," Maya commented.

"Probably, also it may have been that the king's party was pretty wild with a lot of people drinking and she didn't feel safe. Some people even think he wanted her to come to the party in *only* her crown." Lebron explained.

"Ewwww," Maya and Mark said in unison.

"After the party was over, the King brought together his friends and advisors and asked them what they thought he ought to do about Queen Vashti. After all, she had embarrassed him by not coming to the party when he had requested her. His advisors were concerned that all of the wives would think they could act the same way and there would be all kinds of disrespect and trouble and that the king needed to deal strongly with Vashti. They suggested she be banished and the king agreed. She had made him look bad."

Maya broke in saying, "How can they talk about her like that? She was the queen!"

"Yes, but this was a long time ago and women didn't have the same rights as men," interjected Karen.

"That stinks," pouted Maya. Even Mark knew enough to keep silent.

"Later the king thought about what he had done....."

"I hope he was sorry," interrupted Maya.

"...and wanted another queen. One of his attendants suggested that he send his servants out into the kingdom to look for the loveliest young girls in the land and bring them to the palace for beauty treatments, then pick from them. So that is what he did."

"Sounds like The Bachelor," whispered Karen. Jessica and Becky giggled.

"Meanwhile in Susa there was Jewish man named Mordecai who had been raising his cousin, Esther, who had been orphaned."

"What happened to her parents?" Maya asked.

"We don't know," said Lebron.

"How sad," Mark said.

"Esther was a beautiful girl, and was taken to the king's palace and put under the care of Hegai, the kings servant. Esther and

Hegai became friends and he moved her to the best place and got her the best food and beauty treatments. When it was her turn to go to the king, she consulted Hegai on what would be best to wear and bring with her to the king. The king was enchanted by her and made her his queen. Mordecai worried that Esther might be persecuted because she was Jewish, so he told her not to tell anyone. He paced back and forth in the courtyard of the area, asking for news about Esther.

"He must have loved her very much," said Sasha.

"While he was there at the gate, Mordecai overheard two of the guards discussing a plot to kill the king. He told Esther and she reported it to King Xerxes, telling him that Mordecai had told her. The foiled plan was recorded in the history books. About the same time an evil man, Haman, came onto the scene and became close to the king, closer and more powerful than anyone else. The king trusted him and commanded that all the people bow to him, but Mordecai wouldn't bow to Haman. There was a long-standing feud between the Jews and the Agagites, which was Haman's family, but that is another story. Haman was so mad that he wanted to punish not only Mordecai but all of the Jews in the country. He convinced the king that the Jews were bad people and should be destroyed. Haman rolled a pur, which is like a dice, to see which month they should all be killed. The order was put out to kill all of the Jews and on the same day, the 13th of Adar, and take all of their belongings. This was about a year away."

"That's awful!" cried Maya.

"When the Jews heard about this they were shocked and scared and many of them started crying and wailing. Mordecai felt especially bad and wore mourning clothes and cried at the gate of the king. Esther didn't know about the order but heard about Mordecai and sent a servant to find out what was going on. Mordecai sent her a copy of the order and asked her to go to the king and beg for mercy. Queen Esther was afraid to do this because she hadn't actually seen the king in a while and the punishment for interrupting him without an invitation was death."

"Wow," said Mark. "And I thought it was harsh to get a

time-out for interrupting."

"Mordecai sent back his reply to her – he believed that if she didn't act, another way would be provided to save them, but what if she was put in this place for such a time as this?"

"Maybe it was her destiny," said Maya.

"Esther asked Mordecai to have all of the Jews fast for three days, she and her maids would fast too, and then she would go to the king. 'If I die, then I die,' she said."

"So brave," said Maya dreamily.

"So after three days, Esther dressed in her royal robes and went to the king. When King Xerxes saw her he smiled and invited her in by holding out his gold scepter to her. He asked her what she wanted and said that she could have it – even half of his kingdom."

"She should take it and run," said Mark.

"But then what would happen to the Jews?" said Sasha.

"Oh yeah, never mind," Mark said. Lebron smiled and continued with the story.

"'Come to a banquet tomorrow night and bring Haman,' she asked. So the king and Haman came to a banquet that Esther had prepared. At the banquet, the king asked again about her request, and she replied that she wanted them both to come to another banquet, the next day."

"Another banquet? Why didn't she just ask right then?" Maya exclaimed.

"Yeah, it sounds like he was in a good mood. I always wait for Mom and Dad to be in a good mood when I ask for a big thing," said Mark.

"I don't know, but for some reason she must have felt that the time was not right. Anyway, Haman went out from the banquet all happy and full of himself. Then he came upon Mordecai at the king's gate. Again, Haman was enraged because Mordecai wouldn't bow to him. He went home and got his friends and wife together and bragged about his wealth and the honor of having the king treat him so highly and even bragged about how he was the only person Queen Esther had wanted to dine with them at the banquet that day and the next. But none of this made him happy because of Mordecai's refusal to bow to him."

"Pretty petty," noted Jessica. She found herself just as enrapt with the story as the children. "Haman's wife and friends had a suggestion. 'Build a gallows and hang Mordecai on it tomorrow and then you can go on to the banquet and enjoy yourself.'"

"What! Could he do that?" Mark asked.

"Well, as the king's right hand man, he could do pretty much anything he wanted. So he took their suggestion and built the gallows during the night. Meanwhile, the king was having trouble sleeping, so he asked that the history books be brought for him to review.

"Yep, that does it for me every time," Karen commented.

"King Xerxes noticed that Mordecai had never been honored for saving him from the assassination attempt. Right about this time he heard Haman in the court and called for him. The king asked Haman, 'What should be done for a man the king wants to honor?' Haman was excited because of course who would the king be honoring but him? So Haman said, 'Oh you should put one of your royal robes on him, put him on one of your horses with the royal emblem, and parade him around town saying "This is what is done for the one that the king wants to honor!"'

Maya and Mark laughed. "Oh no, he is going to be so embarrassed!"

"Oh, yes. The king said, 'Great idea – go get Mordecai the Jew and do all of that for him. Do just like you said.' And of course Haman had to do it."

"That's what he gets for being such a jerk," Maya said.

"So Mordecai went back to the king's gate and Haman went home and talked to his wife and his friends about what to do now. They were still figuring it out when Haman was called for the banquet. At the banquet the king asked Esther again, 'What is your request? Up to half of the kingdom, I will give it to you.' This time she answered, 'If you care for me, grant me my life and spare my people, this is my request. I and my people have been condemned to death.' King Xerxes asked her, 'Who has dared to do such a thing?'

"Didn't he remember that he had signed the order?" asked

Taylor.

"Well, King Xerxes was a bad guy too, and he may not even have remembered, or Haman may not have told him who the people were he was planning to kill. And remember, neither of them knew that Queen Esther was Jewish."

"Anyway...." said Mark, eager to get on with the story.

"So Esther points to Haman and says 'The enemy is this terrible man, Haman!'"

"Yeah!" cheered Maya.

"The King was so angry he got up and went out to the palace gardens to collect his thoughts."

"Maybe he is finally going to make a decision on his own," said Karen.

"Meanwhile, Haman desperately begged the queen for his life, approaching her on the couch where she was resting. The king came in and saw him that close to the couch and accused him of trying to attack the queen. The attendants grabbed him and covered his head and told the king, 'There is a gallows 75 feet high already built right by Haman's house. He built it there to hang Mordecai, the man who saved the king.'"

"Wow, they really hated him didn't they," Maya said.

"I bet he was mean to them, too," Taylor commented.

"So the king said 'Hang him on it!' and the attendants took Haman to the gallows he had built for Mordecai and he was hanged."

Everyone was silent for a moment. Sasha looked at Lebron with a worried look.

"If this was on TV I don't know if my Device would have let me watch it!" laughed Mark. Maya nodded in agreement, smiling.

"Does it upset you?" Sasha asked.

"We're not babies, Gram," replied Maya, "If God didn't think it was important, he wouldn't have put it in his book."

"Actually my video games are more violent than this. Besides, it's good versus evil and good won!" added Mark. "Please keep going, Gretz!"

Lebron looked around the room and got approving nods from the adults. Becky said, "Ok, go ahead, but how about we leave the story of David and Bathsheba for when they get a little older?" The adults all laughed; the kids looked confused.

"So wait, is that the end of the story?" asked Maya.

"No, it isn't," replied Lebron, "There was still the edict to kill all of the Jews."

"But couldn't the king just take it back?"

"No, in those times a law could not be revoked – not even by the king."

"So what did they do?" asked Mark.

"The king told Mordecai and Esther that they could make any law they wanted, so they made another law that the Jews could fight back if they were attacked. So on the 13th day of Adar, and again on the 14th, they defended themselves and won the battle. The next day they rested and celebrated, and declared that every year they would celebrate the day of rest and they do so to this day. They feast and read the book of Esther, which they call the Megillah. The celebration is called Purim, from the word Pur which is to cast lots, or dice."

"So, did they live happily ever after?" asked Maya.

"Yes, they did," answered Lebron, settling back in his chair. "And that's the whole Megillah."

"But wait a minute;" remarked Jessica, "You didn't mention God once in that story. Why was it in the Bible?"

"To show that even when God is not obvious, he is always there, providing for us and protecting us. Sometimes it is by keeping a king awake at night, or putting a young woman in place for 'such a time as this'".

"Do you think he is watching over us now?" Maya asked in a shaky voice, crawling up into his lap.

"Every minute, sweet child, every minute." Lebron replied hugging her close.

What they didn't know was that outside the window, someone else was watching them, too.

# CHAPTER THIRTY-SIX
··· ◇ ···

Jessica headed to the well, bundled up in one of the coats found at the farmhouse. She had risen early this morning, unable to sleep. Jessica wanted to be like Lebron, trusting in God for their needs, but the previous night's dinner used the last of their provisions and she was worried. They had stretched the emergency packs and the food they had brought for two weeks, but now they needed to figure out a plan for the next few months until they could plant. They had tried foraging, but Jessica had not had time to familiarize herself with the native plants and they were worried that they would poison themselves trying to figure it out. Exploring was difficult since they were not sure where the property lines lay and they were afraid of being turned in if someone saw them.

Jessica tried to focus on all of the things they had accomplished since their arrival. The house was now livable and mouse- free and they had made reasonably comfortable beds from their emergency blankets and parts of the car seats. Taylor had shown a natural ability to use the tools found in shed and so far had made stools for the kitchen table by cutting up a felled tree into pieces and was working on making real chairs. Becky had figured out that the septic tank was still functional, but since they had no power, they had to bring up water to use in the tank to flush every time. Even with all of this progress, the lack of food was constantly on Jessica's mind.

All of these thoughts were preying on Jessica when she came upon the pump. At first she thought she was dreaming or perhaps hallucinating when she saw a bucket under the pump with a glass bottle in it. Jessica approached the pump, looking suspiciously around her as she did, then she knelt beside it. The bucket was filled with cold water and the bottle was full of milk. Next to the bucket was a note on a torn piece of paper.

"Check the root cellar," Jessica read aloud. "What is a root cellar?" Of course they had known as soon as they found the pump that they were not alone, and there had been other times when the ground near the pump was wet before they had been there in the morning. But there had never been contact. Jessica grabbed the milk bottle and ran back to the house, excited to tell the others about her find.

"Milk!" Jessica cried as she entered the kitchen.

Lebron and Sasha were reading their Bibles at the table when Jessica came in. They looked up, startled by her loud entry. They continued to stare at her, the bottle, and each other in disbelief.

"There's more," Jessica gushed, handing them the note. "Do either of you know what a root cellar is?"

"I do," said a voice from kitchen door. Karen looked disheveled and barely awake. "What's with all the yelling?"

Jessica described her find as the rest of the group filtered in. Sasha got their cups out and divided the milk among them, splitting her portion between Maya and Mark who commented that this milk tasted different than what they were used to, but downed all of it. Jessica said that she remembered this flavor from the farm she had visited. This was the taste of raw milk from cows that were grass fed. They all speculated about who their mystery benefactor was, and then began to discuss the note.

"Did you say you know what a root cellar is?" Jessica asked Karen.

"Yes, in the old days before refrigeration people would dig a cellar, maybe five or eight feet square and about as deep. Underground the temperature stays more steady, cooler in the summer and warmer in the winter. They would store their food there."

For a moment they all looked around nodding and taking that in. Then, as if on cue, they all jumped up. Taylor led the way out of the back door to the corner of the house. They had all noticed a small structure only a few feet tall with doors set into it on an angle. When they had explored it they were further baffled by the dirt floor and crude, empty shelves on the wall. Taylor waited as everyone gathered around like Christmas morning. Then he and Karen each grabbed a door handle and opened the cellar. Inside the cellar was food. Taylor jumped in and handed out glass jars of vegetables, a basket of onions and another of potatoes. There were a few carrots, and some white bulbs with the greens attached that Sasha said were turnips. Jessica gasped as Taylor handed her a pint jar of honey, the honeycomb right inside. There was cornmeal and flour in small sacks. The last thing Taylor handed out was a basket of eggs, some blue, some brown and some white. Taylor came out of the cellar and put his arms around Karen who by this time was crying. She was not alone; Lebron had tears streaming down his face, as did Sasha, Jessica and Becky.

"Why do you think they are crying," Maya whispered to Mark.

"I don't know, sometime adults cry when they're happy I think. I know they were worried that we were going to starve to death or something but Gretz said God would provide. I guess they didn't believe it."

Back in the house they took inventory of their bounty. In addition to the things they had initially seen, there were cotton bags containing dried beans and a few pieces of beef jerky. Sasha unwrapped a cloth package tied with twine and found a slab of bacon inside, a find applauded by everyone. The odors of food permeated the kitchen and the natives became restless. Sasha was the voice of reason.

"Now I know everyone is hungry and all of this food looks so good, but we have to ration it. We don't know when or if our angel will return."

Mark looked like now he might cry. "Ok, but the bacon and eggs? Please?"

Sasha looked around at the hopeful faces. "Ok, I think that seems reasonable. Maya, why don't you bring me that pan you cleaned so well. And Taylor, how about building us a fire to cook on," motioning to the fireplace. "Now I have never cooked breakfast over an open fire, my idea of camping is a cheap hotel. Anyone want to give it a go?"

"I would love to help but I don't know if I will do any better," Jessica said. "Anyone who complains has to do all the cleaning up," she threatened.

While preparations were being made for breakfast, George and Becky returned the rest of the food to the cellar. They tied the doors together to keep out the animals, and sat for a moment on the stoop before going back in.

"Do you wonder about our neighbor?" Becky asked George.

"Well, before today I was worried that she would turn us in as refusers. I can't imagine that she would give us food then turn us in. I hope at some point she trusts us enough to introduce herself."

"You said 'she'," commented Becky. "Why do you think this person is a woman?"

"I don't know, just a feeling," George said.

The smell of bacon wafted out of the house and lured them back in. They went back in the kitchen and found Jessica hovering over the fire, the cast iron pan on the grate over the fire, stirring the scrambled eggs in the pan with the bacon fat. Sasha had the bacon on a plate ready to serve. Mark had run to the pump and was pouring water into their cups. No one minded that there was residual milk in them. George and Becky took their places at the table and watched the eggs take shape. When they were ready Jessica placed the pan in the middle of the table and Sasha put the bacon next to it. Everyone started to reach their spoons into the pan when Lebron's booming voice interrupted them.

"Have we forgotten something?" he said. He bowed his head and the rest of the group followed suit. "Lord, thank you so very much for this bounty we are about to receive. We are so thankful. Amen."

"Amen!" the entire group said in unison and began laughing as they dug into their feast.

After the meal was finished and, since no one had complained, they had all helped with the cleaning, they took a moment to relax and chat around the table. They wondered aloud about the identity of the person who had brought this marvelous food and why.

"Well I don't why but I do know his name," said Mark.

"You do? What is it?" asked Becky.

"It's Mason," said Mark holding up one of the jars of vegetables. "See, it is right here on the jar!"

Laughter filled the room. George explained to Mark about Mason jars but commended him on being so observant.

Maya looked at the note left by their benefactor. She took the note and a pencil from the desk in the den and went out to the pump. She thought for a moment and wrote a message and left it under the bucket, then skipped back to join the others.

The ivy parted. A lone figure approached the bucket and noticed the note below it. She read it, smiled, and took the bucket with her through the ivy and beyond.

# CHAPTER THIRTY-SEVEN

··· ◇ ···

Jared surveyed his land from the vantage point of horseback. He was obsessively conserving fuel now that they were counting down the days until the mark would become required for commercial transactions. He and Mary had known it was coming but when the deadline announcement was made they were still shocked. The idea of never being able to purchase another thing was daunting to say the least. Mary had taken it on as more of a challenge, trying to get together like-minded neighbors to start a bartering network. She had been disappointed to find out that very few of their friends were willing to take a stand. She and Jared had organized meetings at their home, assuming that these God-fearing people would naturally be refusers, but few of them were. Many had jobs in town, so they needed to use public transportation, useless without an identity chip. Also, the money that they earned would be inaccessible without it. Jared had implored them to consider homesteading on their property, offering to help them get set up with gardens and livestock, but the idea of taking such a risk scared them. Now all Jared and Mary could hope for was that the few that had agreed would not back down, and that the ones they had trusted to include in the discussion would not turn them in to Homeland Security. A few of them were barely feeding their families and he could see how tempting the reward for turning in refusers could be.

For now Jared and his family would continue to live off of the land. The only difference would be that he would be riding this horse out to check on the fields and the livestock. Soon they would have to transition to a life without electricity, but since the money was automatically withdrawn, it would not be until their bank account was emptied that they would have to deal with that. Mary continued her after-school child care, showing no discrimination against those who had taken the mark.

Jared lived with the knowledge that at any moment an official vehicle could drive up and demand to see his mark. How they had that authority was something he could not understand with his albeit limited understanding of the world legal system, but apparently they did. If that happened their property would be seized and they would either be carted off to a refuser camp or their property would converted into one. Either way would be horrible. He would try to cooperate for the sake of his family, but he knew his temperament and he really couldn't imagine being gracious about it. Jared searched the Bible for help with this issue, and found it pretty clearly outlined in Romans 13. He interpreted it as saying that there is no authority that has not been allowed by God, so follow what is directed of you, pay your taxes, and give honor and respect to your authorities. But what if the authorities are telling you to do something that is against your beliefs? Surely you don't go along with it. It was something he struggled with every day. He reminded himself that the early Christians were persecuted, often having their lands and possessions taken by the government as well. It was apparently coming full circle.

Jared got off his horse at the garden. He now focused all of his energy on these crops since his money crops could no longer bring him money. He suddenly thought of Jessica. He wondered why she hadn't called him to remind him that he needed to order Malhindrone. He didn't need any since he was dropping those crops but he felt a need to let her know now, before his Device became inactive once the deadline passed. Jared looked over his organic garden, sparse now because of the lateness of the season. November crops of turnips and their tasty greens, cabbage, beets and onions were supplemented by their pantry supplies as well as pecans and walnuts from their trees. He gathered a few bunches of turnip greens and a cabbage as requested by Mary and moseyed on back to the farmhouse. Interestingly, producing food for just his family and a few neighbors had lightened his load tremendously. He had a lot more time to spend with the kids and even did a little hunting.

Back at the house Jared decided to give Jessica a call before he forgot. He had never actually called her before, only textmailed her, but since she had come here and he knew of her position on the mark he thought of her as a sister. He spoke her name into his device and found himself looking at an unfamiliar face.

"Business or personal?" the young woman asked.

"What?" Jared said, confused.

"The person you are requesting is not available. Business or personal?"

"Business," Jared said, feeling guilty but not knowing why. The screen changed and Jared found himself looking at the face of a young, smiling man.

"Dacon Chemical, Malcolm speaking, can I help you?"

"I am trying to get a hold of my salesperson, Jessica Morrow. Can you connect me to her?"

"I am afraid that Ms. Morrow is no longer employed at Dacon. I would be happy to help you. I see that you should be about ready to order more Malhindrone. Can I handle that order for you?" Malcolm said with a pasted-on smile.

Jared thought fast. If he denied needing any more Malhindrone, he could be red- flagged for investigation. Better to just buy it even though it would mean fewer months of electricity. They still had quite a few credits left even after they had purchased everything they thought they would need for the next few years. They had purchased only a few items at a time to avoid a fraud alert. Mary had learned her lesson after she encountered a fraud alert after purchasing two cases of Mason jars. She told the agent that a shelf had broken an all of her jars had smashed, requiring her to buy a whole new supply. This satisfied the agent but made Mary feel terribly guilty for lying.

"Yes, I will take my usual amount. Thank you," replied Jared.

"Thank you for your order, you should be receiving your invoice now," said Malcolm, still smiling. "And thank you for doing business with Dacon!" The screen changed to a copy of the invoice. Jared tapped his approval of the transaction and returned his Device to his pocket.

Jared sat in his favorite chair in front of the fireplace and gazed at the fire. Jessica no longer worked at Dacon. Either something terrible had happened to her or she had fled. Jared jumped up from his chair and went over to where Mary displayed the Christmas card that Jessica had sent. He put on his reading glasses and went over to the window where the light was brightest and smiled when he saw the map embedded in the card.

Just then Mary came in from the chicken house with a basket of eggs. "What are you looking at?" she asked Jared, peering over his shoulder.

Jared told Mary about his interaction with Dacon and his suspicion that Jessica had fled to Josh's farm. Jessica had told them about the plan when she was visiting a few months prior. He felt that sending them this card was an invitation to join them there. They briefly toyed with the idea, and then decided that they wanted to stay with their home. If it meant that their farm would become a camp or that they would be forced to go to one, so be it.

Jared and Mary looked again at the card. They discussed what would happen if the Homeland Security team came and found the card in their search. They probably would not recognize it as a map but it was still possible. Silently Jared stood, walked over to the fireplace, put the card in the fire and sadly watched it burn.

# CHAPTER THIRTY-EIGHT

··· ◇ ···

Ellen walked down the rows of her garden, a wicker basket in her hand and her long curly hair pulled back into a grey-streaked braid. Late November gardening was pretty minimal, but she cut some turnip greens and pulled a few radishes and potatoes, putting them in the basket she carried. To that she added some peanuts and a couple of green onions. Ellen smiled as she remembered the contentment she felt the first time she gathered food for the family she had been watching.

Ellen had spotted the family as soon as they pulled in. She had been sitting out on her back porch enjoying the cool day when she heard the first car coming. Since this was an infrequently travelled road, it caught her attention immediately. When the car crossed the bridge, slowed and turned into the driveway of the big house, as she was accustomed to calling it, Ellen became alarmed. Then the second car came and she decided to keep watch. If this was the owner that had returned he would certainly find her in the cabin and toss her out.

Ellen was surprised that this hadn't happened earlier. Surely the owner had been notified when the infrared census had been done a few years back. When Ellen heard about the census in town she tried to devise ways of avoiding it, but since it was done at night and no one knew which night it just wasn't practical to try to hide from it. If she was caught she would just have to figure something else out. After all, it wasn't as though she had set out to live here.

Seeing this family arrive reminded her of when she first came to this farm. She had not always lived like this. In the first decade she was a happily married successful financial planner in New York City. She had helped many clients to maneuver the stock market for their wealth management and retirement. Many high-end clients trusted her and Ellen felt very important and respected in her workplace.

Then came the Great Recession and despite her attempts to shield them, clients lost thousands, some even millions. Even though the collapse of the market had more to do with insolvent banks due to poor lending practices and very little to do with her market choices, clients naturally blamed her. Of course all of her associates were feeling the same pressure. Congenial discussions with clients about retirement funds turned into desperate, angry challenges about how they were to live on what was left. Two of her closest associates chose suicide to escape. She chose alcohol.

At first it was just a couple of glasses of wine to help her sleep. She had been a social drinker before this, only having a few drinks per month. Then it increased to three or four glasses per night, but that started to disrupt her sleep and she awoke with a headache and was groggy. Ellen's husband Ryan had noticed of course, but he didn't say too much because he knew she was under a lot of pressure and he didn't want to make it worse. Besides, he was dealing with his own business issues. With the collapse of the housing market his work as an electrical engineer came to a grinding halt. He was having a hard time keeping up with his half of the rent and utilities, and Ellen had to cover the whole thing a few months in a row. Her clients paid a monthly fee so her income hadn't changed, but that caused a change in the balance in their relationship. She continued to work as usual, taking acetaminophen every morning for the hangover headache, until her assistant introduced Ellen to marijuana. This she could use without the headache and sleep problems, but her judgment became impaired and she was apathetic about her clients, blowing off meetings to smoke pot and forget her troubles. To counter this she added Adderal which she obtained legally from her doctor. All she had to do was give him the list of symptoms for attention deficit that she had looked up on the internet. When Ryan found out about the drug use he threatened to leave her. When the wife of the man she was having an affair with called to let Ryan know about it he did leave her. Ellen promised to end it, stating that the man meant nothing to her, blamed it on her drug use and promised to clean up her act. Ryan was too hurt and she conceded to the divorce. They went their separate ways, each keeping their own bank account and half of the wedding gifts.

Heartbroken and depressed, Ellen considered suicide, but decided instead to pack up her things and drive south until the gas in her Prius ran out. She told herself that wherever that was, that was where she would live. She included in her packing a small full gas can in case she was in the middle of nowhere when that happened. She was secretly hoping for Raleigh, but her car didn't run out until about a hundred miles past there. Exiting the highway on fumes Ellen coasted to a halt at the farm she was living on now. The big house looked like someone might come back any minute and was too big for just her, but she made note of the water supply with relief. She explored the woods and she found a little dilapidated cabin. The back porch overlooked the river and the front porch overlooked an overgrown graveyard. The most recent person buried there died fifty years before, and the oldest grave was from 1856. Instead of being spooky, the graveyard gave Ellen a peaceful feeling that she was not alone.

Ellen settled in, knowing that at any time someone might come and kick her out. When a few weeks passed uneventfully and her food supplies ran out she poured the small gas can into the car and went into town, what there was of it. The locals were very helpful, showing her what seeds to plant in which season. They helped her to pick out tools and survival equipment, not pressing her for an answer when she declined to fill them in on her situation. The hardware store owner, Nathan Cyrus, befriended her and came out to the property to help get her ready for winter. He brought insulation, new roofing, and new boards to replace some of the rotten ones on her porch. In the evenings they sat out on the porch drinking tea brewed by placing teabags in water and putting it in the sun, a trick Nathan had taught her. Before too long the friendship blossomed into much more. Nathan spent his days at the store and his evenings with Ellen.

Nathan taught Ellen about gardening and shared heirloom seeds with her. He explained that the seeds from these plants could be used again to produce the same plants, something that was not true of the commercial seeds. It had taken him a few weeks of observing her before he felt safe sharing the seeds with her. He explained that it was illegal for him to collect seeds since some of them could be contaminated with patented seeds produced by one of the big agriculture companies. Ellen was surprised by that information, and she realized that she still had a lot to learn. Nathan also taught her about composting. She was still amazed every time she turned over the pile of vegetable waste and found it had turned into rich black dirt that she could use for her garden. Nathan taught her what to plant and when, and how to can and dry her extra vegetables. When she bemoaned the absence of hot water he built her a tank on a stand that she could build a fire under and attached a hose she could run to an old iron claw-foot bathtub.

Ellen spent the days gardening and fixing up her little cottage, cleaning and preparing meals. In the past she had paid other people to do these chores which she had considered beneath her, but now she found them quite rewarding. The new skills she was learning were actually more fun and productive than sitting at a computer all day watching stocks go up and down. The sunshine was invigorating and the brisk air of fall had the same effect. When winter came Ellen and Nathan stoked up the wood-burning Franklin stove that had been in the cabin and snuggled under the covers to keep warm. There were a few days when there was enough snow to make driving dicey, so they spent those days relaxing and reading around the stove, dipping into the pantry for food. Ellen thought about snow days in New York. Loss of power, even for a brief time, would cause deaths from hypothermia. It seemed odd, even reckless, to her now to be so dependent on electricity when its supply could be knocked by a storm or even just a car hitting a power pole.

Nathan and Ellen continued to work on the house and the grounds, enjoying each other's company while they worked. Eventually they ran out of projects to keep them busy. Nathan made it clear that he was ready to get married and start a family, but Ellen was reluctant, having made such a mess of her first marriage and never really having had the maternal desire to have children. They realized that they had different goals and went their separate ways, remaining friends. Nathan married a girl in town and they had three children now. Most days Ellen was happy with her solitary life, but the long winter days in the cabin sometimes made her doubt her decision.

Ellen filled her basket with some other pantry items, put a pot of water on the Franklin stove to boil, grabbed a knife and went out to the chicken coop. She expertly grabbed one of the chickens and turned it upside down, slipped its head into the cone made for this purpose, and sliced its' neck through with the knife. After the blood drained out Ellen took it into the cottage. She dunked it briefly in the boiling water to loosen the feathers, then plucked them out in the sink. The feathers she laid out to dry, planning to add them to the others she had been saving for a new pillow. Content with her offering, Ellen gathered up all the food she had collected and headed out of her protected area and across the street.

As she approached the front door of the big house, Ellen realized that she was nervous. She had been so isolated that she wasn't sure that she remembered how to socialize. Voices and laughter drifted out to her and reassured her. She had watched this family for a month now and had enjoyed the stories she heard them tell as she sat hidden in the bushes below the library window. Ellen knew they were decent folks. She knocked on the door, gently at first, and then more forcefully when there was no response. Suddenly there was quiet, then Ellen heard furtive whispers. She could tell that a decision had been made when the door opened slowly and the whole group stared at her, clearly unnerved by her presence. Only the little girl, who she knew was named Maya, was smiling.

"You came!" she cried out. The rest of the family looked at her, obviously confused. "I left her an invitation by the pump to come to dinner and she came!" Maya said, turning to the rest of the group.

Ellen looked shyly at the group as it dawned on them that she was their secret benefactor. They all broke into smiles and Lebron took her by the hand and drew her in.

"Happy Thanksgiving!" he exclaimed.

# CHAPTER THIRTY-NINE
··· ◇ ···

Josh stood at the window, waiting. He felt sweat dripping down his sides, soaking his shirt. Strangely, when he exercised he hardly broke a sweat, but nerves turned it on like faucet.

He was waiting for a knock on the door. It had come to the administration's attention that some of the government employees had not yet received their identity chip. Josh wondered if there were others that were avoiding this moment or whether it was just an oversight on their part. Maybe they were just too busy to go get it placed.

Rachel had not asked him about it since the night that he had discovered that his whole family had taken the chip. That night he had told her about his concerns and she looked at him as though he had lost his mind. After that he caught her stealing a glance at his hand from time to time, but she never said a word about it.

Outside of his door Josh heard raised voices and a scuffle. He went to the door and listened, afraid to call attention to himself by opening it. He could hear a man's voice yelling about the mark, warning people not to take it. The sweating changed from a faucet to a fire hydrant. Josh slipped on his dark suit jacket to cover the sweat stains and sat at his desk, his head in his hands.

Josh could honestly say he still hadn't decided what he was going to do when they knocked on his door. After George called, Josh brought out his printed Bible and began to reacquaint himself with the prophesies that had convicted him so strongly in college. He saw passages he had underlined back then and notes that he had made in the margins. He thought about the world events that had happened since he had last looked at this Bible as well as the current political climate. He realized that prophesies were being fulfilled. The passion Josh had felt in college started to rekindle. He carried the Bible with him in his briefcase and studied it in secret when he had time at the office. It certainly wasn't a crime to study the Bible, at least not yet, but he knew that if anyone saw him it would alert them to the possibility that he might be a refuser. What he found made him realize that George and Jessica were right. This was the mark. It had to be.

Yet he still couldn't decide. He could see advantages to both sides. If he got the mark he could stay with his family. It was important for his children to have a stable family life, and if he was outed as a refuser they would be ostracized. Also, he was the main bread winner. How would Rachel be able to support herself and the kids with her income as a teacher? They could survive on her salary but certainly not at the level that they were accustomed. He had to consider that. Also, with his position he had the opportunity to make a difference in government. With his insight concerning the mark he might be able to affect legislature that could make it easier on refusers. That had to be considered too. Being sent to the refuser camp would be no picnic either.

On the other hand, the consequences of taking the mark were very clear. Eternal death and damnation was the price. That was quite a downside.

Josh heard a knock on the door. He had to make a quick decision. He raised his head from his hands, pasted a smile on his face and called out permission to enter.

"God will understand," he thought.

# CHAPTER FORTY

··· ◇ ···

George awoke with a start. He sat up and looked over at Becky, who was sound asleep. By the amount of light in the room he estimated that it was almost dawn. George wondered how he was going to be able to wait until the rest of the group woke to share this with them. For the last few days he had been bothered by the feeling that there was something important that he was forgetting. It had been on the tip of his brain and now it had surfaced. He didn't want to wake Becky so he lay back down and lost himself in thought.

The past month had tried their patience. The food supply was dwindling and it had everyone on edge, even the children. Although none of the adults had voiced any concerns in front of Maya and Mark, they could sense the tension. Also, it was getting harder to stay warm. George looked over at Becky who was wearing several layers of clothing. The bed that they had made with stuffing from the car seats tucked under a blanket brought in their supplies did little to keep the chill from the floor away from their bones.

Everyone had settled into their roles in the little community based on their skills. George and Taylor had committed to going out each morning to get wood for the fires. With the winter settling in they had a fire burning in the kitchen all day both for cooking and for warmth. Taylor had taken to sleeping in the kitchen in front of the fire and kept it smoldering all night, making it easier to stoke in the morning. On especially cold nights they would start fires in the bedroom fireplaces as well, so a lot of wood was needed. Lebron found a number of tools in the barn which he had cleaned and sharpened until they looked like new, and George and Taylor used them to take down dead trees and split firewood. The two had also become quite handy with repairs to the aging house, using tools found and repaired by Lebron.

Becky and Sasha kept them fed. Sasha said she understood

how pioneer women had kept so busy with the housework. It seemed that by the time one meal was cooked and cleaned up, the next one was being made. Any vegetable scraps went into the compost, plus shells from the eggs they got from Ellen. They had started the compost under Ellen's direction and with a scoop of her compost to give it a jump start. Within a month they were amazed at the black dense soil the worms and bugs had created.

Karen had settled into cleaning the house and creating furniture with Taylor. They would create simple designs then set to work making them from pieces of wood brought in by Taylor and George, who also enjoyed helping with the construction. Lebron turned out to be an excellent whittler, spending hours sitting in front of the fire creating useful as well as decorative items out of scraps of wood.

Jessica's talent was in gardening. She and Taylor had envisioned and then created a little greenhouse using windows and other parts from the defunct cars, which at this point looked like skeletons picked clean by vultures. Luckily the cars were fairly new, with UV penetrating glass. Now they laughed at the need to allow UV penetration, being outside gave them all the exposure they needed, but after the Vitamin D crisis in the second decade, when rickets and osteoporosis were becoming evident even in children due to the lack of sun exposure from staying indoors, it was decided that allowing UV penetration in cars would allow at least some vitamin D production.

Jessica spent hours inside the small greenhouse planning what she would plant after the last frost and nurturing the seeds Jared had given her as well as some donated by Ellen. She had them growing in a variety of containers, most of which she found by the side of the road. Soda cans, broken jars and paper cups all contained seedlings. She scouted out the area that she planned to plant after the last frost. George had started preparing the soil, turning it over with a shovel and adding compost when it was available. Meanwhile there were a few things that they could eat now – bean sprouts and lettuce grew in an old trough Lebron had retrieved from the barn and placed inside the greenhouse, producing enough to feed their group and still share some with Ellen when she came over for supper. Jessica snipped lettuce leaves and small tomatoes from the greenhouse plants for salads more flavorful than she had ever had in a restaurant. She looked forward to being able to plant more substantial crops.

Even Maya and Mark had their roles. Their main job was water management. After breakfast each morning they would head out to the pump and each would carry in a bucket of water. The first bucket was hung over the fire to heat for dish washing and laundry and the second was transferred into clean jugs for drinking and cooking. Then they would take another trip to the pump for water for the bathrooms. After flushing more water would need to be retrieved, causing them to consider Taylor's suggestion that "if it's yellow let it mellow, if it's brown, flush it down". Of course this suggestion caused a lot of laughter and some blushing on Taylor's part, but it was adopted quickly.

Once the water over the fire was warm, Maya and Mark began the laundry. They set out the warm bucket for wash and another bucket for rinsing. These days they did the washing in the mudroom off of the kitchen, but they preferred warm days when they could be outside. After rinsing and wringing out the clothes they hung them carefully on the clothesline, a coated wire taken from one of the cars, using clothespins whittled by Lebron.

Once the laundry was done, as well as any other chores that were given to them by Sasha and Becky, they began their schoolwork. All of the adults participated in the teaching. Sasha created a master schedule for the week and assigned each adult a teaching task. When it was their time to teach, all other chores were put aside. Even Ellen participated with the teaching. Sasha was amazed at how much schoolwork could be accomplished in a short amount of time when it was done this way. She even added in time for art and music, long since abandoned by the school system as frivolous. In her experience that caused all those children who were gifted in these areas to find themselves worthless. It didn't take long to figure out that Maya was a talented artist. Her natural ability to create works of art using things she found in the woods was astounding.

Once the schoolwork was done Maya and Mark were free to play. In the beginning they had to be taught how to play, having relied on their Devices to entertain them with games and shows. Karen and Taylor were not much help, having grown up with mostly Device-related games. Even George, Becky and Jessica had little experience with unstructured play. Only Lebron and Sasha could suggest things to do. At first Maya and Mark whined about being bored, but they discovered that if they whined they were given more chores, so along with games that were suggested they made up their own games, using imaginations that they didn't even know they had. Sometimes they would go across the street to Ellen's cabin and help her with her chores, most times returning home with something good to eat. This was a learning experience, too. The first time they came home with potatoes they set them on the counter and gave Becky a look of disgust, announcing that the rest of the family could eat them but they weren't going to. Becky was stymied.

"Why not?" she had asked.

"She pulled them right out of the dirt!" Maya had said, holding her stomach as if nauseated. After a lesson on the growing of root vegetables, both agreed to partake, feeling foolish.

Ellen had been a godsend. She helped them with food, gave them extra blankets from her cabin to use for the kids, and gave them priceless advice about living without electricity. She seemed to enjoy having company, and she knew she was always welcome at their home. She especially enjoyed the kids. George sometimes caught her looking wistfully at them, and he wondered about her past. They had asked Ellen about her story, but she was not forthcoming. George knew she had been married before, that she came here from New York City, and that she was a stockbroker there. Any more questions and she became uncomfortable, so they stopped asking.

George looked around the room again and noted that the light was turning pink. He would expect the rooster to crow any minute, and for once he was eager to hear its cry. He decided to wait until after breakfast to share what he had remembered since he knew that it could take a while and he hated to miss a meal. These days he was burning calories like a teenager so he could eat all he wanted and still had lost a lot fat, replacing it with muscle. He thought about the gym machine upper body workouts that he had replaced with shoveling as he prepped the garden. He got his cardio workout splitting firewood and carrying it in. It seemed weird to him after only a couple of months that he would expend all that energy at the gym and have nothing to show for it. Plus he couldn't skip it; they would be cold and hungry. In fact, everyone in the group had transformed in differing degrees. He noticed it dramatically in the kids in their body shape. Mark, who once had a hard time carrying an empty pail of water to the pump, now could easily tote two full buckets. His pudgy belly had disappeared and his stamina for playing had grown exponentially. Similarly Maya had slimmed and strengthened, and George noticed that her coordination had improved, surely borne of hours of play, climbing trees, balancing on logs and throwing balls made by Lebron from dead vines.

But probably the most dramatically transformed was Sasha. Even though she never mentioned it, George knew that her Crohn's medications had run out after they had been here only three weeks. He looked for signs that she was worsening, and he noticed Lebron's worried posture when he was looking at his wife. But the worry was unnecessary. Sasha blossomed in the new environment. Whether it was the fresh air and sunshine, something in the fresh food or not in the fresh food he was sure they would never know, but regardless of the cause, this was the best he had seen Sasha look in many years. Her smile was radiant and she seemed to have an endless amount of energy. Everyone noticed and commented on it, even Taylor, but Sasha just smiled, saying they would just have to wait and see. Lebron told George that Sasha had confided that after so many years dealing with the ups and downs of Crohn's and praying for deliverance from it, she was afraid that this wouldn't last. George told Lebron that his gut feeling, no pun intended, was that this would be permanent.

George turned his head toward Becky and inhaled her fragrance. When his kids were little George would find himself sniffing their heads as he held them, taking in that special baby aroma. He recognized this as a throw-back to primitive man when the sense of smell had been so important. Now with the lack of deodorant and limited soap access all of their scents were quite pungent. At first they had all had trouble adjusting to the overwhelming smells of the body odors, finding them embarrassing, but in just a short time they became accustomed to it. The body odors actually seemed to heighten the sense of community in a way that was hard to explain. He could pick out Becky's scent easily and found it arousing. Their sex life had never been so good.

"Cock-a-doodle-do!"

That was George's cue to jump out of bed, waking Becky.

"What has gotten into you?" she said groggily, but with a smile on her face. In their old life Becky slept poorly, tossing, turning and sleep-talking, awaking tired and sometimes grouchy. The hard physical labor seemed to improve her sleep and the absence of time pressure stabilized her mood. Though they never had any serious marital difficulties before, they were closer than ever. Paradoxically, the more physical the labor was during the day, the more energy they seemed to have.

"I have something I want to check out when everyone is up. It may turn out to be nothing at all, so don't get your hopes up," George said cautiously.

"What is it?" said Becky, her curiosity piqued.

"You'll see," teased George. "After breakfast I'll tell everyone."

George and Becky went down to the kitchen, waking Taylor who was stretched out on the table. The fire burned low.

"You guys look like the cat that swallowed the canary. What's going on?" Taylor asked.

"I actually don't know. George has a secret," said Becky smiling at George.

'George has a secret' was the topic of breakfast chatter, making George nervous that his secret wasn't going to turn out to be anything at all. Breakfast cleanup was done in record time, and everyone helped with the water transporting. Then all eyes were on George.

George found he was nervous. Maybe he should have checked this out before getting everyone amped up.

"Ok guys, here it is. I remembered that Josh told me that there is a secret room in this house." Gasps and smiles filled the room.

"Did he tell you where?" asked Karen excitedly.

"Well I've been thinking about that. He said it was in the room that he stayed in when he visited, so I was thinking.."

"Our room!" squealed Maya and Mark, jumping up and tearing up the stairs, the adults close behind. George took up the rear, smiling uneasily. It was fun to see everyone so excited, but what if Josh was just kidding, or if it had been cleaned out. He arrived in the room to find everyone tapping on walls and lifting up carpets.

"Let's be logical," said Taylor. "It can't be on an exterior wall, or a wall shared with another room or hallway. So it has to be this wall," he said, pointing to a paneled wall. Taylor peered behind a bookcase, uttered an excited cry and shoved the bookcase to the side. Then he pushed gently on the wall and, to everyone's surprise, a small door opened up.

"Let me go in first and make sure it is safe," said George, entering the small room, dimly lit with light coming from the bedroom. He carefully stepped in, assessing the situation. "Don't come in," he said. "There is no floor, just beams from the ceiling below. I'll hand stuff out and we can go through it out there."

First came a box of clothes, followed by an old trunk with a lock on it. A box labeled "ornaments" and one labeled "baby clothes" came next. A toy box caught the attention of Maya and Mark, and box of craft supplies caught Sasha's.

"This is a heavy one!" said George. Taylor leaned in to help him haul it out.

"Books!" said Taylor excitedly. "But they all look the same. Odd."

Lebron looked over his shoulder. "Encyclopedias!" he said. Taylor gave him a funny look. "I'll explain later," said Lebron with a smile. Of course Taylor had never heard of Encyclopedias, they had not been published since 2012, before he was even born. Lebron knew Sasha would be excited to use these in her school lessons.

"More books!" cried Karen as she took the heavy box from George. She had not wanted to be a whiner, but the lack of outside distraction was really getting to her. Her life of constant stimulation had come to a grinding halt. In many ways she had found this to be a positive thing. They had filled the evenings with stories. Lebron had continued to tell Bible stories, Sasha knew a lot of fairy tales, and Karen told stories of famous figures from history. They had all come up with stories to tell. George had been the surprising one, telling stories from his imagination that were print-worthy. Often they shared stories from their pasts, some of them funny, some sad. Karen finally heard stories about her father. She had a much better picture of him now after hearing stories sometimes told through tears. The accepting atmosphere had broken the silence. She had also learned a lot about Taylor, who had turned out to be an excellent storyteller. It had been really great to see the acceptance extended to Taylor. It took him awhile to be comfortable with it, but slowly he had come to realize that these people were genuinely allowing him into their fold. One of the stories he told was about a lone wolf who was accepted into the pack even after he accidentally attracted hunters to the lair requiring them to abandon their home and find another. It was a mistake that most wolves would not have forgiven, he had explained. But this story had a happy ending and when Taylor said 'the end' there was not a dry eye in the house.

Even with all these wonderful times, Karen craved some down time alone, enjoying some entertainment. In the past she would have curled up on the couch with her Device and watched a movie, but she was confidant this would be just as good. Some of the titles she read as she pulled out the books were unfamiliar including several in series called <u>Harry Potter</u>. Many of the stories she knew: <u>Huck Finn</u>, <u>Lord of the Flies</u>, even some Shakespeare. She had seen these movies in Literature class. Long ago actually reading the books had been abandoned, and instead movies were shown. It had been determined that the time spent reading was wasted and could be better used studying math and science. Karen's mom had told her that it just wasn't the same, that reading the book was vastly different from watching the movie. Karen was more than willing to find out. She hoped they were as good as the few that had been left in the library.

Maya and Mark had emptied the contents of the toy box on to the floor. They looked disappointed. Sasha broke away from her box of craft supplies and asked them what was wrong. She thought they would be overjoyed with the discovery.

"We don't have a Device to play with these things," Mark said sadly.

Sasha laughed, surveying the booty. She saw board games, Chinese checkers, a chess set, jacks, some jointed army men, and a bag labeled 'little kiddles' containing cute little dolls. There was also a baseball and a jump rope. "None of these require a Device," she explained. Maya and Mark looked at her suspiciously. Sasha laughed at their unbelief. "We will show you."

A small but heavy box was passed out and opened by Sasha and Maya. Inside were small notebooks with neat handwriting covering every page.

"What are these?" Maya asked.

Sasha flipped through the pages. "Journals," she replied, "most likely written by someone long ago. I can't wait to read them."

Maya looked over Sasha's shoulder at the flowery writing. "How will we read them without our Devices?" she asked.

"I know how to read cursive," replied Sasha. "I can teach you how to read it and write it too." Starting just before Maya and Mark went to school it was decided that writing in cursive was no longer worth the time it took to teach it. Anything written in cursive could be read by holding a Device over it and a typed version appeared on the screen. Similarly, foreign languages were not taught because a Device could translate both spoken and written languages.

A smaller box came out and George handed it to Taylor. He watched Taylor open it, look furtively around to see if he was being watched, then take something from the box and put it in his pocket. This was something he was going to have to ask Taylor about later.

A loud sound made everyone freeze. Someone was pounding

on the door, yelling. George tip-toed out of the bedroom and peered through the window at the end of the hall. He thought he recognized one of the voices as Ellen's, and when he looked down at the figures on the porch, he saw that he was right. He also saw a wheelbarrow with a young woman curled up in it, and a young man in overalls desperately yelling and banging on the door.

"It's ok," he called out, seeing the scared faces of his farm family, as he had come to think of the whole group. "Ellen is with them."

George ran down the stairs. The rest followed, lining the stairway to see what was so urgent. George opened the door.

"I'm so sorry but I didn't know what to do. This is Matthew and his wife Ruth. They came to my house because they knew that I had animals that I had helped birth, but I have never.." said Ellen, uncharacteristically manic, wringing her hands and looking frightened. In the make-shift ambulance, an obviously pregnant girl was writhing in pain.

Now it was George's chance to panic. The last time he had delivered a baby was in medical school, 25 years ago. Hopefully it would come back to him.

"Get some clean sheets and put them on the kitchen table," he said. He hoped that he was the only one who noticed that his voice was strained and starting to sound shrill. One look at Jessica and Becky told him he wasn't. "And get any clean rags, towels or shirts you can find." Taylor helped Matthew carry Ruth into the kitchen. Karen helped the young woman onto the table once it had been covered by Maya and Mark, who had scurried upstairs to where they kept the sheets after they washed them.

Becky knew she could help. She had seen births in the villages when she was doing mission work. She ladled some hot water from the pot on the fire into a bowl and, mixing it with some cold water from the pitcher, gave it to George to wash his hands. Then she put their kitchen scissors into the pot to boil. She directed Taylor to get some twine from their supply box. He came back with two small pieces, all that was left. It would have to be enough.

George washed his hands in the warm water with a sliver of

soap left from the supplies they brought with them. His hands were shaking and doubt filled his mind. He felt Lebron's hands on his shoulders and turned to see his friend with his head bowed and his lips moving silently. George took this cue and prayed for focus, for peace, and for God's help with this birth. Lebron stepped back and George moved over to the couple.

"Tell me what is going on," he said in the most authoritative voice he could muster.

"We thought we could handle this at home, you know, the natural way. We don't have a Device," Matthew said in a whisper, furtively looking around the room. "But the baby won't come. I can see the head but it won't be born."

George nodded and took Ruth's hand. She gripped it with a fierceness that was actually painful, but he just tightened his grip and allowed it.

"I am going to help you," he said, hoping to sound more confident than he felt. "Listen to me and follow what I say to do."

The girl nodded, visibly relaxing. After explaining what he was going to do, George placed a sheet over her legs and sat on a stool at the end of the table. Parting her legs he could see that the baby's head was indeed visible. As another contraction started, George was alarmed to see the baby's head pull away rather that push forward.

"Don't push! Breathe!" George yelled over her cries. The father took her hand and modeled breathing for his young bride. George slipped his hand past the baby's head, finding what he suspected. A loop of the cord encircled the neck, drawing tight and cutting off the blood supply from the placenta with every contraction. In the hospital it would have been caught early with 3d ultrasound at the first sign of labor. George prayed that there had not been brain damage from the lack of oxygen as he gently pulled the loop over the baby's head. He checked for additional loops and, finding none, gave the go ahead to push. With the next contraction the baby slid out easily, depositing in the clean rag George had been handed by Becky. They both looked grimly at the silent, floppy, slightly blue infant as Becky rushed to tie the twine around the cord twice. She handed George the scissors and he cut the cord, quickly taking the baby to the counter where a clean t-shirt laid waiting.

"Come on, baby, breathe," he said, rubbing the chest. He glanced up at the parents, whose heads were bowed in prayer as Lebron prayed with them. When there was no response he wiped the baby's face quickly and covered the nose and mouth with his mouth giving two short breaths. As he pulled away he heard a wonderful sound, a baby's cry. The room erupted in cheers, and George found that there were tears streaming down his face.

"It's a boy!" he shouted.

# CHAPTER FORTY-ONE
... ◇ ...

Josh was back in the board room yet again. Now that Identity Chip requirement had been enforced there were a few empty seats around the table, but just a few. This emergency meeting had been called to inform them about new developments from Homeland Security. Josh glanced at Senator Thomas, clean cut and efficient looking as always, rifling through his papers, preparing for his presentation. Senator Thomas' authority had risen greatly in the past few months as lands had been seized and people had been corralled into the camps or "Resident Farms" as they had been instructed to call them when discussing them with their constituency. As predicted, these strong-minded farmers rarely went willingly. Some recognized the need to comply in order to remain with their families, but many had to be chemically lobotomized, allowing for order and for the safety of the government workers. The farms were quite productive, easily meeting the needs of the residents and the guards. The other confiscated lands were being managed by government farm workers, and the products were sold on the open market. At the last meeting Senator Thomas had described this as a "win-win" situation, his chest puffed out and a triumphant grin on his face. An unobtrusive glance around the room told Josh that most of the committee agreed, though he did note one or two members shifting uncomfortably in their seats or frowning intently at the screen.

Today's meeting agenda was entitled "The Threat of Religion to the Levine Peace Accord". Josh knew he wasn't going to like this. He checked his Device for the time. It was just now ten o'clock so he figured he had a few minutes to relax before the meeting began considering the President's usual lack of punctuality. Josh was just about to close his eyes when the door opened and President Sontara entered, looking just a little frazzled. Behind her was a dark-haired older man of small stature who Josh recognized immediately as

Supreme Principal David Levine, the head of the World Government. Josh sat up straight in his seat, unconsciously coming to attention, as did all of the other people in the room. Josh reviewed what he knew about the man by scanning his mental file, wishing he had known about this visit so that he could be on his A game. David Ravi Levine, the most powerful person on the planet, here in the same room with him. It made him feel a little bit giddy. Supreme Principal Levine had single handedly saved the economy of the world by uniting the countries and getting them to agree to cancel each other's debts in a worldwide Jubilee a little over three years ago. Prior to that there had been many countries on the verge of bankruptcy and other countries that had bought so much debt that they were gaining too much fiscal power. The United States of America was so indebted to China that it was destined to become insolvent and had been saved by this man standing before them. Meanwhile there was friction between China and other nations, including the USA, concerning debt from the early 20th century that had never been honored. The situation had become extremely volatile.

The concept of Jubilee came from the ancient Israeli practice delineated in Leviticus that every 50th year debts were forgiven, land was returned to its original owner, and slaves were freed. The purpose of it was to make sure that the land stayed within the original families and that no great debts were amassed. Also it reminded people that the land ultimately belonged to God and they just inhabited it. Jubilee had not been practiced for centuries but at a time when the global financial system had reached its peak of instability, David Ravi Levine, then Prime minister of Israel, somehow convinced the world that the only way out was a Jubilee. He presented his proposition of a ten-member governance with the entire population of the world represented, sharing resources and ideas, and miraculously it was agreed upon. It was as if he had done a Jedi mind trick on the whole world. Since Jubilee they had been in a period of peace, known as the Levine Peace Accord. Levine was made the head of the ten-member governance and given the moniker of 'Supreme Principal'. Statues of Supreme Principal Levine dotted the landscape in every region and his face adorned the universal currency. His presence in the room seemed to make it extremely small. President Sontara looked uncharacteristically slope-shouldered and weak.

"It is my honor to present to you someone who needs no introduction, Supreme Principal Levine. He has asked to speak to you concerning our topic today: 'The Threat of Religion to the Levine Peace Accord'. Supreme Principal?" With a shaky smile, President Sontara took an empty seat, leaving the head of the conference table free for their guest.

Supreme Principal Levine sat at the head of the table and looked around at all of the Senators and finally at the President. His gaze seemed to have a relaxing effect on each of them, taking a stress-filled situation and making it feel ordinary. Calm settled over the group and Levine began to speak.

"Good morning all of you," he said with a smile and just a hint of an accent. It was rumored that Levine was fluent in over a hundred languages. "I do so appreciate your valuable time shared today with me. What I would like to discuss with you is of utmost importance to the cause of freedom."

He did know the buzz words for each country, Josh thought. For Americans it was freedom. For Asia it might be prosperity.

"A committee within the World Government has been studying a threat to this freedom," he continued. "It may surprise you to know that religion is the biggest threat to our way of life." The Supreme Principal paused dramatically and looked around the room again.

"Please do not confuse religion with faith," he explained. "Individual faith is the backbone of our being. No one could ever regulate that nor would I ever suggest trying. No, the threat I am talking about is in the form of organized religion. Organized religions of one type or another have been responsible for many atrocities over the centuries, from the Crusades to the terrorism of Al-Qaeda. Religion was responsible for destabilizing governments in the first decade during the Arab Spring and continues to threaten our way of life now. As I am sure you know, some Christians across the world and even some Jews are refusing to take the Identity Chip in an act of civil disobedience. This threatens to destabilize this world in a way we have not known since before the Governance."

"It is because of this threat that an edict has been passed by the Governance committee banning the gathering of persons, two or more, with the purpose of organized religion. Asia has already begun this transition, and has not found it to be very difficult, but of course their history has been quite different than that of America. The main concept that we must stress is that no one will ever disturb an individual's ability to commune with the god of their understanding because, of course, no one ever could. What we are regulating is only the corporate aspects of worship, such as church services and festivals. These will be replaced with non-religious based self-help and motivational talks by government approved speakers. Some may even ministers if they are willing to forgo the religious portions of their talks. I believe that our citizens of the World Government will find them very enlightening. Senator Thomas has some words to say concerning this matter and the specifics of its roll-out. If you will all excuse me, I must catch a plane to the next nation. I am confident that your President will be able to answer any questions that you may have. Thank you all so much for your attention."

As Supreme Principal Levine stood, all the cabinet members arose as well, as if marionettes on strings. Like marionettes, their heads bobbed and big smiles came upon their faces as he faced each one and nodded to them. Then he was whisked off by his team of body guards to, Josh supposed, an awaiting jet.

President Sontara, having regained her composure and air of competence, reclaimed her spot at the end of the table and asked Senator Thomas to present his plan to expedite this edict.

Josh listened intently to Senator Thomas, thinking about what he could do to help. He found that even though he didn't like the idea of disbanding organized religion, he had to agree that it was a threat to the World Government. Senator Thomas spoke of Homeland Security forces helping with transitioning the churches from faith-based to secular. To enforce the secular nature of the meetings World government flags would be flown and Supreme Principal Levine's picture would be hung in place of the cross and all religious symbols would be removed. The Senator reassured the group that these measures were being conducted throughout the world, even in the Supreme Principle's home country of Israel's National Temple.

Suddenly into Josh's mind came a verse from Daniel prophesying the end times:

"He will confirm a covenant with many for one 'seven'". In the middle of the 'seven' he will put an end to sacrifice and offering. And at the temple he will set up an abomination that causes desolation, until the end that is decreed is poured out on him."

And from Mark:

"When you see 'the abomination that causes desolation' standing where it does not belong – let the reader understand- then let those who are in Judea flee to the mountains."

And from Revelation:

"This calls for wisdom. If anyone has insight, let him calculate the number of the beast, for it is man's number. His number is 666."

Josh had never memorized these verses. How they were coming to him he couldn't understand. Surely God was speaking to him. But what did He want him to do? Josh suddenly felt lightheaded and put his head down on the table. He realized that Senator Thomas had stopped talking and the committee member next to him was tapping Josh's shoulder. Josh jerked his head up and saw that everyone was looking at him. He must look like a madman.

"I am really sorry, I feel sick," he managed to say. He got up from his seat and made his way to the door. Everyone leaned away from him as he passed, whether to make sure they didn't catch whatever was ailing him or to prevent being thrown up on he didn't know. Outside in the hallway he felt like there was more air. He was relieved that no one came to check on him. He made his way into the bathroom and splashed some water on his face, then slipped into his office, hoping to keep from calling attention to himself and having to endure questions about why he wasn't in the meeting. At least he had met The Supreme Principal. Such an amazing man. Josh sent a textmail to Rachel telling her that he had met David Ravi Levine. Just before he pressed send something about the Supreme Principal's

name caught his eye. Why had he never seen it before?
David Ravi Levine
vi vi vi
666

He deleted the textmail.

# CHAPTER FORTY-TWO
··· ◇ ···

Becky ducked through the opening in the vines and peered down the street, checking for cars. Spotting one was a rare event, seemingly rarer all the time. Becky wondered about that. She wondered about what was going on in the rest of the world. She wondered if they had actually put the refusers into camps as they had threatened. That would explain the decrease in traffic if the farmers who clung to their land and their ideals were carted off, since the main use for this road was transporting harvested crops. Seeing no cars she crossed the street, headed for Ellen's place, coffee cup in one hand and cornbread in the other, and a shawl draped across her shoulders to ward off the chill in the early spring air. By noon she would be shucking it off as the temperature rose.

Becky had fallen into the habit of coming over to Ellen's most mornings with leftovers from breakfast and sometimes surplus garden vegetables. Often Sasha, Jessica and Karen would come, but today Jessica and Karen were tending the garden and Sasha was teaching. They would sit in Ellen's comfortable porch rockers and drink tea that Ellen made from tea leaves and mint she grew in her garden, either brewed hot or brewed in a jar of water on the porch rail in the sun and sweetened with honey from Ellen's bees. Becky found that she cherished this time. In her old life Becky had no time to connect with friends. Each day was a rush to the finish, from sunrise to sunset. She had missed the close friendships from her college days. George was wonderful, and she considered him her best friend, but she missed the diversity of opinions and the warmth of girlfriends. Ellen had told Becky the story of her life and how she had ended up here, and Becky shared some difficult stories of her own, ones she hadn't told a soul. Even George didn't know about the sexual abuse she had suffered as a child. She just had never thought there was any reason to bring it up. Becky hadn't realized how therapeutic it was just to speak of these things, like a weight lifted from her.

Today they were discussing a mission trip Becky had taken to Haiti. Becky had always loved the Haitian people, full of faith and love despite their hardships. She had learned so much from them about accepting her circumstances and making the best of them. In addition there were practical things that she had learned that she was putting into practice now. One of them had also been adopted by Ellen, the making of compost tea by putting some compost in a large jar and filling it with water, allowing some time in the sun for the water to leach out the good minerals from the soil, and then pouring the water on the garden. It was a great fertilizer.

As they sat rocking and looking over the garden, Maya and Mark strolled up to them carrying a basket with some more cornbread and a thermos. Mark was munching on a raw turnip and Maya was eating a carrot. Before they came here they snacked on chips and candy. Even the granola bars that she had once thought of as a healthy snack were no more than glorified cookies and yogurt had so much sugar added it should have been classified as a dessert. When they had run out of their processed snacks the children- well, to be honest, everyone- went through a type of withdrawal. They all had sugar cravings and were as irritable as drug addicts coming off the hard stuff. Thankfully after a week or two they found that they no longer desired the sweet, processed snacks. They were quite content with fresh fruits and vegetables.

Becky was glad to see that Maya and Mark were wearing the sweaters Sasha had knitted for them. When knitting supplies were brought out from the secret room Sasha told them that she had been taught to knit as a little girl by her grandmother but she doubted that she would remember how. Surprisingly, she took to it easily and used her free time to sit on the porch and knit. Fortunately there was a lot of yarn but unfortunately not a lot of the same color. Becky struggled to suppress a laugh as her children stood before her in multicolored sweaters. They looked like Joseph in his coat of many colors.

"You guys already done with your schoolwork?" asked Becky.

"Yeah, Gram said she thinks we are already ahead of where we need to be so we should go fishing with Gretz and Taylor to catch supper," said Mark.

"She said we needed to get your OK first," added Maya coming up the steps and sitting in her mother's lap.

"It's OK with me," Becky said with a smile. "Just be careful not to get hooked."

"What's that?" asked Mark, pointing at the jar in the garden.

"Compost tea," replied Ellen.

Maya peered into her mother's cup, and, seeing a dark brown liquid, put her hand over her mouth, jumped off her mother's lap and ran down the steps. Mark seemed confused but followed her with the basket.

Ellen and Becky broke out in peals of laughter as Maya ran away, one hand over her mouth and one on her stomach.

"Should we tell her?" Becky asked, still laughing.

"Maybe someday," Ellen said with a smile.

# CHAPTER FORTY-THREE

· · · ◇ · · ·

"Nice job with these poles, Lebron," said Taylor, admiring the hand-carved fishing poles and the reel made from an empty spool of thread. Ping-Pong balls found in the secret room were repurposed for bobbers and bent wire formed the hooks.

"Thanks. I think when we get the hang of casting it will be a lot better than just the string on a stick method that we have been using. Now where are those kids to dig us up some worms for bait?" Lebron looked back toward Ellen's cabin. He saw the kids running toward them, Maya's braids flapping on her shoulders, Mark just a few steps ahead.

"There you are," called Lebron, smiling at the kids as they come closer. Lebron noticed that the two were barely winded. What a change from their arrival when even walking that far would have spent them for the day. Even their coloring was different, more pink and youthful appearing.

"We were hoping for some worms for bait," said Taylor. "Know where there are any?"

"I do!" They both yelled in chorus. Jessica had been teaching them about bugs and worms, two of her favorite topics. They took the knowledge and ran with it, looking for all sorts of organisms under rocks and fallen logs. They knew exactly where to look for worms. They ran toward a fallen log as Taylor and Lebron baited their hooks with cornbread in the meantime. They cast their lines out in the river and watched the bobbers for signs of action.

"So, Taylor," said Lebron, "What do you miss most about your previous life?"

"Hamburgers. Definitely. Sasha has really perfected the bean burger and I love when we get the occasional meat from someone in trade, but I sure do miss sinking my teeth into a juicy burger," replied

Taylor. Since Ruth and Matthew had delivered baby George on their kitchen table there had been a steady stream of patients showing up at the front door. George had called a family meeting about it, concerned that the continued traffic would call attention to their situation. Sasha voiced that it would be wrong to turn anyone away who was in need, regardless of the danger. All of the family agreed. After George started seeing people in his makeshift office they set up in the library they started having food show up on their doorstep. Baskets of vegetables, sausages, cheese and milk, and one time, a side of beef dried into jerky. The famine at the farmhouse was over. Lebron said that God was providing because of the farm family's obedience concerning God's command to help our neighbors. He told the parable of the Good Samaritan one night for story time and it really drove the message home.

"What about you, Lebron, what do you miss the most?" asked Taylor.

"Hmm. That's a tough one. I guess I would say I miss the church building. Even though God is with us wherever we are, there is something about a entering a church and seeing the cross and the pews and the altar that put me in a reverent mood."

Taylor thought for a moment as they watched for movement of the bobbers.

"We could make one you know. A chapel. It wouldn't be that hard. It would actually be fun. We could make it outdoors with some split logs for pews and a cross and altar."

Soon Lebron and Taylor were drawing plans in the dirt with a stick, each contributing ideas for the chapel. Maya and Mark returned with worms and had to point out to the pair that they both had fish on their lines. Laughing, they took a break to reel in a couple of trout, perfect for supper. Mark looked at the fish hungrily.

"Do you think you might catch some more?" asked Mark.

"Well I would think so," replied Lebron. "Why, what did you have in mind?"

"I was thinking they would make a yummy lunch for us right now!" replied Mark. This would not be the first time a few fish didn't make it back to the house.

"Ok," said Lebron, "You can have these two if you want to clean them and cook them."

Maya and Mark scampered off a little ways away to make their preparations. Working as a team, Maya gathered some wood and cleared an area for a small fire. Mark set to work cleaning, gutting and filleting the fish. From their Device pockets they took their Swiss army knives, treasures found in the secret room and entrusted to Maya and Mark after many promises to take care of them and be careful with them. Before too long the two were squatting by the fire with small fillets cooking on sticks that they had whittled down. They presented Taylor and Lebron with perfectly cooked trout. Again Lebron thought of how quickly these children had adapted to this changed life. After lunch they took poles of their own and a few worms and went downstream a little ways to fish.

"So back to the chapel idea," said Lebron. "If I gave sermons on Sunday would you come?"

Taylor looked pensive. "I think I would," he replied. "I've had a lot of time to think about my beliefs since we have been here. I see you all practicing your faith by leaving your comfortable lives and coming here, by helping people who come to the door even though it may be a risk, and studying your Bibles. I wish I could have faith like that, but I just don't know if I can."

"So where do you stand now. Do you believe that there is a God who created the universe and you and me?"

"Well yes, I think anyone who would say that there is not a higher power just hasn't really thought it through. I just have a problem with some of the beliefs in Christianity."

"For instance..?" asked Lebron gently.

"I don't know, there are a few things that I have a hard time wrapping my head around. Like a virgin birth for instance."

"So you believe that God created the heavens and the Earth but have trouble believing that he could send his son here in the form of a child?" asked Lebron.

"Well when you put it like that it does sound kind of silly. But what about the problem of evil. I have a hard time believing in a god who could allow that."

Lebron laughed. "Who is the created and who is the creator here? Do you think that you can create God to be whatever you think he should be? God is who he is whether you believe in him or not. He wants to have a relationship with us, that much is clear from the Bible. Whether or not you believe in the Bible as the word of God, now that is just something you have search your heart for. What is standing in your way?"

Taylor thought for a moment. "I guess I just want proof. I want to see it with my eyes."

"Look around you Taylor. You can see it with your eyes. The creation around you is so remarkable that no one can deny it. But it does at some point take an act of faith. William Sloane Coffin said 'I love the recklessness of faith. First you leap and then you grow wings.'"

"But I don't know if I could live up to what the Bible says. I am afraid I would fail," said Taylor quietly.

"Ah, so that's it. God doesn't expect you to be perfect, but he does expect you to continue to strive for Jesus' example of perfection by prayer and reading the Bible, his word to us, for guidance."

Taylor considered all that Lebron had said. He sat silently for a few moments and felt a stirring in his heart. He had always felt a certain emptiness there that he recognized now as a lack of faith.

Lebron watched Taylor's face and saw a look of peace overcome his troubled look.

"I am ready. I want to feel what you feel, to feel close to God. What do I do to make that happen?" asked Taylor.

"Just invite him in," said Lebron with a smile. "Pray a prayer to him that says you believe and want him in your heart and in your life."

Taylor closed his eyes. As he prayed he felt warmth he had never felt and found that tears were making their way down his face.

"What now?" he asked, grinning at Lebron.

"Well, I'm a Baptist minister, so there's one more thing!"

**********

"What are those kids hollering about?" asked Sasha to no one in particular. She had just finished canning the green beans that Jessica and Karen brought her that morning. The extra mason jars they had found in the secret room were invaluable for saving their crop. The garden was plentiful even though there was still a nip in the air. Jessica had nurtured her seedlings in the greenhouse so they were ready to plant as soon as the ground warmed up.

Sasha dried her hands and headed outside. Close behind her the rest of the clan came spilling out of the house.

An unusual site greeted them – Taylor walking toward the house soaking wet from head to toe, holding up his heavy jeans by the belt loops to keep them from dropping to the ground, shirtless despite the chill in the air. Behind him danced Lebron and the children, singing a gospel hymn.

Ellen made her way across the street and caught up with Maya at the back of the procession.

"What's going on?" Ellen asked, watching as Karen threw her arms around Taylor, wet clothes and all.

"Taylor loves Jesus!" exclaimed Maya, "And Gretz baptized him in the river. Taylor said he wishes he waited a little longer to figure it out, at least until the water got warmer but I think he was kidding."

"Well isn't that something," said Ellen. "Good for him."

Maya took Ellen's hand as they strolled toward the jubilant group.

"Do you love Jesus?" asked Maya.

Ellen thought for a moment. She wanted to be truthful, but was not sure what to say to the little girl.

"Well I don't know if I love him, but I don't hate him," she said, hoping that would be enough to satisfy Maya, but it wasn't.

"But Gretz says that the Bible tells us that the only way to see God in heaven when you die is by loving Jesus and trying to live like he did. What do you think?" said Maya, a worried look on her face.

"Well, he might be right, but maybe you just have to be the

best person you can be and that is enough. I guess you would call me agnostic."

"Is that like being Presbyterian?" asked Maya.

Ellen laughed. "No, it just means that I am still considering all the options. Who knows, maybe one day it will be me strutting home in soaking wet clothes," Ellen said with a smile. She had recently been asking some questions of her new family, and she did like what she heard. Still there were some things holding her back. She had a hard time believing that she could be forgiven for her past mistakes, or that the maker of the universe would care about her personally. Ellen just felt she could keep on her new path and God would see that and take her in when the time came.

Maya seemed satisfied for the moment. Everyone was piling back into the house, singing and praising God. Maya let go of Ellen's hand and ran to catch up with them. Ellen stopped, turned around, and made her way back home.

# CHAPTER FORTY-FOUR
··· ◇ ···

Mary worked next to her husband kneeling in the field, picking green beans. She still called him her husband even though he bore very little resemblance to the man she married. She watched Jared methodically pluck the beans from the plants, his eyes vacant. She rubbed his back and he smiled at her like a small child. She absently stroked his head like she might pet a dog. He looked down at the bush and continued to harvest the beans.

Agents from Homeland Security came early one morning before the children went to school. The children screamed when they heard the shouts of the agents and the banging on the front door. Before they could unlock it the door flew open, the code overridden. They were told that they were being evicted due to their refusal to take the identity chip. Jared and Mary were both asked if they would reconsider taking the chip, and did they realize what it would mean to their children? Mary cried and the children surrounded her and clung to her legs as she repeated the required three times that she refused. Jared spoke quietly through clenched jaws as he also refused. Each member of the family was given a small box in which to put a few personal items. They were to be taken to a nearby farm which had been designated as a Refuser Camp. Their farm was to be reassigned for operations and government farming.

Jared and Mary had known this was eminent and had discussed their plan to make the best of it and keep their family safe. They knew that there would be many of their neighbors at the camp and that they would be allowed to farm their own food. They tried to see it as more of a refusers' commune than the prison it obviously was. Mary could see Jared struggling to keep his temper and she prayed that he would succeed. The Agents had been very clear that should any of the refusers resist them in any way they would be chemically lobotomized. As a former psychiatric nurse, Mary was very familiar with the procedure. A specialized chemical was given which targeted and destroyed the frontal lobe of the brain, the area that dealt with personality and aggression. In the mid-20th century surgical lobotomies, actual surgical removal of the frontal lobes of the brain, were performed on difficult or aggressive psychiatric patients as a last resort. In class they had watched 'One Flew over the Cuckoo's Nest', an old movie from that time period, which showed the devastating effect of such a surgery. The patient was turned into a docile sheep. The currently used chemical means sounded less barbaric but had the same effect. She had described this to Jared in hopes that it would keep him from resisting the demands of Homeland Security. A few of the Agents were sympathetic to their situation and tried to shield them from other agents who seemed to have no sense of justice or morality. They seemed to get pleasure from degrading these proud, strong-willed farmers. It reminded her of what she had read about the Holocaust.

One day a particularly sadistic Agent came up behind Jared as he was in the field digging postholes. Jared routinely volunteered for duties that would give him some isolation, knowing that it would be the safest way to keep from becoming defiant. He focused on the task at hand rather than the unfairness of the situation. He found himself praying for patience in an almost constant way. Mary watched from kitchen of the converted farmhouse as the agent snuck up on Jared and leaned in to say something in Jared's ear. She saw Jared startle, then stiffen, then spin around and swing the posthole digger at the Agent who easily ducked the awkward attack and laughed as he tasered Jared, calling over other agents to help him. Mary would never know what the Agent had said to provoke Jared but she could guess that it was something disgraceful about her or one of the children. A personal insult would have been brushed off.

Jared had been taken away immediately and when Mary was allowed to see him she had to stifle a gasp. He sat in a chair, looking toward her but not seeming to see her, a thin trail of saliva dribbling out of the side of his mouth. She flashed back to One Flew Over the Cuckoo's Nest and for a moment she considered suffocating him, like on the movie, but knew she couldn't. So she took him back to the room they shared with the children, and cared for Jared like he was another child. Mary was so angry. She divided her anger among the Government who created this situation, her husband who had succumbed to it, and God who was allowing it. At night she read her Bible, one of the things she had put her in box, especially devoting herself to the study of Revelation. She could see that so many of the prophesies had come to pass and found herself yearning to see the beautiful heaven that she read described there. She closed her eyes and thought of Revelation 4 and pictured a rainbow, resembling an emerald, encircling the throne of God. The description of the colors was so vivid she could almost see them. The mark of the beast had clearly come to pass and she felt in her heart that it couldn't be long before Jesus brought his faithful to him with his sharp sickle. She would opened her eyes and looked around at the dreary surroundings, her children crowded into one bed, the shell of her husband next to her, and prayed as John did at the end of Revelation.

"Come, Lord Jesus," she prayed, "Come."

# CHAPTER FORTY-FIVE

 ··· ◇ ···

Jessica came up the stairs with an armload of laundry. Laundry dried on the clothes line was at first difficult to get used to since it was much stiffer than laundry out of the dryer. Jeans could almost stand up by themselves. But the smell of the fresh laundry was so wonderful. It was different depending on what was blooming, what crops were being brought in, or even when it was about to rain. Jessica thought about the laundry detergents she used before which promise. "Mountain Fresh" or "lavender scented". She realized now that the whole purpose of these scents was to make the laundry smell like it had been dried outdoors.

Jessica knocked and then entered Karen's room.

"What's wrong, Karen," Jessica said as she sat down on the bed setting the laundry down next to her. Karen was curled up on her side, crying.

"Oh, Mom, I just don't know what is going on with Taylor. He is acting so strange lately, and he is gone for such long periods of time during the day," said Karen, wiping her eyes with the corner of her sleeve.

"Honey, you know he has been busy with George and Gretz building the chapel," Jessica said soothingly. The chapel was coming along beautifully. It was great to see Lebron so happy.

"But that's the thing, when I went down there to bring them some lunch it was just George and Gretz. They made some excuse about Taylor but I could tell they were uncomfortable. I think he wants to leave this place and go back. I know he misses his family," said Karen letting a sob escape from her throat.

"I think you have this all wrong, honey. Taylor loves you. I know he misses his family, but you are so important to him. I really don't think he would leave," reassured Jessica.

"Are you just saying that?" asked Karen, looking at her

mother with searching eyes. "Do you know something that I don't know?"

Jessica took a deep breath. The truth was, she did know something that Karen didn't know but it was not her place to tell.

"No, I don't," she lied. She gave Karen a hug and got up from the bed. "Now come on down and help me with the rest of this laundry."

"Give me a minute," replied Karen, trying to smile a bit.

"Alright, don't be long," said Jessica closing the door as she left.

As soon as the door shut, new tears streamed down Karen's face. Her mother was a terrible liar.

********

When Karen finally came down she heard whispered voices in the kitchen. She crept up quietly into the doorway and saw her mother and Taylor having a quiet but heated discussion. They both startled when they saw her there observing them.

"Is there something you want to share with the whole class?" quipped Karen, her voice quavering.

Taylor looked at Jessica who nodded almost imperceptibly.

"Karen, can we talk outside?" asked Taylor.

"Of course," said Karen, trying to hide a shuddering breath. She looked at her mother and noticed that she was smiling. Of course that didn't mean anything, she had known her mom to smile or laugh at completely inappropriate times.

Taylor led Karen out of the house and down the path toward the back field. He took her hand in his and glanced at her as they were walking. He made small talk about the weather and the crops until Karen thought she would scream. He was clearly nervous. If this is how he had acted at the Homeland Security meeting it was no wonder that he had been made.

"Karen, you know I love you, right?" said Taylor, his voice strained.

Here it comes, Karen thought. The big "but". "Well, I thought I did, but you have been acting really weird lately, and now I don't know what to think."

They had come to a clearing in the path. Karen had never been this far down the path before, and was surprised to see a small cabin in the clearing. It was an old cabin, but there were flowers planted around it and it looked like it had been cared for. She was curious about the cabin and when she turned to Taylor to ask about it, he smiled and knelt down on one knee. He pulled a small box from his pocket and opened it. Inside was a diamond ring in an antique setting.

"Karen, I love you. You have changed my life and I will be forever grateful. Will you marry me?"

*************

The farm family gathered on the porch step nervously awaiting the return of the lovebirds.

"She thought he was going to leave?" Sasha asked Jessica, incredulous. "How could she not know that boy thinks she hung the moon?"

"I don't know," Jessica replied, smiling. "I had to tell him. I couldn't bear to see her suffering like that. I know he wanted everything at the cabin to be perfect before he showed it to her, but it just wasn't fair to her."

"There really isn't much left to do," said Lebron. "It really is ready to move into now."

"Well I don't know about that," interjected Sasha. "I wanted to get those curtains done, but I didn't want Karen to see me working on them."

George was quiet. He had been the first to know Taylor's intentions, having asked him about the box from the secret room that George had seen Taylor slip into his pocket. Taylor had sheepishly showed George the ring, explaining that he hadn't known how he could ask Karen to marry him without a ring. Then Taylor found the cabin while on a run in the woods. It was barely visible under a cover of kudzu vine. Taylor brought George with him to tear down the vines and what they found was that although the cabin was dilapidated and had some rotten areas, it was charming. Taylor worked diligently on it with the help of the rest of the family, wanting to be able to present it to Karen when he proposed. He even made furniture, working late at night after everyone else was in bed.

"Do you think she is going to be mad that we all knew before she did?" asked Maya. She and Mark had been sworn to secrecy by Taylor. They had helped clean inside and plant flowers around the little cabin.

"I am guessing that nothing is going to make her mad today," said Ellen with a laugh. Becky had run over to fetch her when word got out about the proposal.

"Here they come!" cried Mark pointing down the path.

"She said yes!" cried Taylor as soon as they were in earshot. Karen was grinning from ear to ear.

"Congratulations!" everyone shouted and rushed to hug the couple.

Karen approached her mother, who had hung back from the group, and saw tears streaming down Jessica's face.

"Are you ok, Mom?" she asked.

"I'm just really happy," she said. "I'm sorry I had to lie to you. I hope you understand."

"I do. I guess I need to practice saying that huh?"

Jessica laughed and put her arms around her daughter.

"I wish your dad could be here. He would love Taylor. He would be just as happy for you as I am," Jessica took a deep breath and then let go of Karen. "I want you to have these," she said, opening her hand to reveal two wedding bands. One was small and delicate, one larger and thicker.

"Oh, Mom, I couldn't take those," said Karen.

"I want you to have them," said Jessica, smiling. "And this is the perfect time to give them to you."

Jessica caught Taylor's eye and gave him a smile. She had always wanted a son.

********

"Make sure he doesn't come in here and see me!" exclaimed Karen.

"He wouldn't dare come up here," reassured Becky. She was working diligently on Karen's hair, twisting it and braiding it into an up-do while interspersing white baby's -breath flowers among the strands.

"All done," said Becky. "See what you think." She gave Karen a hand mirror, the edges silvered with age.

"It's perfect," proclaimed Karen. "I don't think the best salon at home could have done any better. Thank you." She gave Becky a hug.

Jessica and Sasha came in with Karen's wedding dress on a hanger. Sasha had found the dress in the secret room, wrapped in plastic and in its own box. As soon as she spied the box Sasha knew what is was, having left a box much like it at home with her wedding dress in it. Sasha had quietly taken the box out of the room and had slid it under her bed, foreseeing this possibility even then. The dress had turned out to be made of beautiful antique lace, just the kind of dress Karen had dreamed about. It had required very little altering to make it perfect for Karen.

"It's time," Jessica said, smiling.

Karen stepped into the dress and the ladies fluttered around her, straightening this and plucking that. Maya stuck her head in. She was taking her role as maid of honor very seriously.

"They're waiting!" she exclaimed.

Jessica faced Karen, taking her hands and squeezing them.

"You are so beautiful. Taylor is a lucky man," said Jessica, eyes filling with tears. "Now let's not keep him waiting at the altar." They stepped out of the room and found George, dressed in a vintage double breasted suit, standing outside.

"I'll take it from here," he said, extending the crook of his arm to Karen, who beamed back.

Becky and Jessica met Ellen at the back door and headed out to the chapel, built only about a hundred yards from the house, a newly laid path of pine straw showing the way. As they drew close they saw Matthew playing the guitar and Ruth singing. The baby, named George after the doctor who delivered him, bounced on her knee. No one was really sure who would be attending the wedding since they had put out the word that all were invited. Jessica smiled and squeezed Becky's hand, then Becky and Ellen took their seats next to Sasha. Jessica took a deep breath and walked under a trellis covered with flowers and down the aisle. There were about a hundred people sitting in the pews, their heads turned to watch. These were people who the family knew through clandestine trading of goods and services, here to share this special day. Knowing the risk they were all taking by gathering like this nearly broke Jessica's heart with humble gratitude.

After Becky and Jessica sat down next to Sasha, Mark and Taylor stood and took their places next to Lebron at the altar. They both looked so handsome in their borrowed suits. Taylor wore his running shoes since no one they knew had a size twelve foot. Jessica had never seen Taylor look so happy. If he was at all nervous, it didn't show.

Jessica took a moment to look around at the chapel. The split logs used for pews and for the cross were perfect for the forest setting. Taylor had made the altar and Lebron had carved engravings into it. Instead of stained glass there were vibrant flowering plants, and in place of a painted ceiling, a beautiful blue sky. Lebron had started preaching here just a few weeks ago, first to just the family but as word got out, more and more people arrived to worship with them on Sunday morning. Jessica had noticed that Ellen was there every week, sitting toward the back.

The whispering quieted when Matthew began to play the wedding processional. They looked back to see Maya, dressed uncharacteristically in a dress, pass through the arch. Sasha smiled, remembering a moment taken from The Sound of Music, her favorite movie as a child, when she had found some old curtains and made the dress from them, just as Maria had in the movie. Maya held her head high and scattered petals from a basket as she walked slowly up the aisle.

Then came Karen, her antique gown looking as if it had been made just for her, the off-white lace accenting her mocha skin. The oohs and ahhs rose from the pews as she walked slowly down the aisle on George's arm until she arrived at the altar. George nodded at Taylor and, after giving Karen a peck on the cheek, passed her hand to him. Lebron gave a brief but poignant discussion of marriage and

God's role in their lives. They exchanged rings, and then came the vows.

"Taylor, do you promise to love and honor Karen until death do you part?"

"I do," replied Taylor.

"And Karen, do you promise to love and honor Taylor until death do you part?"

"I do," replied Karen.

"Well then, in front of God and all these people, I now pronounce you husband and wife. Taylor, you may kiss your bride," said Lebron, wiping a tear from his eye. The onlookers stood and cheered as the two kissed and then made their way down the aisle.

Lebron announced that a feast was set out in the kitchen and all were invited. Everyone made their way in and they were amazed by the amount of food. Each guest had brought food based on what they had, and each brought a gift, wrapped in scraps of paper from old feed sacks and bound in twine or bits of vine. Of course none of the people that came had taken the mark, so there were no store bought gifts among them. Karen and Taylor would later open the gifts and marvel at the time and effort put into these handcrafted items. Some generously gave of their few possessions, the sacrifice not lost on the new couple.

A few of the guests had brought musical instruments and they started playing in the corner. The cake had been made by Sasha using the last of their flour. Karen had fussed about it but was shushed by Sasha, who stated that there could never be a better use for it.

Karen and Taylor held hands and observed the happy group. For just this moment, there was no fear, no hiding. For just this moment they were all free. Karen had a sudden thought.

"Taylor, we're never going to have any wedding pictures," she said sadly.

Taylor smiled. "Why would we need them? We will remember this day for the rest of our lives."

As the party wound down, Lebron circulated among the guests and handed them torches. They made their way out of the house and lit the torches from a small fire that Mark had set up outside, then they lined the path. Taylor and Karen passed between them smiling and thanking the guests as they made their way to their little cabin. Jessica was the last in line. She gave each of them a kiss and passed her torch to Taylor, who took it and led his new bride home.

# CHAPTER FORTY-SIX
··· ◇ ···

Lebron glanced around to make sure no one was watching and slipped into his bedroom. The strain of keeping up appearances was taking its toll. He gently pulled up his pants leg and examined his calf. The angry red infection had grown since he last looked at it just a few hours before. Now the center was black with white surrounding it giving the whole lesion the look of an ugly bloodshot eye. Red lines were tracing up his leg, a sign he knew was not good. He was hoping he could handle this himself, that it would just drain and heal but it hadn't. It had been a week since he had first noticed the small red spot that had grown into this monster.

Lebron limped over to the bed and lay down. So far he had been able to convince Sasha that he was alright, that the summer heat was just getting to him and making him tired, but he had caught her eying him suspiciously. Lebron wasn't sure how much longer he could hide the infection. He shivered despite the heat and then fell asleep.

Sasha had seen Lebron sneak into their room and shut the door. As hot as it was, no one was shutting any doors, preferring to catch any crosswind through the windows. He was acting very strange. She was suspicious that there was something wrong with Lebron that he was keeping from her. She gave him a few minutes of privacy, using the time to work on a baby quilt that she was making from scraps of fabric. No one was particularly surprised when Karen relayed her suspicions that she was pregnant since there was no access to birth control in their community. Everyone was excited and now that she was near delivery the nesting had begun. Sasha had taught both Jessica and Karen to sew and they were enjoying their newfound skill. Becky had proven to be surprisingly inept at any needle craft, a skill which she felt took a lot of patience which she claimed not to possess.

"Well that's enough privacy for you," thought Sasha. She set aside her quilt and opened the door. On the bed was Lebron, cuddled under the blanket, his face strangely flushed. Sasha touched his arm and found him to be burning up. She pulled back the covers and he didn't wake up, but she noticed his pant leg was pulled up revealing an obvious abscess. After trying unsuccessfully to wake him she called frantically out the window for George who was working in the garden. He came running in, recognizing the panic in Sasha's voice.

George took in the scene and ran to get his bag. He listened to Lebron's heart, beating strong and fast, and examined his leg.

"It's an abscess alright," he said agreeing with Sasha's diagnosis, "But his fever is very high and with these red streaks I suspect the infection has reached his blood. Sasha, would you go to the pump and get some water? We need to sponge him down and the water is cool straight from the well."

By this time Becky and the kids had heard the commotion and had come running.

"What do you want me to do," asked Becky, quickly switching gears from reading a story to the kids to assistant.

"We need to drain this and we might as well do it while he is out of it with fever. Maya and Mark, you might want to leave, it is going to be pretty gory."

"I want to stay," insisted Mark.

"I'm out of here," stated Maya, "I'll go down and tell Taylor and Karen what is going on."

"Ok, Becky let's get this done before Sasha gets back with the water." He took betadine from the bag and washed the area carefully. Then he took the scalpel and cleaned it with an alcohol swab.

"Becky, go up by Lebron's head and hold his hands. I am afraid he is going to wake up and grab my hand. Mark, you hold his leg still."

Once they were in place George deftly sliced into the abscess, releasing a fountain of pus which he caught in the sheet. Lebron let out a moan but didn't move.

"Cool!" cried Mark, forgetting for a moment the dangerous situation Gretz was in. "Oh, sorry," he said, embarrassed by his own enthusiasm.

George smiled at his son. "It's OK, Mark. I think it's cool too. Unfortunately that was the easy part. We are going to need to really clean this out, and it is going to hurt." He began to apply pressure to the area around the abscess, draining more pus and bloody fluid.

Sasha heard Lebron screaming from out by the well. In a way she was relieved, at least he was conscious. She had known that George was trying to get her out of the room but she was perfectly willing to go. Illness and injury were not her strong suit. When Michael was little it was Lebron that tended to those things. Seeing even a little cut made her woozy. By the time Sasha was inside the screaming had stopped.

"Is everything alright in there?" she asked, unable to get her voice much louder than a whisper.

"You can come in, Sasha, we have the wound covered," Becky called out. Everyone knew this was not Sasha's cup of tea.

Sasha entered the room with the bucket of water and a few towels. She averted her eyes from Lebron's leg, briefly taking in the bandage covering it, already starting to seep through with blood. Lebron was barely conscious, his eyes fluttering. She dipped the towel in the water and sponged his face and neck.

"You stupid old man," she muttered.

"Why would he conceal this, Sasha?" George asked, bewildered. "He had to know that this needed to be treated."

"Well, I can tell you why. I know how he thinks. He didn't want to use your last few doses of antibiotics on him, and he knew you would. He felt that medicine should be saved for younger people."

"I suspected as much. Sasha, I would use whatever I had to make him better. I gave him a dose of antibiotics, but the main treatment was to drain that abscess." George had seen this before. Rationing of care made people question their worth as they aged.

"Sasha, you stay here with him. Call me if you see any

change. I'll be right back." George motioned to Becky and Mark and they stepped out just as Jessica and Taylor burst into the house followed by Maya, with Karen waddling behind.

George explained the situation to them and told them that he was worried that the infection was too far advanced for Lebron to fight off with just the medicines that they had available. They were all stunned into a solemn silence.

Sasha sat on a stool by the bed. Lebron would wake for a few minutes at a time and try to speak but then would lapse back into unconsciousness. George came back in and suggested that Sasha talk to him explaining that even though Lebron appeared to be unconscious, he might wake enough to be able to take some fluids if he heard her voice. George felt so helpless without his IV fluids and medicine. He explained gently to Sasha that the next several hours would be critical. Sasha considered what she could do to try to engage Lebron. Knowing his affinity for music she began to sing. Amazing Grace was the first thing that came to mind. As she sang the family outside started to file in until they were all singing.

"How precious did that grace appear the hour I first believed," they sang. Lebron opened his eyes and Sasha got him to take a few sips of water. The song reminded her of a time before she lost Michael, a time when she first believed and she felt a stirring of that passion rising up in her. They continued to sing and Lebron would intermittently wake and take sips of water. Suddenly Lebron became limp and struggled to breathe. George was alarmed to find that Lebron's blood pressure had dropped dangerously low. Sasha felt a wave of despair.

"We need to pray," she stated. She put her hand on Lebron's head. His fever had broken, but the clammy feeling of his skin was almost as bad. Everyone followed suit, laying a hand on Lebron and bowing their heads. Becky began the prayer with an appeal to God to heal Lebron, and around the group it went, each one lifting up Lebron who they loved so much. Even Taylor, who was so uncomfortable with public prayer that he stumbled over saying grace at meals, cried out to God for His healing power. Finally Sasha spoke, quietly admitting her anger at God all of these years and asking for his forgiveness.

"Please Lord," she prayed, "if both your will can be done and Lebron can live, please let it be so." At that moment she felt a peace that she had forgotten existed and she knew that whether Lebron survived or not, everything would be alright. She opened her eyes and Lebron was gazing at her, smiling. She touched his face gently and encouraged him to drink some water.

So it went, with everyone taking shifts, forcing Lebron to take sips of water and changing his bandages every few hours. Ellen brought over food and tea when she found out about Lebron's illness. She sat by his bed and forced him to eat just a little bit of chicken soup that she had brought for him. After a few days it appeared that Lebron had turned the corner. Once Lebron felt better George gave him hell for concealing his plight. Lebron confirmed Sasha's suspicions that he was trying not to use precious supplies, and the whole family tried to explain him that his life had value equal to any of theirs. He was appreciative of their kind words but appeared unconvinced.

Ten days after the abscess was drained Lebron was finally able to leave his bed. Things were returning to semi-normal now that the whole family didn't feel a need to be close to Lebron's bedside. Taylor took Maya and Mark down to the creek to fish and swim and the rest of the family were scattered doing their chores while Lebron and Karen sat outside enjoying the breeze on the front porch. Karen was due any day and suffered greatly from the summer heat. Lebron sat in a chair with his leg propped up while Karen read Huck Finn aloud. She was shocked that the book used the words "nigger" and "Injun Joe". She felt sure that she would have noticed that when she watched the movie in high school. Lebron told her that the words had been changed so as not to offend, but that he had disagreed with that. As a black man he welcomed the discussion that reading literature from that time period caused. Changing a work of literature allowed the injustices to be ignored and thus forgotten.

Karen was about to resume her reading when they heard shouts.

"That sounds like Maya and Mark," said Karen, alarmed. The

shouts brought everyone to the front porch. Tensions were still high from Lebron's illness.

"Is Lebron OK?" said Ellen breathlessly as she reached the porch. They turned their attention to the shouting and moved toward it. Out of the woods emerged Maya and Mark struggling to carry Taylor.

Karen froze and George ran and got his medical bag while everyone else ran to help Taylor.

"Lay him here under the tree," instructed George. Taylor looked like he was in shock, his face was extremely pale and his body was limp. When George touched Taylor's leg he cried out in pain.

"What happened? " George asked the kids, who were kneeling by Taylor and crying. "I need to know what happened!" he yelled, shocking them into responding.

"A snake," sputtered Mark. "I turned over a log and there it was and it went to bite me but Taylor got between me and the snake and it bit him."

"What did it look like Mark?" asked George.

"I know what it was, Daddy. We just studied snakes in the encyclopedia. It was a rattlesnake," said Maya solemnly. She had also studied the results of a rattlesnake bite. She knew that Taylor would need the anti-venin and she also knew they didn't have any.

Taylor was barely conscious. "It's not good is it, Doc?" he said, attempting a smile. Karen had finally mobilized and dropped by his side. Lebron was at Taylor's feet fiercely praying.

"No, it's not," said George quietly.

"Do something!" pleaded Karen.

"There's nothing I can do. If we could get him to a hospital..." his voice trailed off. There was silence as everyone absorbed what George was telling them.

Becky knelt at Taylor's side and took his hand. "Taylor, I want you to know that I love you and I am so glad that you came with Karen. Your strength and your sense of humor will be missed so much."

Jessica, taking her cue from Becky took Taylor' hand from her and looked him in the eye.

"Taylor, I will always be grateful to you for the love you have shown all of us, especially Karen, I want you to know that we will love your child so much and we will make sure the baby hears wonderful things about you."

Each member of the family took a turn at Taylor's side, sometimes having to raise their voices above the prayers and sobs of the others. When at last Karen took Taylor's hand he had to struggle to stay with them.

"I love you so much and I wish I could stay with you," Taylor said.

"I will always love you," replied Karen. As he started to drift away Karen reminded him about the gazebo when they had professed their love in the rain, and told him that they would see each other again someday.

Suddenly, Taylor opened his eyes and appeared to be focused on something just passed them.

"Oh, the colors!" he whispered, "It's amazing!" He closed his eyes and smiled. And then he was gone.

An almost inhuman sound erupted from Karen. She lay awkwardly over Taylor's body as if she could somehow keep him from leaving. Jessica gently pulled her back and held her. She knew the pain Jessica was feeling, worse than any physical pain imaginable. Pain that, despite what everyone said, time never heals. They all knelt around Taylor, too stunned to move.

Lebron prayed for strength for those who had loved Taylor and slowly they began to do what needed to be done. Jessica stayed with Karen by Taylor's body. Becky and Ellen went into the house and found a sheet to wrap him in. They had to convince Karen to let go of his hand but before she did she took off his ring and put it on her finger, the two rings flanking her engagement ring as her mother had worn hers most of Karen's life. Jessica sobbed at the sight.

George and Mark carried Taylor's wrapped body to the root cellar to keep it cool and protected until the grave was ready. George put his arm around his son who was shaking with sobs.

"Why did he do that?" wailed Mark. "He would still be alive if it wasn't for me."

"He loved you," said George, stroking his son's head and holding him close. "The Bible says that 'greater love has no one than this, that he lay down his life for his friends.' It wasn't your fault. It was Taylor's choice and he chose you."

******

Lebron stood in the front of the church, next to the coffin that held Taylor's body. Ellen had gotten the word out and the community had built Taylor a pine coffin and brought it over as an offering of sympathy. A new grave was dug in the graveyard by Ellen's cabin. Now they all gathered again, the same group who, almost exactly one year ago, had gathered for the happy occasion of Karen and Taylor's marriage. The mood was somber and there were sniffles and occasional sobs rising up from those gathered. Karen sat in the front row with her family, a look of bewilderment on her face.

"Thank you all for coming," said Lebron. "We are all sad to lose Taylor, but we know that he has donned his white robe and is with his Father in heaven." Lebron felt some of the crowd become uncomfortable. Although all of them were refusers, not all of them were believers. Some of them, like Ellen, refused the mark because they felt their freedoms were being violated. Lebron worried for their souls, feeling that it was likely that they were rapidly approaching the time of Jesus' return.

"Those of us with him in the end can testify to his strength and to the wonderful vision that he gave us in his last words. 'It's amazing' he said. 'The colors' he said. We know from Revelation that heaven is alive with color and light that we cannot even imagine. Taylor saw that. Of course we wish he could have been here longer but we can rejoice in the knowledge that we will be with him again someday. As Paul says in 1 Thessalonians 4:16-17 concerning the end times – *The Lord himself will come down from heaven, with a loud command with the voice of the archangel and with the trumpet call of God, and the dead in Christ will rise first. After that, we who are still alive and are left will be caught up together with them in the clouds to meet the Lord in the air. And so we will be with the Lord forever.*"

Lebron talked about getting to know Taylor and what a

special man he was. He talked about Taylor's love for Karen and his excitement about becoming a father. Lebron asked the community if anyone had anything they would like to say. Several people rose to say wonderful things about their experiences with Taylor, kind and sometimes funny stories about him. Then Karen rose and Lebron, surprised that she would be able to speak, asked if she had something she wanted to say.

"My water just broke," she announced.

*************

Cock-a-doodle do!

Karen awoke and stretched her arm out to Taylor's side of the bed, feeling nothing. She opened her eyes and saw on her left hand three rings, one masculine and one feminine, flanking her engagement ring. After three months she still cried every morning when she awoke. Her mother had honestly told her that she still thought of Karen's dad every morning when she awoke. She told her that the pain was still there, just not as debilitating. Jessica had told her that what got her through it was Karen, and she understood. Karen looked over at the crib, handmade by Taylor with intricate carvings added by Lebron. Taylor Michaela was already awake and smiling at her. Karen brought her into the bed and fed her, enjoying the close bond of breastfeeding. Karen gazed at her baby's beautiful face; the blue eyes so much like her father's that it almost brought her to tears every time she looked at them. Karen looked at the little hand wrapped around her finger, the soft baby skin just a little lighter in tone than her own. Karen kissed the top of her head, breathing in the intoxicating baby smell. Taylor's hair was lighter than Karen's but to her chagrin, just as curly.

"If only we could pick the genes we passed on I would have chosen your dad's hair for you, sweet baby," Karen murmured. Taylor was such a good baby, rarely crying at all. Of course there was never really any need, someone was always holding her and playing with her. Lately their circle had tightened as more of their neighbors had been taken away by Homeland security. Karen had been saddened to hear that Matthew, Ruth and baby George had been turned in by his parents for the reward money. Karen couldn't imagine turning on her family like that but Lebron said that it was just more evidence that they were in the last days.

Karen had moved back to the farmhouse after Taylor died, unable to handle the memories, but she hoped that at some point she and Taylor Michaela could live in the home that Taylor had made for them. Once she finished nursing, she changed the baby's diaper and Taylor started cooing happily. Karen put the baby back in the crib long enough to change her clothes and then picked her up and headed down to the kitchen. Sasha had breakfast already started and Lebron was having a quiet time with his Bible. Everyone was already up and doing their chores. Maya set some freshly picked flowers on the table. Sasha waved off Karen's offer to help so she went out on the front porch and wrapped herself and Taylor up in the patchwork quilt made for her by Sasha. The autumn mornings were getting a little chilly. Karen sat on the porch swing and watched Taylor's face. Before she had a baby of her own she would never have believed that she could spend hours just smiling at her baby and watching her every expression. Taylor suddenly shifted her focus to something up in the sky and her face revealed that she was delighted with what she saw. Karen turned to see what had caught her attention.

*************************

Mary was out in the chicken coop gathering eggs for breakfast. Months of hard work and rough, sometime brutal treatment by the guards had demoralized her. She had to keep strong for her kids, she knew, and for Jared. As she stood among the chickens she suddenly felt a presence, and a peaceful, joyous feeling overcame her. She turned her face to the heavens and smiled.

# CHAPTER FORTY-SEVEN
··· ◇ ···

Things were not going well in Josh's world. The Supreme Principal's announcement barring religious practices had produced unrest rather than unity. Rumors of resistance and even war were being circulated, especially in the American regions. It seemed that some of those that were not strong enough to resist the identity chip were pushed to the brink by the abolition of religion. There were protests in front of churches and government buildings requiring Homeland Security to intervene. This stretched the agency to the maximum and it had been suggested that students who had Homeland Security commitments be asked to postpone their education to do their service now. Senator Thomas hoped that they would have enough volunteers but discussed the necessity of a draft if that wasn't the case.

Josh sat at his desk with his head in his hands. He just couldn't believe that things had gotten so out of hand. Josh had been so consumed by his grief and guilt that he had not been very available to his family. Rachel had repeatedly asked him if he was alright, finally confronting him one night and asking if he was having an affair. He couldn't help but laugh, which did nothing to lighten the mood. If only it was that simple. He finally told her about the fears he had about the Identity Chip. Rachel seemed relieved; apparently the thought that he was unfaithful was harder to take than the thought that they were doomed to burn in Hell. Silly.

One evening Ben sat down next to him while Josh was brooding on the couch. Josh had been startled by Ben's attention, his Device nowhere in sight.

"I need to talk to you, Dad," he said.

"You can talk to me about anything," Josh said. He felt tense, but was glad the boy felt his father could be trusted.

"Don't laugh," said Ben, glancing over at Josh who shook his head solemnly. "I have been having these dreams. Well not dreams exactly, because I am not asleep. I feel like I am losing my mind."

Into Josh's head came Acts 2:17 "In the last days, God says, I will pour out my Spirit on all people. Your sons and daughters will prophesy, your young men will see visions, your old men will dream dreams."

"Tell me about these visions," Josh said with trepidation.

"Well, like yesterday I was just watching a show on my bedroom screen and I could see the screen but in front of it was like another scene. There were men on a boat and they were terrified because the ocean all around them was red and the fish were floating on top, dead. Other times there are battle scenes and other times terrible storms. They are always scary, Dad. What is happening to me?"

Josh assured Ben that he was not losing his mind. With Ben's permission he asked Hannah and Rachel to join them and began the most difficult discussion of his life. He told them about his understanding of the book of Revelation and his thoughts on what might be in store for them. He took out his Bible and read about the seven bowls of God's wrath and how they related to Ben's visions. Josh's family was silent as he read about sores, the sea and the rivers turning to blood, the sun scorching, darkness, the Euphrates drying up and the battle of Armageddon. He told them about the final bowl with massive earthquakes and hailstorms with 100 pound hail. He opted to leave out the punishment for those taking the mark. He told them about the verses that kept coming into his head, his grief over not keeping them from taking the mark and how sorry he was. He explained that even though he believed that these things would eventually come to pass, no one could know the day or time except God, so they should continue on as they had been. If they had any more questions he promised to be honest with them to the best of his knowledge.

"So just go along to school and act as though the world is not about to end, that's what you are saying?" asked Hannah, incredulous.

"What's the other choice?" asked Ben, "Sit around at home and wait for it? Dad, I appreciate your honesty." He stood up abruptly and sauntered off to his room, a teenager once again. Hannah followed, branching off to her room and quietly closing the door.

"Do you really believe all of that?" asked Rachel.

"I do," replied Josh. Rachel looked toward her children's' rooms and a tear escaped from her heavily made-up eye, traveling down her cheek leaving a faint black trail. Finding that he had no soothing words, Josh drew her near to him and held her.

Now back at his office he found himself mindlessly picking at his chip. The NA tattoo overlying it had changed over the last few days from black to a brownish-red color and had become itchy. He kept meaning to ask whether anyone else was noticed this too. An alarm sounded on his device, advising him of an emergency meeting of the Homeland Security Committee. Josh could not remember a time when this had happened before and it worried him. He made his way to the board room, wondering what the issue was and whether President Sontara would be present.

The room was about half occupied when Josh arrived. Worry and confusion were evident on all of the senators' faces. Senator Thomas burst into the room and quickly took control of the meeting. He glanced around the room and took note of who was present and asked them to be seated. The President, he relayed, was on her way to a Skype Governance meeting. Senator Thomas explained that he was meeting with this committee today to keep them in the loop.

Senator Thomas took a deep breath. It appeared that he had the weight of the world on his shoulders. His hair was uncharacteristically messy and he ran his hand through it in a nervous gesture.

"The situation in the world is very unstable," he began. "It has come to the Governance's attention that certain factions have retained nuclear capability." He paused for a moment, letting this fact sink in. Part of the agreement at the time of the Jubilee was that all of the nations would disarm themselves of nuclear weapons. Until this moment Josh was sure that they had all done so. A look around the room told him that the others on the committee had thought so also.

"At this time there is evidence that in the area of the former Iran, militants are preparing to launch missiles at multiple targets. We believe that they have the capability to launch but are unsure of the range of their missiles. They may fall harmlessly in the ocean."

Josh thought of Ben's dream and of the prophesies. Maybe falling into the sea was not so harmless.

"Is there anything we can do?" asked a junior senator on the committee. Senator Thomas paused for a moment.

"Pray," he said. He looked embarrassed, as if he had accidently let a swear word slip.

Senator Thomas adjourned the meeting with the admonishment not to tell anyone about this, even their spouses. They were each given research to do concerning future preparations should they be faced with this disaster.

All of these things weighed heavily on Josh as he took the train home. His research assignment was the prevention of radiation poisoning. Every three-day pack included Iodine pills as well as antibiotics and antivirals in case of bioterrorism. He would need to make sure they were still good and when to recommend them.

As Josh finished the short walk from the train he noticed the itching of his hand had increased. He examined the tattoo and realized that there were small blisters on his skin around the area. Rachel greeted him with a hug and a kiss, and the kids lifted their eyes from their screens and greeted him as well. One thing about having a "the world could end anytime" discussion is that it did make you more appreciative of your time together. Rachel had the news on as she prepared dinner. One item caught his attention.

"In medical news, it has been noted that some people have been having some sort of reaction at the insertion site of the identity chip. If you are experiencing any discomfort or rash you are advised to see your physician as soon as possible," the anchor said with a smile.

"Hey, I have that – how about you guys?" asked Josh.

Rachel looked at her hand and shook her head. "Nope, all clear."

"Me too," said Hannah after glancing at her hand.

"I don't know, Dad, what do you think?" Ben asked, looking carefully at his hand. Josh saw that Ben's hand looked a lot like his.

"I will make us both appointments for tomorrow," said Josh, feeling vaguely uneasy. He took a minute to make the appointment on his Device. "9 am tomorrow with the triage nurse, and then I will take you to school." He tousled the boy's dark hair as they sat down to eat. Everyone's devices were put away and Rachel turned the screen off. Josh hated what had caused it, but he was enjoying the new family dynamic. Even so, the talk was light and centered on events in school and with friends rather than the more scary aspects of life.

Josh thought about the meeting he had been in today and how a nuclear war would affect his family. They had been lucky that during the last conflict none of United States, as it had been called then, was affected. India, North Africa and Europe took the brunt of the destruction and contamination, killing a third of the Earth's inhabitants and contaminating vast expanses of the ocean as well as rivers and wells. The Middle East had been the source of that nightmare also. Under the noses of the United Nations, Iran had built a nuclear weapon and had almost immediately used it against Israel, beginning the Middle East war. The whole world had chosen sides with enormous devastation within just a few months of the first missile. The loss of life and property had been huge and had been partly responsible for the acceptance of Jubilee. In order to maintain order and to help those in need the whole world had to come together and cooperate. Iran had been defeated and its leader had promised to comply with all of the demands to disarm. Apparently even in this era of enhanced drone surveillance they had found a way to squirrel away weapons. Unbelievable. How anyone who had lived through that time could even consider detonating a nuclear weapon again was beyond him. At least there was not the stockpile of weapons that there once was in the rest of the world. Or at least he thought there wasn't. He couldn't imagine that it could be worse than the war they already lived through. There was only so much destruction that man's inhumanity against man could produce. Through his recent study of Revelation he realized that he had already lived through the time of the seven seals and seven trumpets that had come earlier in the prophesy.

After dinner Hannah suggested that they watch a movie together. Josh was so shocked it took him a moment to respond.

"Well, if you don't want to," Hannah said, averting her eyes.

"I would love that," said Josh, recovering. "You pick."

Josh and Rachel sat on the couch and the kids sprawled on the rug at their feet. Hannah picked a light-hearted comedy and that had them all laughing. Josh glanced around at his family and smiled. All felt right with the world at that moment. Maybe he was overreacting. Maybe there was nothing to be so worried about. He didn't really believe that but he did know one thing, worrying was not going to accomplish anything. Josh deliberately pushed the anxious thoughts out of his mind and enjoyed the movie with his family.

# CHAPTER FORTY-EIGHT
··· ◇ ···

Josh and Ben arrived ten minutes early to their appointment but there was already a line that extended out of the door. He had expected a wait, there always was, but this was unusual. He observed the patients for a minute and noticed that they were all looking at their right hands, some wincing in pain. One man had his whole arm wrapped in gauze. Since making the appointment Josh had noticed that the rash had spread. The backside of his hand was covered in blisters and Ben even had some on the other hand. The sores were tender to touch and oozed clear liquid. Before they left the house Josh checked Hannah and Rachael, but they didn't have any rash yet.

The line was moving fast as the receptionist tapped each of the patients' Devices and then directed them back to the triage nurse. When it was their turn Josh and Ben held out their Devices, got checked in and followed the person ahead of them. Once in the triage office he realized why they were moving so fast. The nurse took a picture of the rash, tapped their Device to save it in their file, then told them that they were investigating this symptom but as of yet had not identified the problem. They would be textmailed when more information was available. Until then she recommended keeping the lesions covered and handed each of them a pack of gauze and Band-Aids and sent on their way. Josh and Ben drove to school in silence. Josh wondered if Ben remembered the Bible reading from the night before. Revelation 16:2 foretold of sores that would break out on the people who took the mark of the beast.

"Do you think the angel has poured out the first bowl?" asked Ben as if reading his thoughts. Ben looked out of the window while he spoke, trying to appear casual, but his shaky voice relayed his true feelings.

"Impossible to know, Ben," said Josh. "There have been many instances through history when people thought they knew that the end was near and then it wasn't. Many people thought that Hitler was the antichrist and that the world would soon end but it didn't. It is not for us to know."

Ben nodded. He opened the door as soon as Josh stopped the car at the school and got out. Josh called after him but Ben didn't hear, or at least pretended not to.

On his way into the Capital, Josh received a textmail requesting his presence in a Homeland Security briefing. He let Senator Thomas know about his medical issue and was told to alert the Senator as soon as he arrived. These meeting were becoming more and more frequent, almost daily. Josh wondered what it was about today. Perhaps there was more information about the nuclear threat from the Middle East. He thought about his discussion with Ben and thought ahead to the devastation that the further bowls could bring.

The meeting was called as soon as Josh arrived. He rushed down to the conference room without even stopping at his office. Around the table were all of the rest of the committee members. He quickly noted that about half of them had bandages on their hands.

"This meeting is called to order," stated Senator Thomas before Josh could even take his seat. "As many of you are obviously aware, we are experiencing an outbreak of blisters that seem to originate at the site of the identity chip. This has happened in the past twenty four hours, with all ten regions reporting similar symptoms. The blisters are painful and are spreading from their original site to the rest of the body, at least in some. The best scientists around the world are working on this but so far we don't know whether this infectious, an immune reaction or what else it could be, so we don't have a treatment." Senator Thomas looked down at his device, gave it a tap with a bandaged hand, and the main screen lit up with a document titled 'Press Release'. At the same time Josh's Device lit up with the same information.

"This is the release that will be given to GTV. It is an honest discussion of the possibilities of what is causing the outbreak. The Governance feels that honesty would serve us well here, feeling that what people might imagine would be even worse than reality. At this time it does not appear to be an act of terror since all of the regions have been affected. I will be delegating responsibilities to all of you concerning tracking and identifying the source or cause of this outbreak. Any questions so far?"

Josh raised his hand like a schoolboy and was called upon by Senator Thomas.

"If there is evidence the blisters originate at the site of the identity chip, then has anyone looked at the refusers to see if they are also experiencing the blisters?" he asked.

"We have not been able to confirm whether the identity chip is causing the problem as we have not had access to any of the refusers to check their status." Senator Thomas looked uncomfortable and changed the topic immediately. He gave each of them assignments and asked the two senators who were overseeing the refuser camps to stay behind. Clearly there was information that was currently on a "need to know" basis. Josh, because of his medical training, was assigned to filtering all of the information coming in from the scientists in every region and would be reporting to the committee the following day. Josh called Rachel to let her know that he would be staying at the office all night.

"All night?" she asked. "What is going on Josh? Should I be worried?"

Josh wasn't sure how to answer that. He settled on telling her the truth, that he was in charge of helping figure out what was going on with this outbreak, and that there would be more about it on GTV if she wanted to watch. She told him that she had noticed that her tattoo had darkened, as had Hannah's. Josh wished he could give her some answers but he had none.

Worries of war were eclipsed by the possibility of a pandemic. His research into radiation treatment was put aside and Josh spent the day and well into the night reading information that was coming in. There was no evidence of an infectious agent and no sign of radiation. Biopsies were showing that the blistering was caused by the skin just separating with no inflammation, ruling out an autoimmune cause. Blistering was spreading throughout the body with no other abnormalities noted in blood work. There was no known disease that they could compare it to. Puzzling.

Notably absent was a discussion of the refusers. Why didn't they have "access" to them? Josh shuddered at the thought that they may have all been killed. He thought about George and wondered if he would have any idea about the blistering. In reality he wanted to know if George was alright. Even though it was midnight he spoke George's name into his device using the private line. Immediately his screen lit up with red letters. REFUSER it said. He knew if he had dialed through the regular line there would have been a government employee who would have answered and tried to ascertain his relationship to the refuser and to obtain information about them both. Josh had mixed feelings about getting this information. He was glad that George had stuck to his principles and that he and Becky and the kids may not be affected by this blistering, but he worried about their safety. He laid his head down on the desk and drifted off to sleep.

Josh dreamed about the farm. In the dream he walked through the farmhouse and saw evidence of human occupation. In the kitchen there were dishes in the sink and eggs in a bowl on the counter. There were ashes in the fireplace and some flowers on the kitchen table. He walked around taking note of a board game in progress and books in the shelves. He pulled one out and turned in over in his hands. *Huck Finn*, he read on the worn cover. He wandered upstairs and saw a crib in one of the rooms. He ran his hand along the top and noticed some carvings. He didn't remember a crib in the house before but it could have been put away in the secret room and he hadn't noticed it as a kid. One room was messy, toys strewn about, some that he remembered playing with as a child. He wandered back downstairs and out the back door. A garden and a makeshift greenhouse were visible from the back porch. He walked over to where he remembered the pump to be and pumped some cool water which ran over his hands. Josh awoke with a start, recognized where he was, and wiped the drool off of his face. He stretched and remembered his dream, so incredibly vivid. He thought about all of details of the farmhouse. Just before falling back to sleep he had a startling thought: *Where were the people?*

# CHAPTER FORTY-NINE
··· ◇ ···

Josh awoke to the sound of sirens. Completely disoriented, he sat up quickly and looked around. He remembered that he had stretched out on the couch to catch a few minutes of sleep before the rest of the staff came in. He had set the alarm on his Device but this was not it. This loud sound was coming from his Device but was unfamiliar to him. It reminded him of the air raid sirens on old World War II movies. Josh got up and peeked out of his door, looked both ways down the corridor but saw no one. He looked at his Device which was now scrolling: WARNING TAKE SHELTER IN THE CAPITOL SAFEROOM.

Josh took the stairs two at a time as he descended to the Capitol safe room. There were safe room drills twice a year since the Middle East War so he knew exactly where to go. Glancing at the time he noted that it was only 5 am, so he doubted there would be many people here. Apparently his Device's GPS had alerted the warning system to his presence in the building.

Trying to push down his feelings of panic, Josh made his way down the hallway to a solid metal door. He touched the pad with his device and it opened, let him in, and started to close as soon as he passed through. The room was large with several screens on the walls and a long table facing them. He knew that the room was run on a generator and was lead lined in case of nuclear attack. No one else was in the room when he entered but just as the door was almost closed it opened again and a middle-aged black man dressed in a security uniform slipped in. Josh was relieved to see him. The idea of being trapped in this room alone was just downright scary no matter how safe it was. He recognized the man as Larry, the security guard of the night shift. When Josh was there late Larry would stop by and check on him. A few times he had brought Josh coffee and had spent a few minutes chatting with him as he made his rounds.

"Senator," said Larry, nodding his head toward Josh respectfully.

"Do you know what is going on, Larry?" asked Josh.

"Not exactly, sir. I was watching GTV and they were talking about some unusual activity from the sun and that there could be disruptions to the Devices and not to worry. Don't worry that there is unusual activity from the sun. What do they take us for, Senator? Idiots? Anyway, they cut to some fishermen in Asia who were showing video of the sea and I know this sounds crazy, but it looked like the boat was floating in blood with dead fish all around them. I was watching that when outside it was suddenly bright like it was noon even though it was the middle of the night, and then the siren went off. I checked the security screen and saw that you were on your way down. We are the only two in the building," said Larry, obviously trying to control his agitation.

Josh processed this information while he tried to call Rachel. His Device was operational but he couldn't call out due to the lead lined walls. Larry tried also with no luck. He told Josh that his wife and teenage daughter should be at home, just a few miles away. As he was considering the possible ramifications of what Larry had told him, he heard a phone ring. Instinctively Larry and Josh looked at their Devices, but the ringing was not coming from them. Larry followed the sound to a red telephone in the middle of the long desk. Josh noted that the phone was attached by a cord to the wall. He hadn't seen a phone like this in decades. He remembered there was one like it at the farm, but in black.

"Well, answer it!" shouted Larry, shaking Josh out of his reverie. Embarrassed, Josh picked up the phone.

"Hello?" he said timidly. It had been a long time since he had answered a call without knowing who was on the other end.

"Hello," said a voice he immediately recognized. "This is President Sontara, President of North America calling from the

245

White House Bunker. Who is this?"

"This is Senator Josh Davis. I am here with Larry, a security guard. We were the only ones in the building. I am glad to hear your voice. Are you alright? Can you give me any information?" Josh knew it was bold to question the president but he was desperate.

"We are still sorting things out but it appears that an asteroid passing between the Earth and the sun has caused a solar flare. The World Government scientists have been tracking the asteroid and felt that it was not a threat but they did not count on the solar flare that was caused by the asteroid. There was no time to warn people and I fear we will have mass casualties."

Josh was amazed at the president's ability to remain calm in this situation. He would never be able to keep it together so well. Mass casualties. Josh wondered what that meant. He thought about his family and his friends. He thought about George and Jessica and their families. The president's voice aroused him from his rumination.

"Senator? Are you still there?"

"Yes, Madam President, what can I do?"

"Stay close to the phone. It appears that the solar flare has caused power outages throughout North America and likely throughout the world. Our communications are spotty but we have some satellite intel of dead animals and people concentrated in the Middle East and lessening from there. It would have been noon in the Middle East – and closest to the sun. Rumors of rivers full of the blood have been circulating."

Josh was startled by the openness of this discussion. He was used to hearing only what was deemed necessary for him to know, always having only part of the puzzle. Now all of the puzzle pieces had spilled onto the table.

"I am telling you all of this in case our communication is lost. The line we are on is a direct line which was run between the White House and the Capitol. I am here with my family, my secret service agent and his family, and Vice-President Hallerman and his secret service agent."

Josh was not surprised to hear that the vice-president was there. John Hallerman was known to have very little need for sleep and was the first to arrive at his office in the morning. During these unstable times Josh would not have been surprised to find out that he spent most of his nights in his office in the White House. His family had remained in Idaho; his wife ran the family hardware business.

"Senator, I am glad to know that you are alright. I am not sure of the status outside. I will get back to you." The line clicked and there was a sound that he remembered from his youth. The dial tone. Josh set the phone in the cradle.

"Well, what do we do now?" asked Josh, more to himself than to Larry.

"Sir, I would like permission to go see what is going on outside," said Larry.

Josh thought about that for a moment. He also wanted to know what was going on out there, but he certainly didn't want to risk Larry's life. On the other hand, they were of no use to anyone holed up in this room forever.

"OK, Larry, I am going to put a clock on you," said Josh, looking at his device. "Fifteen minutes is enough time to go up, get to a window, and then get back down here. No heroics, agreed? Just a look and then come right back. I will stay here in case the president calls back."

Larry nodded and then slipped out. Josh set the timer on his device. Looking at the Device count the time calmed him somehow. He noted that it was now 5:30 so it should be starting to get light. Fifteen minutes ticked past, then sixteen, and Josh was beginning to panic when there was a knock on the door. Josh flung the door open and Larry came inside, panting.

"I did just as you said sir, sorry if it took longer. I am not a young man anymore and those stairs wore me out. Anyway, it looks like noontime out there. People are walking around like zombies. They all look confused. Some have burns on their skin and some are kneeling in the middle of the street screaming at God. We have to find a way to warn them, Senator. They are going to get burned up!"

Josh agreed but didn't know how to inform them. He didn't know how long this flare would last and then how long the power outage would continue. He thought about the bowls from Revelation. He knew that the fourth angel poured his bowl on the sun and allowed it to scorch the people, but for how long? The bowls were being poured much faster than he had thought they would be. He thought about the food and water supply. How would anyone survive this? The ringing of the phone interrupted his thoughts. This time he picked it up immediately.

"Senator?" Josh recognized the voice of Vice-President Hallerman.

"Yes, sir, I am here."

"We have sent out an agent and it appears to be safe to leave the bunker as long as you remain indoors. All communication is down however, except the direct lines between here and the presidents of the other nine nations and the Supreme Principal. The Supreme Principal seems to think that we are at war. At this point he is gathering forces to fight the enemy."

"Who is the enemy?" Josh asked reluctantly, closing his eyes and bracing himself for the answer.

"God," Vice-President Hallerman replied. They were both silent for a moment, both pondering the absurdity of the statement. Josh could hear a lot of chatter in the background while the vice president whispered into the phone.

"Josh, I know you to be a good man. I also know your family is nearby," his voiced cracked and he took a moment to continue. "I have to tell you that you are to stay where you are and wait for further orders. But I know that we are on the wrong side of a battle and if you left…"

"I hear you and I wish you and your family all the best," replied Josh and quietly hung up the phone.

"It's Armageddon," said Larry. Josh wasn't sure if Larry was asking him or telling him. They looked around the safe room, assessing the availability of supplies. Larry went into the supply closet and found some canvas bags that they fashioned into backpacks. He also found raincoats with hoods and sunglasses that they could use for protection from the sun's rays. They packed up as much of the food and water as they could carry and ventured out into the street. A wave of heat rushed to meet them, like opening the oven door to check on the turkey at Thanksgiving. Josh felt ill-prepared for what he saw. There were people lying in the street with blisters on their exposed skin. Others looked like him, some wrapped in sheets, some on their balconies observing the chaos. Josh and Larry agreed to go to Larry's house and check on his family first. They were unwilling to part ways quite yet, as if they had been friends their whole lives. Larry told Josh about his family, his wife Eden and his 12-year-old daughter Amanda. As they walked on Josh felt guilty for hoarding his supplies, knowing that the people on the streets needed them, but he had to be practical. One look at Larry and he knew his new friend was having the same issue. Soon they arrived at Larry's apartment, their step quickening despite the heavy load they carried. Larry called out to his wife and she opened the door, tears streaming down her face, and his daughter rushed out to hug him. Josh choked up at the homecoming scene and prayed that his would be similar. As they had made their way to Larry's home he had looked out in the direction of his house and had seen smoke billowing toward the sky.

"Thank God you are alright," cried Eden.

"I am so sorry," sobbed Larry. "You were right, I should have listened."

Josh didn't have to ask what Larry was talking about. He knew. The mark had trapped them all. But this wallowing in self-pity was not going to get him home to his family.

"Larry," Josh said loudly in his most authoritative tone. "What's done is done and we have to move on from here. Do you have a car?"

Larry straightened up, responding to Josh's tone. "Yes, but will the Device turn it on?"

"We'll just have to try," replied Josh. He instructed Larry and his family to bring only what they needed for survival, keeping in mind the weight of the car and the energy it would need for the trip. His house was only about ten more miles, and they could figure it out from there.

"You have to hurry," he said to Larry. "Right now people are still trying to figure out what is going on but soon the roads are going to be full and traffic lights are out. It's going to be a mess. Let's go," he urged.

Larry, Eden and Amanda took what they could easily carry and headed down to the apartment garage. They slipped into the car and Larry closed his eyes as he pushed the on button. The car revved to a start and they all breathed a sigh of relief. Larry made his way out of the garage, carefully avoiding the people lying in the street. Some people walking along called out to them, some even grabbed onto the car as it passed, but Larry looked straight ahead and kept going, gripping the steering wheel and speaking only to ask directions from Josh. Amanda buried her face into her mom's shoulder to avoid seeing the devastation and Eden stared vacantly as her tears dripped into her daughter's hair.

The slow progression gave Josh plenty of time to come to grips with what he was heading toward. As they entered his neighborhood he saw that many of the homes were on fire, most likely sparked from the power surge, he thought. He closed his eyes as he instructed Larry to turn onto his street. The car stopped and Josh opened to eyes to see that every house on the street had burned to the ground. He got out of the car and staggered toward his house, Larry close behind. When he neared the house he saw a figure partially obscured by the smoke, kneeling in the street. The figure turned and Josh realized it was Ben. Josh ran to him and threw his arms around him but Ben would not allow himself to be consoled.

"They're dead, Dad. Mom and Hannah, I couldn't save them," he sobbed.

The elation of finding Ben followed the devastating news about Hannah and Rachel was more than Josh could bear. He collapsed beside Ben and they both sobbed. This time Larry had to take charge.

"We can't stay here, Senator. Remember? We have to get out of here."

Josh tried to get back on track. "But I don't have a car, how will I go?" he replied helplessly.

Larry considered his options for moment, looking back at his family and then back to Josh.

"If you have somewhere to go we will go with you. Just lead the way," he said.

Josh thought about the Christmas card from Jessica with the embedded map.

"I know the way," he said, and they made their way back to the car.

# CHAPTER FIFTY
··· ◇ ···

Larry's car ran out of fuel just a few miles from the farmhouse. Larry, Josh and Ben pushed it into the woods after removing a few items they might need right away. They had passed miles of scorched farmland, but the flare seemed to have settled down, and the temperature was returning to normal. They had passed very few cars on the road. There seemed to be a tacit agreement that no eye contact would be made. At one point Josh thought he could feel the ground trembling and he wondered if he would survive to see the earthquakes and the hailstorms. It was hard to hope for that.

They approached the farmhouse and saw a woman with a long grey braid sitting on the stoop. He wondered if she was the person who had triggered the alert so long ago. She appeared wary and he couldn't blame her. They were a bedraggled band of misfits. He asked about Jessica and George and their families.

"Don't you know?" she said, incredulous. "They were right all along. And no they are not here. They have gone. All of them." She looked down and a sad smile crossed her lips. "I thought I had more time to decide."

Josh put his arm around Ellen's shoulders and led them all into their new home.

Made in United States
Orlando, FL
28 March 2024

45243720R00152